THE BABY HONEY SHOW

NANCY BAGSHAW-REASONER

FourCats Press

For Katie and Cathy

This useful
nut
now argues
with persuasive lunacy
that truths are cyanide
to human beings
body and soul.

It is lies
and superstitions
he says
that make human
beings
bloom.

—discovered written on the inside cover of an old paperback copy of *Cat's Cradle* by Kurt Vonnegut

Nothing in this book is true.

Everything in this book is true

Contents

Act Three

Day By Day

Act One

Chapter 1 – The Day by Day Café

The Day by Day Café, now in its seventh decade, is wedged snugly between a dry cleaner's and a Dollar Store on 75th Street, not far from Broadway on Manhattan's Upper West Side. It is an unremarkable presence on an ordinary street. To be fair, the café doesn't get a lot of direct sun and is open during hours when many people are still abed, so it is entirely possible to walk by day after day, year after year and never take notice. But if you happen to be on the street around 3 a.m., you might find yourself standing in front of a square picture window that perfectly frames a golden interior, warmly lit by an assortment of table lamps—all of them different from one another, all purchased at the local Goodwill many years ago. You might find yourself counting the mismatched kitchen tables; there are eleven of them. Each is accompanied by two mismatched chairs. And like the lamps, the tables and chairs were procured at the Goodwill long ago. It is likely that you will see patrons already seated at the tables; the place is nearly full even now at 3:02 in the morning.

You will feel compelled to enter and take a seat. Then you will note that the lamps are distributed one per table and that they focus a romantic spotlight on the faces of the patrons, making them more attractive than they actually are. You notice now that everyone, including yourself, is taking notice of their reflections in the strategically placed mirrors throughout the room. And you feel dreamy, seeing yourself this way. It makes you unself-conscious, frees you to imagine what might have been and what might still be.

On the windowsill by the front door sits a lavish *Philodendron* in a large ceramic pot. You can't help but notice it, especially if you are inside the café. This plant is lush with shiny heart-shaped leaves promenading along the entire length of the windowsill. But the remarkable thing about the *Philodendron* is that it's deathless. They say this plant was placed on that spot on a June day back in 1951 when the café first opened its door and even now, sixty-five years later, the original plant continues to generate new growth. For years, customers were encouraged by the owner to take a cutting home and many did. But it is said that the stems just don't survive outside the café no matter how much care is taken to nurture them.

There's a large blackboard on the wall behind the cashier's station that features the daily menu, handwritten each morning by the owner, who is also the cook. The only other distinguishing feature of the Day by Day Café is the back wall covered with bookshelves—open ended faux-wood planks starting at eye level; the highest ones are placed within fourteen inches of the ten-foot ceiling. Each shelf is stocked end to end with old paperbacks, which form a lending library for the customers. A ladder stands at the ready for anyone inclined to browse the upper shelves. Borrowers aren't expected to return a book ever, but they always do. It's the only honest impulse in the place. Otherwise, the Day by Day Café is a place of untruths.

It's said that the hula hoop was invented at a table in this café. An idea had bounced around the antic imagination of a customer named Rodolfo while he was eating a fried-egg sandwich with a side of fresh pineapple spears. Those spears made him think about Hawai'i and then he thought about the way the hips of the women dancers moved. And voilà. He came up with the hula hoop. That was in 1953. It is said that Rodolfo was actually credited in *Popular Mechanics Magazine* that year with reinventing the wheel, but Rodolfo modestly shifted all credit to the Day by Day Café, a place that, according to him, "cradled single men in inspiration." They say Rodolfo became super rich. But he never returned to the Day by Day. He moved into a fancy suite in the Ansonia a block away; it was still operating as a hotel then. Thereafter all of his meals were provided by room service. He even had a servant. Once that story started making the rounds, the café took on a reputation as a place where highly creative people ate breakfast. It began to attract storytellers.

The café was open two days each week in the early decades of its existence. The first owner, a young guy named Pete, soon realized that the café wasn't much of a money maker. He needed a conventional Monday-through-Friday job to finance his lifestyle, which eventually included a wife and kid. But Pete couldn't just walk away. He said the café was worth its weight in gold because of the customers it attracted and the stories they told. Pete said it was his labor of love, and he looked forward to being there even if the café could only be open on weekends. It was in the Day by Day that he heard about an underground zoo where the animals roamed unfettered. One of the customers claimed to have volunteered there. He told Pete wonderful stories about the albino zebras.

Pete couldn't get that story out of his mind and over time, he wrote a bestseller called *My Friend Whitey*. Pete dedicated the book to America *"where men and women live proud and free to do whatever they want. Where everyone is prosperous, where no one is hungry, where animals are safe and happy. And where everyone admires their Congressman and Senator and loves the President.* The book, written in 1955, was shortlisted for the National Fiction Award the following year. It was Pete's one and only book but he was happy to have written even one. And he loved the Day by Day all the more for making it possible.

Pete set the hours for the Day by Day and they would never change. When the café opened, the front door was unlocked promptly at three in the morning. Even at that hour there were always a couple of guys waiting to get in. Three a.m. is the prime creative time if you are a writer of fiction, the bewitching hour. It's the time you find yourself awake after you've had your "first sleep" of the night. Yes, "first sleep." In medieval times, people acknowledged a "first" and a "second" sleep. References can be found in lovers' diaries written during the Renaissance. And it's said that Shakespeare glorified "second sleep" in a sonnet in 1599.

The "first sleep" typically began at sundown and lasted until three in the morning, at which time families would awaken and go about their chores. Women would cook and weave and whatever else they were inclined to do during the day and men would tend the animals and carve stuff. No one felt obliged to converse. This allowed everyone to think. To go deep inside and imagine. Then at 6 a.m., everyone would climb back into their beds and sleep for three more hours. Those three hours were reputed to be the most relaxing, the most healthful sleep of the whole night. It was said that during second sleep, blisters healed and children grew.

Regardless of the verity of those historical facts, in 1951, the Day by Day Café opened at 3 a.m. for kindred spirits to share their dreams. After the success of *My Friend Whitey* five years later, the café acquired a reputation among professional writers. It is said that the editor of the *New Yorker* began to eat breakfast there every weekend.

In the early Sixties, Pete sold the Day by Day to a poet named Lou, a single guy who would update the place. Lou didn't change the hours; he needed to be "up and at 'em" by 3 a.m. and back in bed by 8 a.m. in order to maximize his own literary output. So the café's hours were ideal for him just as they had been originally established by Pete. But Lou expanded the number of days. Now the café was open seven mornings a week. Other than that, Lou didn't change a thing. Not the furniture, not the lamps. Not the bookshelves or the menu. Or the *Philodendron*.

Lou wrote his poems in between cooking and serving, sometimes on the blackboard by the cash register. He'd stand on the ladder and try to fit his poems around the daily menu and maybe that is why all of his poems seemed to be about sandwiches.

It is said that Truman Capote became a regular during this time. They say he sat at a table morning after morning, absent-mindedly playing with his corned beef hash and rereading an old newspaper clipping that he carried in his wallet. A report detailing the gruesome murders of a family in the farming community of Holcomb, Kansas. Then one morning, Truman suddenly jumped up and, in his distinctive, babyish drawl, yelled *Eureka!* They say it was a morning in 1964. On that day, Truman began to write *In Cold Blood*. It was a true story. One based on fact. But Truman added alternative facts to fit the story he wanted to tell and, in doing so, he created a new literary genre, the Non-Fiction Novel. Readers couldn't tell the difference between the true facts and the alternate facts even when the critics pointed them out. Even when Truman admitted he fibbed. The fact is that the Readers didn't care about truth. In fact, they were impressed by Truman's lies. They said it made Truman's story seem even "realer."

Of course, it was only a matter of time before the café became a magnet for sophisticated drunks who had stories to tell. I was among them. Feeling diminished by a decade of rejection by *The New Yorker*, among other publications, feeling disparaged as a lover by too many one-week stands, I had found a community of peers at a nondescript bar on the Upper West Side, not far from the Day by Day. There I was embraced as a writer and given a reason to get out of bed every afternoon.

I had been making ends meet by proofreading articles for an American history publication. I was a history buff. And I was not without talent as a wordsmith. The same can be said of my barfly friends. Some of them had shown great promise—at least at one time. But as success continued to elude all of us, it was easier to drink booze and whine than it was to write. We lived in a fugue state—fueled by bourbon and marked by random blackouts and incredulous envy in a city that seemed endlessly to discover and nurture new and extravagantly gifted talent. But not us. Never us.

We were meeting early most evenings now and drinking ourselves almost blind. Then, clinging to one another, we would shuffle
down the damp early morning streets in search of breakfast. That
particular morning, the barflies literally carried me into the Day by
Day. They heard that other drunks would be there who liked to tell
tales, and frankly, we were all in need of some new material.

Three o'clock in the morning. How well I remember, despite
my stupor, the welcoming warmth of the lamplight, the regardful
faces of the patrons, the good coffee. I found a sympathetic ear in
the newest owner—not the poet—a different guy now named Ray.
I didn't realize that he was gay at first. I'm always so slow to pick
up on that in men. Even when I'm sober. I flirted shamelessly with
him that morning. He was quite handsome, you see. And lucky for
me, he was kind. And intuitive. He offered me his guest room until
I could get back on my feet. And he encouraged me to discipline
my habits. He said that he sensed that I had "the third eye of a true
writer." I became an habitué of the café, arriving just before 3 a.m.
and leaving just before eight—every morning of the week, week
after week. There in the forgiving lamplight of the Day by Day, I
committed myself to sobriety.

By the way, the original name of the café, written in yellow paint
on the picture window that faced 75th Street, was One Day at a
Time. But one of the drunks was an impatient fellow. He short-
ened the name, started telling people to meet him at the Day by
Day. And it caught on. Finally, Ray painted the new name on the
window—this was in the Eighties—and the name change became
official. It was now the Day by Day Café. But the hours and days
remained the same. And the lamps on the tables and the books on
the wall and the blackboard menu and the *Philodendron*.

As I noted, all of the drunks were raconteurs, hoping to find someone to turn their lost weekends into bestselling novels. But the ambitious writers were heading to L.A. now, chasing a punchier story
style and a contract with a TV studio. The drunks' stories were too
predictable. A guy down on his luck. The gal who did him wrong.
The mom who never loved him. And the dog that was hit by a cab.

Too much like life. Eventually even the drunks got bored and stopped showing up. And the magic faded. The café settled into anonymity.

But I remained. I made a modest living editing other writers' work. And I wrote a few short stories that first year. They were published in literary journals. Ray made a fuss each time that happened—a big dinner, candlelight. Once he let me kiss him on the mouth. I was also beginning to get lucrative assignments for historical magazines. That allowed me to travel extensively. So, I left the Day by Day. I lived in Argentina and Chile. I fell madly in love often. I even married briefly. Years passed. Decades. Then in 2010, I returned alone to New York City and found myself awake one morning at three. I went out for a walk and muscle memory took over. Unthinking, my feet carried me to the door of the Day by Day Café. I entered.

A new owner now, a fellow named Bill, had bought the place. He and I were instantly compatible. He was gay, and, to be honest, I was relieved to hear that. I'm sure that you have already intuited that I have an impulsive libido. Which has created chaos in my life and the lives of others. I was ready, at last, to be celibate.

I immediately reclaimed my table at the window and spent the mornings thereafter reading history and taking notes. I had it in mind to write an historical novel. Maybe something set during a tumultuous time. A popular uprising. Resistance. Revolution. And finally the humiliation and destruction of a malignant king.

Bill often sat across from me, silently culling the dictionary for impressive words to expand his vocabulary. Words like *borborygmus, sabulous,* and *niggardly,* which he discovered meant something altogether different from what he had feared. I suggested that perhaps we could join forces—work on a project together. And he said he would consider it. Another five years passed. Life moves so slowly when you are waiting for something to happen.

Then on May 17, 2016, something happened. An elderly man entered the café. It was three in the morning, Bill had just unlocked the door and turned on the lamps. Strangely enough, for the first time in years, there were other strangers arriving at that hour, as if they were anticipating something special to happen in the Day by Day Café that day.

The elderly man, wearing a trim navy blazer over a pale pink polo shirt; khaki slacks, a bit baggy in the seat; and a pair of loafers, ordered a poached egg and a cup of decaf at the counter and then took a seat at one of the tables. He put his head in his hands. The lamplight showered his bald spot with gold. He seemed burdened. Bill brought the man his order and said, "Mind if I join you? You look like a guy who has a story to tell."

The man looked up into Bill's gentle eyes and laughed wearily. "Yeah," he said. "I have a heck of a story all right. If you're willing to hear it."

Bill said, "I sure am." And took a seat.

The man said, "I was once a star of the vaudeville stage." He shrugged and gave a sheepish grin, "You ever heard of Little Sammy Turner?"

Bill shook his head.

Sam nodded and continued. "Well, it was a long time ago. This story starts back in the '30s. The 1930s. Wonderful time in America. I was a child vaudeville star. Little Sammy Turner. I was famous. I played the circuit from the time I was four. My mother is credited with being the original stage mother. She was briefly married to W.C. Fields. She said he was a louse but I tell you——he woulda done anything for me. Gave me my first break in show biz. Taught me the ladder bit. And Fields and I did it in the Catskills—two shows a day—one entire season—even after he and mom split up. Audiences couldn't get enough of the ladder bit."

The patrons in the café that morning would later report a sudden deep rumble followed by a flash of forked lightning that ricocheted around the room and was magnified in the surrounding mirrors. The lamps on the tables flickered. And you could actually smell the sizzle of imagination in the air. It had been years since there was magic in the Day by Day, but this was bona fide. The patrons turned their faces to Sam Turner. Then they turned their chairs creating a small horseshoe of an audience around the soft-spoken man. "Tell us more," they said.

He obliged. He talked for the next three hours. I watched and took notes.

"W.C. Fields once let me use his toothpaste in his dressing room. He imported it from Spain. It was red toothpaste. Tasted like ginger snaps." Now the patrons were assured. There could be no doubt that this little old man was the true and legendary Sam Turner. Who else could possibly know a detail that intimate?

"I worked with Jack Benny. Nicest man in the world. Not at all cheap. He used to buy me sacks of penny candy. Licorice whips and Mary Janes. He'd tell the girl at the cash register to keep the change." Again, such details as only the true Sammy would know. The audience was hooked. The man continued, "The Marx Brothers? All of them smart. My favorite, Harpo, taught me to play chess. He said I could have been a grand master if I applied myself but I was into sports. Baseball. I was Lou Gehrig's guest at the World Series in 1933. He dedicated one of his homers to me. This was of course before he got sick. I forget what he had. Anyway, it killed him."

Sam took a swig from his coffee cup and went on. "Mickey Rooney was hyper. Drove everyone nuts. Judy Garland was sweet. Jackie Coogan and I were up for the same role in *The Kid*. The director was Charlie Chaplin and he was courting my mother at the time. He sent us on a three-month trip to Europe on the Orient Express so I wasn't available for the filming. But I saw Paris in the '30s. I met Hemingway. He took me fishing. What a man!"

Word spread about this storyteller who had been a vaudeville child star and the café was filling up every day now. One morning three weeks later, after a great deal of coaxing by the standing-room-only crowd, Sam agreed to do some of his favorite bits. He got out of his chair and stood with his back to the picture window. He leaned back and plucked a heart-shaped leaf off the *Philodendron* and tucked it in the buttonhole of his navy blazer, like a boutonniere. His face flushed with happiness. He struck a pose— there were some giggles—and began, "I'll meet you on the corner. If

I get there first, I'll put a blue spot on the sidewalk. If you get there first, you can rub it out."

Appreciative Laughter.

"Slowly I turn … step by step … inch by inch…."

Excited Squeals.

"Hey, anybody got change for three nickels?"

Enthusiastic Applause. Encore, they yelled. Then Sam grabbed the ladder and did the bit he had done with Fields.

STANDING OVATION!

The following day, Sam Turner died with a smile on his face. He was ninety years old. Bill and I collaborated on a loving obituary based on all that Sam had shared in the past three weeks. Bill was inspired to add a few things that he made up just to make the story even more interesting. Like he added that Sam was married to an Italian movie star in the late '40s. A real tempestuous gal who loved him like crazy but didn't want kids so Sam eventually left her and settled down with a nice girl named Carol, in Pennsylvania, and became a fuel-oil salesman. Stuff like that. Bill figured Sam wouldn't mind if we stretched the truth.

Anyway, Bill sent the obit to the *New York Times* and they published it! Then they sent a feature writer to the café to interview the patrons about Sam. Everyone it turned out had a story about him. Bill immediately got a hold of Sam's son, Sam Junior, who lived in Jenkintown, Pennsylvania. The son sobbed on the phone and thanked Bill for calling. He said, "I wondered where the heck Dad had gone this time." And then Bill announced to the patrons in the café that there would be a memorial service. On June 14, 2016.

Now Destiny stepped in.

Chapter 2 — The Lie

On Tuesday, June 14, 2016, Mark Reynolds, a passably nice-looking, thirty-six year old, unmarried New Yorker, out for his daily run, came upon the Day by Day Café for the first time—which seemed odd to him given that he lived just around the corner—in a two-bedroom apartment with his best friend Eleanor with whom he was no longer having sex. It was 3 a.m. He was having trouble sleeping that morning. Yesterday afternoon he had quit his job in a fit of pique and now he was having second thoughts.

Mark had spent the last five years at a small ad agency on 35th Street in the Garment District writing copy for a client that specialized in medical devices for the elderly. Back braces and hernia-support underwear. All day, every day, Mark was forced to cram impossible amounts of technical jargon into sixty-second commercials that would air on local news programs that only old people watched. The client was convinced that technical words were impressive and persuasive. Mark tried to tell him that TV was a visual medium and words didn't matter, that people just needed to see images of backs straightening and tummies being flattened. That's the way you reach a customer—subliminally—with images of health, of youth restored.

Yesterday their exchange had become more animated than usual. Mark asserted that given the chance he could expand the appeal of BackAbility Products, Inc., to a whole new demographic. Mark insisted, "Young customers will find the trusses and hernia belts sexy, Mr. Miller, if they associate them with looking buff and fit."

Mark had a point. It was an especially seductive sell for those thirty-year-olds who spend their days seated in front of a computer screen at work and their weekends seated in front of a video-game console. "It's an expanding market, Mr. Miller. Pun intended." Mark smiled and leaned in. "I swear to you, this generation is going to need back support before they're forty. I can lure them to your products. I can make even an umbilical support cummerbund sexy! Give me a shot." But the normally passive Mr. Miller grimaced with discomfort and said, emphatically, "Let's just stick with what works." And Mark lost it. He quit his job.

He went home and told Eleanor that he had never felt so old and used up. He said his creativity was leaking out of his soul like air out of a limp balloon after the party was over. And because that was such a lame analogy, Eleanor understood that Mark had had no choice but to walk away from BackAbility Products, Inc. immediately before he completely lost what was left of his mojo. Eleanor said, "I'll quit my job, too! This will be an adventure, Mark! Something we can do together."

Now on this June morning, as Mark ran past the Day by Day Café, he had a sudden urge to pee. Realizing then that the café was the only thing open on the street at that hour, he turned back and entered. The café was packed. Mostly men—of—every age. Dressed in dark suits and neckties. A few women stood among them. Each patron wore a heart-shaped leaf. The men had it tucked into a buttonhole on their suit jacket lapels. The women had it pinned in their hair. Mark got directions to the restroom from a guy standing just inside the door. It was 3:15 a.m.

When Mark came out of the bathroom, he figured he should buy some breakfast. It wasn't right to use the bathroom at a café and then leave without buying something. That is basic New York City etiquette; Mark was a native. He stepped to the counter and looked up at the blackboard menu. That's when he read:

IN OUR HEARTS NOW AND FOREVER!
REST IN PEACE, SAM TURNER
1926-2016

Mark caught a glimpse of himself in a mirror and was surprised that he looked so terrific given the stress in his life and the hour of the morning. *Wow. I'm young,* he thought. *Young and Restless. I have my whole life ahead of me.* He noticed that everyone else in the room looked good, too. Even the older people. Mark began to relax. For the first time in years, he felt optimistic, which was odd given that he now realized he was at a funeral.

A man approached him and handed him a drink. "It's a Manhattan. It was my father's favorite cocktail." Mark accepted it and gestured to the words on the blackboard. "Your dad?" The man nodded. Mark said, "I'm sorry. My condolences. This is my first time here so I never met him, but obviously your dad was ... uh...." Mark scanned the crowd. "Very well liked." Mark took a sip of his drink and winced at the sweetness. It reminded him of cough syrup.

The man smiled at Mark. "Yeah ... my first time here, too." He extended his hand. "Sam Turner, Junior."

"Mark Reynolds, advertising copywriter."

Mark didn't know what made him introduce himself that way. It wasn't his habit to announce his job when meeting a stranger. But he noticed that Sam Turner Junior took a heightened interest in him.

Sam said, "Hey, I need some air. Care to join me outside?"

Mark followed Sam out the front door and waited expectantly for him to talk again.

Mark was prepared to listen and offer comfort. Instead, Sam started to laugh. Mark watched him, but said nothing. It is a fact that people act irrationally sometimes during bereavement. Mark knew that. He had a vocational interest in psychology.

Sam lit a cigarette, took a drag, and sighed. "I don't know what to do, Mark. This is ... all of this...." He waved his arms toward the mourners inside the café. "It's a lie. Every bit of it."

Mark shifted his weight. "Oh ... so your dad is still alive?"

"No ... no. He's really dead. That's a fact. But ... well.... Look, my dad was a great guy, nicest guy in the world. Conscientious husband and father and grandfather. Successful salesman. A friend to everyone. But he was no child star in vaudeville. Okay? That was all made up. By Dad."

Mark didn't react, he merely listened and nodded from time to time. Sam took a deep draw on his Marlboro, exhaled, and continued his story. "After Mom died ... that was about ten years ago ... Dad struggled, couldn't seem to find something that engaged his time let alone his mind. He gave up golf and bridge. His friends were dying off. Or worse—being warehoused in those assisted living places. Then suddenly two years ago, he gets a girlfriend and starts dancing every night, even taking lessons. The Charleston. The Black Bottom. All these dances from the 1920s. Dad could always dance."

Mark nodded. "Good for him. That's good exercise."

"And then he and his lady friend started binge-watching old movies on the Turner Classic Movie Channel. Dad used to tell us that we were related to Ted Turner...." Sam chuckled.

Mark brightened, "Are you?"

"No. Dad made that up."

Mark shrugged, "Good story though. You should keep it." Mark took a large swallow of his drink.

" Anyway...." Sam resumed. He tipped his head back and blew a perfect smoke ring at the fading moon. "Not long after that, Dad ran off. Not with the girlfriend. He took off on his own. I went nuts trying to find him. See, he lived with us, my wife and me. And then I get a call from Bill—he's the owner of this place. And he tells me how thrilled he was to have finally met the legendary Little

Sammy Turner, the vaudeville child star. And how Dad had a whole new fan club here at the Day by Day. And sadly, Dad was dead now but he was deeply happy here in his final days and Bill hoped that gave the family peace. But well ... Jesus, Mark, here's the thing. The Little Sammy Turner stuff? It was all made up! Dad was never in vaudeville. He was just a normal little boy who grew up in a normal family. And Dad wasn't senile. So, this was deliberate. Dad reinvented himself. And being that he was a salesman all those years—well, he was able to sell these people a big lie."

Now Mark was intrigued. Now he wished he had known Sam Turner Senior and had heard his stories. He seemed like such a cool guy. Mark didn't even care if he was a liar. At least his lies were interesting.

Sam Junior took a final drag on his cig and dropped it to the sidewalk and crushed it under his broad foot. "So, here's my dilemma. Should I tell these people that it's all a lie? Would you do that to your dad?"

Mark shrugged, "My dad has zero imagination so I would never be in this situation. But I see your point."

"I guess he just wanted to be famous, Mark, just once in his life."

"Yeah. I'd say that's probably pretty common in America."

"I mean he never told us that, but I guess Dad was harboring this dream, you know ... to be Somebody ... and he turned ninety last January and it was now or never. And I guess he thought he had to get away from me because he doubted I would play along. See— that's the part that hurts. He thought I would betray his reinvention. You know ... he probably thought I would laugh at him." At this point, Sam Junior started to cry.

"Would you have done that, Sam?"

"I don't think so. But he was afraid I'd blow it for him, Mark. Like my mother—if she was still alive. I mean she loved him. But she would have said, 'Oh Sam, you are so silly.' Right in front of his new friends! Damn ... I mean she didn't do that, but that's only because he waited 'til she was dead.... But if she hadn't died, he would have never realized his dream. The thing is, Mark ... this lie meant more to him than dying in my arms."

Sam Junior wiped away a tear. Mark studied his face. Frankly, Mark saw the lie as benign. Who hasn't exaggerated? Who hasn't tried to impress? What's the big deal?

After a long pause, Sam spoke again. "I loved him, Mark. And obviously, this is what he wants his legacy to be. His last hurrah. He would want me to play along with the lie. Right?"

Mark took a sip of the Manhattan; he was sort of getting used to it now. He said, "Yeah. I think you should play along. I mean ... where's the harm? You don't have to see these people again."

Sam Junior shook a warning finger in the air. His eyes were dry now. "Oh, but here's the scary part. Lies have legs, Mark. They travel. One lie spawns a hundred more. There's an obituary in the *New York Times* this week—about a famous vaudeville child star named Little Sammy Turner. It's got all kinds of made up shit about Italian actresses and a Stage Mother who screwed every big shot in Hollywood in the '30s. It's all false, but before you know it, some writer will get a hold of it. Next thing you know, there will be an entry in Wikipedia about my dad. And a biography at Barnes and Noble. And then a cult following. And when I die, I'll be remembered as the son of the famous vaudeville child star. I'm going to have to prepare my kids now. You see where this is going? I guarantee— this will be part of their bio, too, if I don't act immediately. I have to make a choice right now. Do I set the record straight? Or do I embrace the lie? Make it *my* lie, too? Make the lie eternal?"

Mark followed Sam back into the café. Mark asked Sam what sort of business he was in. Sam replied that he was a detective in a large suburb of Philadelphia. Still working, but he would be retiring in the fall. "After forty years on the force."

Mark nodded, "Congratulations. So, what's next for you?"

"I'm going to try my hand at acting." Sam flushed and shrugged. "My dream is to appear in a commercial. People tell me I have a face for commercials."

Mark smiled. "I'll keep you in mind."

"Oh, that's right! You're Mark Reynolds, advertising copywriter! Talk about your serendipity, huh?"

"Actually, Sam, I'm a screenwriter and movie producer," said Mark. That was, of course, a lie.

"Wow!"

Inside the Day by Day Café, patrons were now taking turns sharing fond memories of Sam Turner Senior. Some of the older people claimed first-hand experience with the vaudeville child star, telling the crowd that they saw Little Sammy's act at the Palace Theater in 1939 when he was working with George Burns and Gracie Allen. Mark watched with interest as the lie took hold.

Mark and Sam found themselves standing on the perimeter of the crowd next to a nice-looking older couple who suddenly turned and smiled at Sam Junior. The woman lightly touched his sleeve and said, "You are Sammy Turner's son, aren't you?" She had an accent. And eyes like melted chocolate.

Sam Junior nodded. "Yes, I am," he said breathlessly.

She smiled again. "Ah, I can feel the connection."

"You knew my dad?"

"I know everything that happens here in the Day by Day. I am a sustaining patron."

Sam Junior figured she was in her fifties. Or maybe her sixties. Whatever her age, she was beautiful. Sam stood up straight and sucked in his gut. He glanced at himself in one of the café mirrors. He was sixty-two but could definitely pass for fifty-nine. And that wasn't just his opinion. The desk sergeant at the precinct, a gal named Judy—just last week she had said to him, "What are you now, Sam? Fifty-nine?" He hadn't corrected her. He let her believe that lie; it made him feel good all day.

The beautiful woman continued to look directly into Sam's eyes. There was an air of unreality about her. Her voice sounded like a song. "Such a dear man, your father. You resemble him, you know?"

Sam Junior grinned and nodded. "Yeah ... well ... I've heard that before...." His face was red as an apple.

The woman purred, "My, you must have grown up with a lot of storytellers, Mr. Sam Junior. Given that your father was an entertainer."

Sam shrugged. "Well ... yeah ... I guess."

She continued. "So, I wonder … you wouldn't happen to know the name of a highly creative advertising copywriter, would you? You see we own a line of children's clothing." She gestured to the man beside her. "My husband here … his grandfather founded the Children's Dry Goods Company back in the Thirties. When I eventually came into the family—that was in 1990—we updated the name of the company. It became The Baby Honey Corporation. But we think it's due for another refresh." She laughed. A charming laugh. Sam Jr. felt weak; he felt himself dissolving in her gaze. She continued, "We want to do something bold and unexpected. We want to shake things up. We want to introduce these baby clothes to a whole new generation of young mothers." She paused. Sam hung on her silence in the same way that he had hung on her words. She lightly touched his lapel. "You understand reinvention, don't you, Sam?"

The woman's husband suddenly said, "Perhaps I had better track down some coffee, Susana."

Susana laughed and said, "Champagne for me if they have it." She watched her husband step into the crowd and disappear. She turned now to Mark, who had remained at Sam Junior's side, quietly mesmerized by this woman's astonishing charisma. Now she addressed Mark directly. "So, where was I? Oh yes. I'm looking for a clever ad man to create a campaign for the Baby Honey line of children's clothing. If either of you gentlemen know someone imaginative…. Money is no object."

Sam Junior said, "Well … as a matter of fact…." He suddenly threw an arm around the shoulders of Mark. "Allow me to introduce my friend here. He's Mark Reynolds, advertising copywriter and movie screenwriter."

"And I also write for TV," said Mark. His face was flushed.

"My goodness. A triple threat? Is that what they say about someone with your imagination?

"I would say it's mainly nerve." Mark grinned.

Now Sam jumped back into the conversation. "He and I have been working together for years. He's the best I ever worked with.

I'm an actor!" Sam winked at Mark and added, "Believe me, Mark Reynolds is just what you're looking for."

The woman's husband returned with her tea and was introduced to our gifted party. He smiled and said, "I'm a billionaire."

Bill, standing beside me, watching this scene unfold from across the room, squeezed my hand, and said, "You know—I'm thinking there might be a story here."

Chapter 3 — Mark & Eleanor

Mark left the Day by Day Café that morning at eight o'clock just as Bill was locking up. I watched from the window. As the other customers quietly dispersed into the city—Sam, Mark and the older couple remained together on the sidewalk. Sam exchanged phone numbers with Mark, said a warm "Until we meet again" to Susanna and her husband. Then Sam Turner Junior strolled to the corner. He waved one last time to Mark, called out a cheery "Until we meet again," and then stepped into a cab. The cab immediately vanished into thin air. Or so it seemed to me.

Mark and the older couple agreed to meet the following morning, same time, same place, to discuss the specifics of their new business arrangement. Everything had happened so quickly that it wasn't until they all said goodbye that the older couple finally turned back and officially introduced themselves as Bob and Susana Rowland. Then Mark watched the Rowlands cross the street and disappear around a corner, after which Mark raced back to his apartment. He couldn't wait to share his news with Eleanor, his longtime girlfriend, who wasn't actually his girlfriend anymore but the apartment was so great and neither of them wanted to give it up. So, they were working things out. In separate bedrooms.

By this time I had dropped back into my chair at my table by the window of the Day by Day Café. I covered my eyes with my hands and touched my third eye with both forefingers. Immediately, with no effort at all, I could see Mark entering his apartment. I could see Eleanor. I could smell coffee and I was able to hear every word they said.

Mark found Eleanor standing at the kitchen sink with her eyes tightly closed. He was overwhelmed with an intense longing for her. After a moment, he said, "Good morning."

Keeping her eyes shut, she turned her head towards him and replied, "I'm doing a scientific experiment. Well ... quasi-scientific. I'm forcing myself to make my very good coffee without benefit of my sight. I am making myself rely on my hunches and then I evaluate the coffee I create. If I am convinced that it is as good as my typical coffee—something I know absolutely can't be true ... then I see that I am vulnerable to a counterfeit reality."

Mark noticed there were sprays of coffee grinds covering the counter and the linoleum floor. And every measuring cup and tablespoon was dusted with the dark stuff. Eleanor, still with eyes tightly closed, added, "I am reading Hannah Arendt's thoughts on totalitarianism. You know? You should read her, too. Times being what they are."

Mark sighed. "Ahhh ... of course."

"She makes a valid point, Mark. That ideological thinking can become emancipated from the reality we perceive with our five senses. And when that happens, it leads to a situation where people begin to insist that a truer reality exists which is concealed behind what is perceptible with our five senses. For example, if we no longer believe our own eyes, that opens the flood gates. That's when we get all these conspiracy theories. Like the 9/11 attack on the Twin Towers 'never happened' even though we in New York watched it from the street. There are people who believe that in spite of all the evidence to the contrary. And worse there are people who *want* people to believe that. Why, you may ask?"

Eleanor turned in Mark's direction, her eyes remained closed. She took a sip of coffee. "Because they want to conquer reality. And they are succeeding. Americans are super lonely, Mark. Rather than going next door, they go online to find friends. And those friends are robots in a warehouse. But people fall in love with them. As Hannah Arendt notes, 'a dynamic of isolation and loneliness creates conditions that give rise to totalitarianism.' We are screwed."

Mark sighed again. "Uh huh."

Eleanor continued. "All I'm saying is that we need to get very tight with our five senses and make sure we recognize what's real every moment of the day. Personally, I think I'm in deep shit. I like this coffee I'm making. All three versions. They all taste exactly like my regular brew. But I know that's not possible."

"Eleanor, open your eyes. I've got big news! We have a client."

Eleanor opened her eyes. "One other thing, Mark. I just want to add that I have great admiration for blind people."

Mark and Eleanor sat at the kitchen table now and drank Eleanor's coffee—a fresh pot that she made with her eyes open. It was excellent. Mark detailed his experience at the café that morning. "You're coming with me tomorrow. We are going into business together," Mark said. "You'll get to meet the Rowlands and Bill. And maybe Sam will be back. His father was a vaudeville star when he was a kid. He knew Hemingway!"

Eleanor studied Mark's face. He was a changed man. Happy. Enthusiastic. Optimistic. In other words, a stranger. It made her remember the creepy movie she had watched at a sleepover at her friend Janie Weiss's when she was nine. She was never able to forget it. The horror story took place somewhere in the center of the country. A creeping blob of orange vapor suddenly emerged from a mountain top and descended onto this small town. It engulfed all the humans and transformed them into an army of robots...."

"Eleanor! Are you listening to me?"

Eleanor said, "Yes. You—Mark Reynolds—are going to sell baby clothes."

"No. I am going to create an image that will make people want to buy baby clothes." Mark grabbed a broom and began to sweep up the coffee grounds on the floor. He kept talking. "See Eleanor, advertising is about motivation. You seduce people with their own desires. It's tapping into people's dreams...."

Eleanor made a face. "Oh God, Mark.... Are adults going to wear these baby clothes?"

"No ... No! Not that kind of desire ... There's nothing kinky about Baby Honey clothes.... Look it's a legitimate old company. These are real kids' garments. For real kids. That's all. I'm going to design a whole new campaign to sell these clothes. I have complete autonomy, Eleanor. It's the chance of a lifetime to show the industry what I can do."

Eleanor took a deep breath. "How in heaven's name did you get picked to create a commercial to sell baby clothes? You don't even like babies."

"It isn't required that I like babies."

"In fact, Mark——as I recall—you told me you can't stand babies."

"I didn't say that ... I said I didn't want to be a father."

There was a pause. Eleanor stood and crossed to the cupboard. She grabbed a bag of Oreos and returned to the table. She opened the package, grabbed two cookies, handed one to Mark, and dunked the other. They stared at each other long and hard.

She had met Mark on a blind date set up by a friend six years ago. She liked him instantly. There was an innocence about him that you rarely saw in men anymore. He spoke kindly about his family. He loved dogs and never swore. He laughed easily at her jokes. He appreciated her curiosity and intelligence. And he had big dreams—to be a creator/writer/director of movies. To live in L.A. and go to the beach on weekends and attend the Cannes Film Festival. And always with Eleanor by his side.

When, on their third date, he told her he loved her—she knew he was sincere. And after having been guarded about love for so long after so many dismal relationships, Eleanor finally allowed herself to feel in love with him. They moved in together. And they were happy. Until this past year.

Mark suddenly changed. All his innocence seemed to disappear. He worked all day and at night, he watched TV network news obsessively—at 6 and again at 11—to make sure his hernia-truss commercials aired as scheduled. And then silently he went off to bed. He rarely talked anymore. He never laughed. Of course, she blamed his dead-end job at BackAbility Products, Inc. for aging him prematurely. But she wondered—was Mark's true nature emerging? Was he a pessimist? He was making her doubt the future.

Eleanor tried to change the trajectory of Mark's life by suggesting they backpack through Europe for a year. They were both barely into their mid-thirties, after all. Teenagers, actually, by American twenty-first-century standards. No American was expected to be an adult until hitting forty-nine or their parents died. Eleanor figured they had years left to just be kids.

Because Eleanor was working at a travel agency at the time, she had access to brochures that featured the most obscure destinations. She brought several home, and she and Mark studied them over dinner. They mapped out routes that would take them away from America—to Setenil de las Bodegas in southern Spain, to the Algarve in Portugal, to Montenegro, to Albania. They talked excitedly and made love passionately.

Then the following morning over coffee, Eleanor had mused aloud about her favorite baby names. The words seemed to tumble out of her mouth—casually, spontaneously—incautiously. "I love the old fashioned names, don't you, Mark? Like Mary. Like Ivy. Like Amy. If we had a little girl...." Mark, looking stricken, interrupted, "NO. I DON'T WANT TO BE A DAD!!" Eleanor countered, "But you love dogs!" And Mark said "Well, that's hardly the same thing." And Eleanor said, "But if we settled down and got a dog, the dog could help take care of the kid. I mean we wouldn't have to raise her all by ourselves." And Mark said, "THE WORLD IS A HORRIBLE PLACE, ELEANOR. HAVEN'T YOU BEEN

PAYING ATTENTION? YOU NEED TO WATCH THE NEWS WITH ME! YOU NEED TO SEE WHAT'S HAPPENING! HUNGER AND VIOLENCE AND RACISM AND SCHOOL SHOOTINGS AND CLIMATE CHANGE. THESE ARE DESPERATE TIMES. I CAN'T BRING ANYTHING I LOVE INTO THIS WORLD. NOT EVEN A DOG. AND CERTAINLY NOT MY OWN CHILD."

Eleanor moved into the spare room that night to think things through. She agreed with Mark that this was probably not the best time to bring a baby into the world. But her longing for a child only increased in the days that followed. It's always that way. The more you deny yourself something, the more obsessed you become with securing it. Like being on a diet and, even though you never used to think about eating a Baby Ruth candy bar, now you can't think of anything else. But Eleanor was clear on one thing. She loved Mark. And she knew he loved her. That left her with only one option—she had to make the world better. And she had to do it fast if she wanted to be a mother. She was thirty-five.

Eleanor grabbed another Oreo cookie out of the bag in the cupboard and returned to the table. She giggled and said, "I froze another batch of my eggs yesterday at the clinic, Mark. Just so you know. My biological clock is eventually going to run down, of course, but I don't want to rush you. And I totally understand that we live in rotten times, but I am planning for any possibility. Because I have decided to be hopeful about the future."

She bit down on the cookie. Mark looked at her but resisted speaking.

"By the way," Eleanor said with a grin. "I call my eggs—'my caviar.' I told the nurse and she laughed."

Mark leaned in and kissed her on the lips.

Mark went to bed early that evening and had his recurring dream—the one where he was about to present a pitch to a new client and suddenly forgot everything he was going to say and just stood there flushing with humiliation, and then he realized he was 'buck naked too. He was relieved to finally wake up the next morning at 2:30 a.m. in time to shower and dress and literally drag Eleanor out of her bed in the guest room.

At 3:15, they entered the Day by Day Café and found the Rowlands had pushed two small, square tables together, placing the two lamps side by side at the seam. Bob Rowland stood as Mark and Eleanor approached. Susana Rowland smiled.

Mark said, "I want you to meet Eleanor. She is the love of my life." He said it matter-of-factly, but Eleanor almost gasped. Mark wasn't the kind of man who expressed his private feelings about her to anyone. He barely expressed them to her. He never even held her hand in public. But she knew he wasn't being facetious. He just wasn't that kind of man. Eleanor looked at Mark and noted that he was actually glowing with a serenity that revealed that he too had been going through some soul searching in the last couple of days. And he had decided that he loved Eleanor. It was written all over his face. Eleanor took his hand and gently squeezed it.

Susana said, "Lovely to meet you, Eleanor. Please sit here next to me. I ordered breakfast for all of us. Family style. Because we are going to be a family now. The Baby Honey family."

Mark caught a glimpse of himself in the mirror behind Susana's head. He looked tan. And handsome, surprisingly handsome, which freed him from all the nagging insecurities he usually had when he was forced to be around people. Once the food arrived, Mark began to talk. Over the next two hours, he laid out an advertising campaign that startled even him with its detail, originality, and sheer possibility. The Rowlands listened with rapt attention as did Eleanor.

"See...." Mark began. "The trouble with commercials is that if they are entertaining, the viewers forget what they're for. I mean, how many times have we all laughed at the one with the young bride and her father-in-law ... you know ... and then her kid sister is in the car eating the sandwich and wearing the hat ... you know the one?"

The Rowlands laughed heartily. Susana said, "Oh my goodness—that is Bob's favorite!" Bob chuckled, "It's true. I always make everyone stop talking when it's on."

Mark nodded, "So, Bob, in that commercial ... what is the product they are selling?"

There was a pause. Bob and Susana looked at each other. Bob said, "Uh ... the hat?" And Susana said, "No, Darling. They were selling lunchmeat." And Mark said, "Actually that's a commercial for deodorant." The Rowlands looked at him aghast. And Mark nodded, "Yes, it's true. That copywriter wasted his client's money. See, that's the danger. If your commercial is boring, people talk through it or go to the bathroom or to the kitchen for a snack. But if your commercial is too entertaining, people watch but completely miss the point. You walk a fine line if you're a copywriter."

Mark scratched his ear and continued, "So what's the solution?" The tone of his voice suggested he didn't know the answer. He inhaled and exhaled dramatically and then he said, "Before I lay out the new Baby Honey campaign in detail, let's talk money." Mark leaned in toward the Rowlands. "For a national campaign, for each individual sixty-second commercial to be on the air in enough major TV markets to saturate the country, we are looking at a minimum of a half million ... just for the airtime. Maybe a million bucks. And that's per each new commercial in the campaign. And we are going to need a lot of them to reestablish the Baby Honey brand. We have to saturate the airwaves in the beginning. It's going to cost a lot of money."

The Rowlands nodded. Mark went on. "But if it's successful, the potential to make a billion this coming year is in reach. I mean these baby clothes haven't been purchased outside of Alabama in sixty years. They are so retro ... they are forgotten. Lost to time. Which means they are poised to be new! Young couples with kids throughout the rest of the country will now look at the little sunsuits with the rickrack trim and the little yellow corduroy overalls with the stripey t-shirt and somewhere in the back of their brains, they will remember a photograph and think to themselves, holy smokes—I think my grandmother wore those in the '50s. Boy, I loved my grand-mother. She was way cooler than my mom. Where do I get these clothes for *my* baby? But we don't want to do nostalgia. No, no.... We want to wrap these clothes in twenty-first-century hipness. In fun. In youth! In sass!"

The Rowlands watched, wide-eyed. Mark continued, "See, we want to be unpredictable. And addicting. We don't want anyone to take their eyes off our commercials. Ever." Mark gulped his water and, feeling suddenly fortified with confidence, declared, "So I'm suggesting that we forego commercials altogether. As I've already noted there are too many risks. You write a conventional ad and peo-ple go to the can during the commercial and miss the whole thing. You write something clever and funny, and the audience totally for-gets the product. My plan bypasses all of these problems by not be-ing a commercial.

"Our vehicle for selling Baby Honey clothes will be a show, a real TV show, an actual situation comedy. Thirty minutes every week with a lovable, attractive young family. And a baby who wears Baby Honey clothes. Word will spread and people will tune in every week on the same day at the same time. Our target audience will come to us. And they won't go to the bathroom or the kitchen while it's on. They will watch it. And they will talk about it. And they will buy Baby Honey clothes, I promise you.

"And *The Baby Honey Show* won't cost any more than a whole campaign of individual Baby Honey commercials would cost. But it will be effective. How do I know? You ask how I know?" Mark stood now, kicking his chair back behind him. He raised his arms like an evangelist preacher and finished his pitch, "Because the time is nigh!"

Now every eye in the Day by Day Café was on Mark. Applause began to ripple through the room. Tears rolled down Bill's face as he smiled at the young man with the amazing plan to sell baby clothes. I, myself, sitting by the window, felt a lump in my throat. It had never been done this way before in the annals of advertising. Never ever. This was pure inspiration. And Bill and I understood that everyone in the café that morning was witnessing history. But more than that—this was magic. The magic of the Day by Day Café was back!

To be honest, Mark didn't know where this idea had come from. It was like he committed to it as the words came out of his mouth. Simultaneously. He certainly hadn't had this idea in the shower that morning and he hadn't had it on the short walk from his apartment. It just sort of fell into him the minute he entered the Day by Day.

Others inside the café would later report that there was something special in the air that morning. A frisson of excitement. They would remember how they had been unable to resist the urge to watch the carefully dressed young man accompanied by a girl wearing cut offs and red flip-flops enter and cross the room. Some of the patrons would later admit that they had eavesdropped and heard every word Mark said, but that their eyes had never left Mrs. Rowland's face. They said that she was actually glowing.

Bob Rowland now stood and announced, "You are hired, Mark Reynolds, advertising copywriter. We want you to create the Baby Honey television show!" Applause rippled throughout the room. The Rowlands had a quick whispered exchange and then stood again and said that they would be committing ten million dollars to the project on the spot—just to kick things off. Now the café patrons were on their feet. Some cheered. A few even joined the Rowlands and Mark and Eleanor at their tables and patted them all on their backs.

When Eleanor and Mark returned to their apartment later that morning, she tore off his clothes and attacked him. Lovingly. It was without a doubt the most amazing day of Mark's life.

Chapter 4 – Kip Barrett

On Friday, Eleanor and Mark had breakfast at the Day by Day. She and Mark held hands now whenever they were together. It was awkward during breakfast as it meant that Eleanor had to eat her scrambled eggs with the fork in her left hand. She was right-handed, but that was the hand that Mark always held now with his left hand because he was right-handed, too. She spilled a forkful onto her lap and finally let go of Mark's hand so she could cut her Canadian bacon. She was famished that morning. She ordered a double serving of the bacon to compensate for the pieces that had fallen to the floor.

When they finished eating, Mark set his laptop on the little table and set to work writing the pilot episode of *The Baby Honey Show*. Eleanor left the Day by Day but not before she took Mark's face in her hands and, in full view of everyone in the café, kissed him sensually on the mouth. "That's for luck. Have a great day." She then headed to the Dollar Store next to the café. She had an appointment with the owner, Mickey.

Eleanor was what one might call an habitué of the Dollar Store and over the past five years, she and Mickey had grown quite close. Early on they discovered that they shared a love of rock-and-roll music and French movies. And esoteric ideas. Furthermore, Mickey admired Eleanor's personal fashion sense which mixed high- and low-end accessories to such dazzling effect. Eleanor wasn't a conventional beauty but she had style and Mickey knew style. So, he never failed to hide something from the other customers if he thought Eleanor might put it to fabulous use. He always gave her first dibs. That's how she got the red flip-flops. And a long strand of multicolored plastic "pop-snap" beads that resembled the originals from back in the '50s.

Eleanor had called Mickey the night before after Mark fell asleep. She told him she was in immediate need of a large empty open space, something that could serve multiple purposes. Mickey said he had just the thing and told her that he would open his store early the next morning. They could meet there.

Eleanor entered the Dollar Store and embraced Mickey in a friendly hug. Then she brought him up to speed on the breathless developments in the Baby Honey project. She said that she and Mark were now in need of space for rehearsals and for meetings with TV executives. Mickey said, "Like I said on the phone, I have just the thing."

As it happened, Mickey not only owned the Dollar Store but owned the space beneath it as well. He led Eleanor down an aisle densely lined on both sides with rolls of cheap wrapping paper, curling ribbon, and brightly colored metallic balloons. Eleanor fought the urge to browse and stayed close to Mickey. At the back of the store, he unlocked a door and led Eleanor down a flight of stairs into a well-lit and spotless basement. She marveled at the large, empty, open space, the clean cement floor, the paneled walls. Mickey said, "They used to make movies here back in the Fifties. You ever heard of the Underground film industry? This is where it all began. They say Andy Warhol was an intern here when he was a teenager."

Mickey opened a closet door on one side of the large space and turned on an overhead light. "There's all this stuff, too." Over the next hour, Eleanor and Mickey pulled old lighting and sound equipment out of storage. Huge microphones wrapped in felt hung at the end of metal arms on large poles. There were shuttered lights suspended along other poles. Everything moved easily on wheels. Mickey said, "This stuff is pretty old. The new technology is much more compact." Eleanor replied, "But it's cool, Mickey. Just having it around will give the studio a very funky vibe."

Eleanor had Mickey draw up an open-ended rental contract for the space, and she signed it on the spot. Then Mickey said, "Not to be pushy, but my new girlfriend Sandy knows her way around a TV studio. She was a camera girl on an early-morning weather program in Duluth for several years. And if you know anything about Minnesota, you know it has weather—lots of it. She became quite adept at filming reporters during blizzards and tornadoes and even on the occasional nice day. Nothing throws her. Sandy can work spontaneously on the side of a highway or in a studio with a script. And she has her own cameras."

Eleanor said, "Introduce me." Mickey nodded and took out his phone. He quietly talked into it while Eleanor sorted through a shelf of new air fresheners. She selected one and bought it, dropping it into her large tote. She always bought something when she was in the Dollar Store.

Meanwhile, back at the Day by Day, Mark was struggling. He had never written dialog before and since the entire show was composed of dialog, he was paralyzed. He stared at his laptop screen. He had written the word ACTION so confidently at the top of the page. And then there was nothing. Mark knew what he wanted the story to be. He could see it like a little movie in his mind's eye. Mark had decided to base the characters on himself and Eleanor. Only they would be a more attractive version. And in the show, they would be married with a baby. Eleanor would like that part.

The actress who played Eleanor would have to have a perfect body though, better than Eleanor's—that's what television audiences in America demand–but she would have Eleanor's smile and sunny disposition which is what Mark loved most of all about Eleanor. They say that happiness is an aphrodisiac, that it is the crowning source of a woman's allure. And that was sure the case with Eleanor. Mark had fallen in love with her the first time he saw her laugh.

Mark sighed and stared at the laptop screen again. He closed his eyes and typed, *Darling, I'm home.* He envisioned his fantasy Eleanor walking through the door of the little house where Baby Honey lived. She would be breathtakingly pretty with a little waist and a heart shaped bottom that was apparent even under her polka dot sundress, the skirt of which would sometimes swing sideways when she was happy because she would twirl in a circle and that would make the skirt flip up. Then you could see her perfect plump thighs. And her lacy underpants. Mark swallowed hard. Then he typed *Darling? Are you here? I'm home!* The fantasy Eleanor would have a sweet voice and large brown eyes like Eleanor's that look at you with longing. With long lashes. And she would have full lips that were naturally red like strawberries.

Mark closed his eyes and visualized the next scene. Now an incredibly handsome man appears at the top of a stairway. Bare chested and wearing perfectly tailored jeans. Tan with chiseled features, really white teeth, and blonde hair. This fantasy version of Mark now descends the stairs into the foyer. He smiles a dazzling smile at the fantasy Eleanor. *Hi,* he says in his sexy voice. The fantasy Eleanor throws herself at the fantasy-Mark and they kiss wildly. Then they stagger to the couch where he powerfully lifts her onto the cushions and climbs on top of her. They look at each other with tears in their eyes, tears of love. CUT.

Mark sat back and tried to slow his heartbeat. He reread what he had written and then remembered that he had to get the baby clothes into the scene somehow. He had a sudden epiphany. The fantasy Eleanor *has been shopping that day* and has returned home with her arms full of shopping bags and boxes, all bearing the brand name Baby Honey. Yes, that's it! Fantasy Eleanor was shopping for their baby! And she would unpack the bags later after she and Fantasy Mark had finished screwing (off screen, of course) and were making dinner. A really healthy dinner. Like models eat—with a green salad and broiled lobster.

So, the baby clothes problem was solved. Mark could now write the entire pilot episode.

As he was about to resume typing, Mark felt a slight breeze and looked up. A young man had just entered the Day by Day Café. Every patron now turned to look at him. This young man was so astonishingly handsome, so spectacularly gorgeous that Mark was certain that he was a Ralph Lauren model who had somehow wandered off a runway, gotten himself turned around in a tangle of city streets and ended up at the Day by Day. His dark blonde hair was cut to look wind-blown. His sapphire blue eyes managed to be mysterious and friendly at the same time. He had chiseled cheek bones. Perfect lips and teeth. A powerful but graceful physique. Just under six feet tall. Mark figured him to be thirty-five—Mark's own age—in the prime of his youth. The young Adonis looked at Mark, and Mark immediately sensed something beyond his physical perfection. Mark sensed vulnerability. The young man actually seemed forlorn. It made him interesting. Mark stood up and beckoned him to his table. The young man dipped his chin shyly, slipped his hands in his pockets, and crossed to Mark's side. The two men shook hands.

"I'm Kip Barrett, Ralph Lauren model and..." He stifled a sob. "... former actor."

"Mark Reynolds, TV writer and producer."

Then unprompted, Kip began to speak of intimate matters. "I recently broke into commercials. I was finally on my way to a lucrative career as a professional actor with union benefits. But today I walked away from it all. I gave it all up for a woman! I'm ... I'm ruined." Now there were real tears in Kip's eyes. "But I'd do it all again." He blotted his eyes with a napkin.

Mark offered him a chair at the table. "You can tell me your story, Kip. I promise you I will understand. I, myself, walked away from a job on Wednesday. And it has turned out to be the best thing I ever did."

Bill arrived at their table with a fresh pot of coffee and a mug for Kip. He poured coffee into the mug and set it before the attractive young patron. Kip thanked him and took a sip. Then Bill quietly lowered himself into a chair at the table next to Mark as Kip began to talk.

"I know this girl. We had the same agent. She was a model like me but she was also an actor and a recent graduate of the Julliard School. You know the Julliard? It's really primo. You've got to be the best to even get in. Anyway, right after graduation, my friend was cast *on* Broadway! You know how crazy that is! Like she was immediately on her way! And at the same time, she was modeling. And I was a model. But we needed to do a TV commercial where TV producers would see us and put us on a TV series so that movie producers would see us and put us in a movie. And then we'd be set. We'd be on our way to international stardom and then even if we got old or fat, we could still work in England. You know?"

Mark nodded but said nothing. Bill murmured, "Uh-huh...."

Kip resumed. "Well, we both finally got a break. Six months ago, we were hired to do the Family Safe and Secure Home Alarm System commercial—the one with the zombies? I'm sure you saw it. It was a national."

Mark nodded and Bill said, "Wow, you were in *that*?"

Kip continued, "Anyway, the day of the shoot came and there were about a dozen of us playing zombies and my friend ... I'll call her Jill. That's not her real name but you know she probably wants to remain anonymous after what happened."

Bill said, "Sure."

"So anyway, Jill and I were Zombies. As I said, there were about a dozen of us on the set. And it was great, a really great shoot. Really long ... you know ... they can be long days. And hot cause we were dressed like zombies. Lots of makeup and wigs. But fun. Really fun! So anyway, at one point, we were on break, and Brenda coughed ... I mean Jill coughed. Shit!" Kip smacked his perfect forehead.

Mark patted his arm. "It's okay, Kip. We'll forget her name anyway. Just go on."

Kip sighed and continued. "See, Jill might have had a cold that day. Just a small cold. But she only coughed during the break. And I didn't even realize that she had a cold. I thought she just swallowed a hair. She was a model and that happens a lot with models. Anyway, so Brenda coughed.... GODDAMNIT! I MEAN JILL!"

"It's okay ... it's okay. Go on...."

Kip swallowed hard. "So, this is what happened. The commercial was a total success. It was so successful that the producer decided to do another Family Safe and Secure Home Alarm System commercial—a sequel if you will—with the zombies again. And everyone who was cast in the first one was hired back. Except for Brenda." Kip stood up and pounded his chest. "OH, FUCK ME! FUCK ME, FUCK ME, FUCK ME!"

Everyone in the café now stopped chewing. We all focused on the intense psychodrama playing out at Mark Reynold's table. Bill stood and rubbed the young man's shoulder, pressing him gently back down in his chair. "It's okay, Kip. Don't beat yourself up. We know you mean Jill."

Kip started to cry. He wiped his eyes on his napkin and sniffed, "So you know. Jill was like upset—she's like what happened? Why am I not getting called back for the Family Safe and Secure Home Alarm System zombie sequel? All the other zombies were. And she talked to our agent who called the producer and this is what he said, 'We don't want Br ... Jill. Because she's *sick* all the time.' SICK ALL THE TIME?" Kip jumped up out of his seat again. "SICK ALL THE TIME? THAT'S A LIE! SHE'S NOT SICK ALL THE TIME!"

Bill guided Kip back into his chair. Mark nodded at him sympathetically. Kip continued, "She's never sick, Mr. Reynolds. And for crying out loud, they only worked with her once so how would they even know and besides, she only coughed on the break! It's not like she interrupted the shoot. And I've known her for two years. She's never sick. She really isn't. That's why when I heard the cough when we were on break, I thought wow, Br ... Jill must have gagged on a hair. SHE'S A MODEL FOR CHRISSAKE!"

Now Kip sobbed openly. Deep heaving sobs. Mark watched the young man and his heart melted at the display of raw emotion. This kid made him think of a young Marlon Brando or a James Dean in his day. It is a fact that most men aren't comfortable with their feelings. Mark himself could never cry in front of strangers. He could barely cry alone in the shower. Oh, how often he had wished that he could cry. That he could feel that release. Let go of that stifling rigidity of the culture's idea of masculinity. Anyway, Mark knew in his bones that this kid should be an actor. Kip had the whole toolbox. Fabulous looks, devastating charisma, and boy, could he cry!

Kip blew his nose, sniffed, "Now here's the truly rotten part of the story."

Mark and Bill leaned in.

"Those producers told other people about the cough and the word spread through the whole industry—that Jill was sick all the time. Now she can't get work anywhere. Because everyone believed that lie. Those producers have ruined her career with a lie! And today they are shooting the sequel to the original commercial with all the original zombies except Brenda and me. Yes, I walked away in solidarity with Jill. I can't let these producers get away with being so casual with another person's reputation. I Hate Liars! Someone has to hold them accountable and it might as well be me. You know?"

Mark nodded. And Bill said, "You bet."

"So, I went on the set first thing this morning and, in front of everyone, I looked the producer in the eye and I said, 'You know, man, you're a lying piece of shit.' And then I said, 'And you can't have me in your commercial either. I have too much integrity.' And I'm the handsomest one they had. I hope losing me really burns them. I hope they learn something from this bitter experience." Kip blew his nose again and said "So, same as Brenda, now my career is over, too. And I didn't even cough. I was perfect." He wailed, "MY FUCKING LIFE IS OVER! BUT I LOVE HER!"

Mark looked around the café and noticed that everyone was still watching Kip, mesmerized; their forks, piled with scrambled eggs, stalled in midair. Mark thought *wow, I have to get this kid on camera. He's a dazzler.* He grabbed Kip by the shoulders and said, "Heck no—your life isn't over! Your life is just beginning! You, Kip, are going to play one of the leads in the brand new hit TV series—*The Baby Honey Show.*"

Kip looked up. "I've never heard of it."

Mark said, "You will. It's brand new. You are going to be the star."

Kip shocked everyone in the café by screaming an over-the-top whoop! Like he was at a football game. Then he grabbed Mark's hand and pumped it energetically. "Thank you, Mr. Reynolds." Then he looked at the ceiling and said, "And thank you, Universe, for giving me all my personal assets!"

Mark smiled warmly at the young man and said, "Furthermore I intend to hire Jill to play the other leading role. You will be together again."

Kip said, "Her name is Brenda."

And Mark said, "Oh that's right."

And Kip said, "You won't be sorry, Mr. Reynolds. Jill and I will pledge all of our personal assets to your service. I mean Brenda."

And Bill, who had seen so many miracles play out at the Day by Day over the last few weeks, was so overwhelmed with happiness at this one that he had to run into the kitchen and cry into a tea towel.

And me? I remained at the window, anonymous, writing hurried notes on my yellow lined note pad, so I wouldn't forget a single detail of this marvelous day at the Day by Day Café.

That night, back at their apartment, Eleanor and Mark talked excitedly over take-out Thai food. Eleanor gushed, "We have the cast. We have our own all-in-one rehearsal space and movie studio—courtesy of Mickey. And we have the camera operator, Mickey's girlfriend. Her name is Sandy and get this—she's a DREAMER, Mark. A real one. She was born in Guatemala, but sneaked into the United States by her parents as an infant. She didn't even know she was here illegally until she tried to get a driver's license at sixteen. I guess Minnesotans are super nice though and everyone has helped her and her family stay under the radar. Mickey figures that when Hillary Clinton gets elected this November, there will finally be a permanent path to citizenship for the DREAMERs. Then Sandy can go to NYU and get a degree in Photography which is one of *her* dreams. Mickey says she has a lot of dreams. And she and Mickey are totally in love."

"Look, Eleanor, I don't want us to run afoul of the Federal laws regarding who we hire. The Rowlands won't like that."

"Oh, Mark. Don't be so cold. Sandy is a woman without a national identity. Can you imagine how weird that would be? It's almost literary! We have to step up and protect her. I know Mrs. Rowland will feel the same way when I tell her."

"Why doesn't Mickey just marry her?"

"Because marriage is a big commitment. It has to be considered at length and these two have only known each other a short time. Besides, she's twenty-four and he's fifty-four."

"God...."

"But I don't think Mickey is bothered by the age difference. He's very youthful, you know. And he says she's mature for her age. And they are both film buffs. They have so much in common. I think they are meant for each other. Frankly, the only issue I can discern is that Sandy wants a baby." Eleanor looked at Mark and said, pointedly, "You know."

There was a moment of silence.

Then Eleanor remembered how excited she was about the Baby Honey contract with the Rowlands and she couldn't stay sad. A wide smile returned to her lips and she said, "Guess what else, Mark? Sandy has a good friend Roger who does sound recording for that station in Minnesota. She says he's a genius. And he's married to a textile artist—her name is Louise–I hired them both. They're on their way here from Duluth. This is going to be outrageously fun!"

Eleanor took a bite of her drunken noodles and chewed. She washed it down with a sip of beer. She grinned at Mark. "The way I figure it we have all our bases covered now. Mickey will help me design and build the set—we've been talking and we have some cool ideas. And Mickey will be great at helping you with the final edit. He's got a great eye. Louise can do props and costumes and any upholstery stuff we need done. Roger will do sound. Sandy on video and publicity photos. We have our leading man. Tomorrow we will meet our actress. You already finished the pilot script. You will direct it. And the Rowlands will provide the dough-re-mi! We're ready to roll." Eleanor dug down in her oversized tote and pulled out a can of air freshener. She stood and spun in a circle, spraying the room.

Mark said, "What's that?"

"Karma in a Can. I picked it up at the Dollar Store this morning. I couldn't resist." Eleanor read from the label. "It says this stuff 'will intensify the results of all your actions in this lifetime and bring you the destiny you deserve.'"

"I'm not sure I want what I deserve...."

Eleanor laughed. "And it comes in three fragrances. This one is called Catasophistry. Which means to outwit by deceit. How perfect is that for an ad agency?"

"Eleanor, we don't intend to deceive anyone."

Eleanor sprayed again. "Mmmm ... it smells nice, doesn't it? This will be our signature smell."

Mark sniffed the air and said, dreamily, "I hope our actress likes it. We get to meet her tomorrow. Kip says she's really pretty." Eleanor shot him a look. He quickly added, "And she's never sick."

Eleanor continued to study Mark's flushed face. He stammered, "She has to be pretty, Eleanor! She's going to be playing you in the show!"

Eleanor laughed and climbed onto his lap. "Well in that case, she better be a knockout."

Chapter 5 – Brenda Beacon

Brenda Beacon, professional actress, has an interview scheduled with Mark Reynolds, writer and producer of the nascent Baby Honey television series. She is to meet him at 5:00 a.m. at the Day by Day Café. Kip Barrett, a fellow-actor, had called her the night before and told her that Kip and Brenda were going to star in a new TV sit-com and all she had to do was "come and meet the producer who is totally nice." Kip had added that Brenda should probably wear something sexy.

Brenda appreciates the loyalty that Kip displayed when he stood up for her over the cough incident on the set of the Family Safety and Secure Home Alarm System national commercial, when she accidentally inhaled a loose hair that was hanging off her zombie costume. But Brenda is far less concerned about being left out of the sequel than anyone might imagine. She has her eyes on a bigger prize. Her acting career is but a means to that goal. Brenda Beacon feels destined to save America from itself.

So, while commercials are a bit of a step down for Brenda Beacon, she is perfectly cognizant of the national exposure a national commercial provides. Furthermore Brenda understands that had she not done the Family Safety and Secure Home Alarm System national commercial, she would never have met Kip, and he never would have set her up for an interview for a TV sitcom. Which could make Brenda Beacon a celebrity and a household name in America.

So while she isn't keen on doing a TV sit-com any more than she was keen on doing a commercial, she recognizes that it is clearly her destiny to do so. Therefore, she has agreed to the interview with Mark Reynolds this morning. Besides, she feels she owes Kip something for his loyalty. She wonders if Kip will be there. She summons a memory of his face.

Now Brenda realizes she's sweating. She blots her forehead, then she takes a second shower. No, she isn't nervous. Brenda doesn't get nervous. She is a formidably intelligent young woman, quite in command of herself. This flutter in her stomach is owed to something else. She dries herself carefully and her mind, once again, drifts. To Kip. His eyes, His voice. His shoulders. His.... She feels a sweet nausea travel from her stomach to her throat. *Am I in love?* she asks herself. *Is this what love feels like?* She has no way of being certain. She has never been in love before.

Brenda was in her late twenties when she entered the Julliard School in New York City, having already achieved a law degree and a budding career as a public defender in Argentina, her home country. She had grown up surrounded by luxury, but something deep inside her told her the world was unfair. Even as a small child she read history books and spent time with the elders, often posing piercing questions about the military junta that had terrorized her country in the years surrounding her birth in 1981. Many of the top brass were now in prison serving life terms. But they had been close friends of Brenda's parents at an earlier time. Brenda had seen evil up close and understood that it could look very ordinary.

As a teenager, Brenda exhibited a sober and single-minded discipline when it came to her studies. She seemed not to care about the usual delights of young girls. She had no close friends, she rarely attended parties. In spite of her ravishing beauty, she never encouraged the attention of any potential suitors. She graduated high school at sixteen, then attended university and obtained a degree in Political Science, graduating summa cum laude three years later, then entered law school where she also distinguished herself and again graduated in record time.

Immediately after graduation, she accepted a position as a public defender in Buenos Aires, the youngest public defender in the history of the country, and committed herself to vigorously protecting the rights of the accused, particularly those who were vulnerable due to their status in society. But over the next four years, Brenda made a disturbing discovery. Juries were increasingly unlikely to find facts and evidence persuasive. In fact, a defense based on drama and emotion was far more likely to get a defendant acquitted.

So Brenda decided to study acting in the certainty that it would make her a more effective lawyer. She immediately applied to the esteemed Julliard School in New York City and was accepted. The day after graduation, she was cast in a limited Broadway run of a new British play called *Yawn*. Reviews were good and Brenda was singled out by the *NY Times* as a "newcomer to watch." That resulted in her signing with an agent at William Morris and that led to a national commercial.

Now there was the possibility of a TV series. Brenda took the string of successes in stride. She was not one to get a big head. And she wasn't vain in the least. Beneath her creamy breasts beat a determined heart. She would stay true to her mission to become a star so that she could eventually return to the courtroom and dazzle the juries and win every case. She would do this in America. Because even in America, Brenda was surprised to discover, there were victims of vicious corruption, bigotry, and cruelty. Brenda would take on the vulgar and powerful. And America would embrace her. She would save America! And if you saved America, she reasoned, you saved the whole world. Brenda hasn't had the chance to mention the TV sit-com to her agent yet; she wonders if Kip has. They have the same agent although she always assumes that Kip's value as an actor is likely to fade as he ages and his incredible looks begin to be warped by the inevitable decay of the flesh. She assumes the same fate will befall herself in time. She thinks of her mother's wise admonition: "Looks are fleeting, but intelligence and curiosity will serve you all your life."

Of course, that presumes you don't get a brain injury or Alzheimer's Disease. Brenda would personally rather be disfigured by a random bomb attack than lose her mind which, in spite of her exquisite face and fabulous body, she considers to be her best feature. Therefore, because she might be falling in love with Kip, she will encourage him to return to college and attain advanced degrees so that he can be a professor someday. That will be something meaningful and satisfying to fall back on as he ages and becomes physically unattractive. Plus, taking classes will be good exercise for his brain. And it will make him interesting to talk to, which is important to Brenda during the times they aren't having sex. Which they will have often after they move in with each other. She pauses and allows herself to enjoy this vision of her future.

Now she dresses. Simply, in a navy suit with a white silk shirt, unbuttoned to the waist, revealing more than a peek at her bosom, unencumbered as it is by underwear. She buttons her suit jacket over the shirt but will release the buttons at some point during the interview with Mark Reynolds. She understands how the audition process works, and she knows that her breasts are just another tool in her toolbox.

Brenda had studied the French Revolution during her senior year of college. Her final paper dissected the solemn lessons of a society that allows the gulf between rich and poor to stretch beyond the limits of toleration. Brenda did not include a detail regarding Marie Antoinette's anatomy in that thesis. (She thought it might be regarded as frivolous.) Nevertheless, it made a lasting impression on Brenda. According to Marie Antoinette's personal diary, her "elegant breasts filled two Champagne coupes fully and to the rim, but no more." Upon seeing that in print, Brenda had retrieved two classic champagne glasses from her father's bar and, in the privacy of her bedroom, leaned over and placed her own breasts into them. She slightly overfilled them—but was nevertheless very close to perfection. That gave Brenda the confidence to attend the interview at law school the following week and wow the interviewers. Of course, she was immediately accepted.

Brenda applies no makeup to her face. She doesn't need adornment. Her dark eyes are naturally lined by a fringe of long lashes. Light bounces off her shiny, black hair. Her full lips are naturally red like strawberries. Her complexion is fair and unblemished, except when she has her period. And her cheeks are slightly burnished—a honey glow that seems to emanate from within her. Now Brenda faces the bathroom mirror and makes her daily vow to live a life of fidelity to America, to Justice, to Animals, to Poor People, and to … to what? What is the other thing? … um, the WORD! … the word she is seeking is … oh my god, she draws a blank. This isn't like her. WHAT IS HAPPENING HERE? She screams. OH MY GOD! WHAT IS THE WORD??? WHAT IS THE WORD???? She clutches the sink basin and moans and thrashes and wrestles with her brain. She cries. She begs the Universe for relief … it is on the tip of her tongue.… Exasperated, she finally falls back on her native Spanish, and there it is, tucked into a corner of her brain that she is no longer relying on. Honradez. Yes, that is the word. Honradez. Honesty. Brenda Beacon will be a Champion of Honesty.

It should be noted that Brenda Beacon isn't her real name. In fact, she doesn't know her real name. She was adopted by a well-to-do childless couple in Buenos Aires on a balmy day in February 1981, immediately following her birth. The couple gave her the name Julieta Christina Maria Raquel Elena Isabel Rosati Morales which included most of the names her adoptive mother had held in her heart as she tried and failed—year after year—to conceive. Within weeks, there was a christening at the Basilica y Convento de San Francisco in Buenos Aires and Baby Morales was introduced to the community of the faithful, among them many of the most powerful families in Argentina at the time. President-for-Life Videla and his wife attended along with his top generals. A celebration followed at the most expensive restaurant in the city.

It didn't matter and certainly no one had taken notice, but Brenda's birth mother had named her Camilia Alexis Rosa León Doran in the fleeting moment, the only moment, during which she had seen her infant. The mother had not held the child but had kissed her infant's cheek, deeply inhaling the primal smell of her baby. She had whispered, Mi bebé con piel como el miel—tan resplandeciente! Tan dulce! The nurse who carried the newborn out of the room, cuddled her close and repeated, "bebé con piel como el miel." Baby with skin like honey. But of course, Brenda had no knowledge let alone memory of her birth. And no one ever knew what happened to the birth mother.

When Brenda was ten, her mother confessed to her that she had been adopted at birth but that didn't faze Little Brenda. She was a wise child and having once seen a poster of Madonna wearing a shirt that said *Shit Happens*, she was prepared to engage with the zeitgeist of the late twentieth century into which she was born.

When Brenda moved to the United States at the age of 26, her first official gesture as a newly minted American was to change Julieta's name. She chose Brenda Beacon. It sounded optimistic. Of course, she will always be Julieta Christina Maria Raquel Elena Isabel Rosati Morales on the phone to her parents still living in Buenos Aires. But she only talks to them now on Sundays. They seem so far away but Brenda comforts herself with the fact that they are merely an hour ahead of New York City, in an adjacent time zone. Of course, that strikes her as surreal because in terms of the time on the clock in Brenda's kitchen, her parents are already living in her future. One hour ahead. *Oh my*, says Brenda to herself. *The world is so strange.*

Brenda stands outside the door of the Day by Day Café. It is three minutes before 5:00 a.m., Eastern Standard time. She considers pulling out her phone and making a last-minute call to her mother in Buenos Aires. She assumes that since her mother is living in Brenda's future time, she has already received a call from Brenda after the meeting that hasn't taken place yet in Brenda's time zone—so her mother is likely to already know the outcome of said meeting.

Brenda is nervous now. She hates not having control over every minute of her life. She comforts herself by thinking about atoms. She reminds herself that we, the people—every one of us—after billions of years—are still made up of atoms. In every country of the world. And in the Day by Day Café? Those people waiting to meet her? They are made up of atoms, too. It is the one thing all human beings have in common. In fact, atoms may be the only thing that Americans, in 2016, still have in common.

Brenda's thoughts return to her mother. Again she asks herself if she should ring her mother and ask, 'Did I get the job?' Knowing her mother, she will simply say, "Guess."

Brenda's hand tightens around the doorknob, she turns it and tries to calm herself. She inhales deeply and steps across the threshold of the Day by Day Café. She forces herself not to fixate on The Big Bang.

A group of people smile at her with welcoming eyes. One of them suddenly jumps out of his chair and calls out, "WELCOME, JILL!"

Brenda looks at him curiously. "Jill?" she asks.

Kip Barrett, who is sitting next to the man, rises from his chair now and says, "No, Mark. I told you.... Her real name is Brenda. Brenda Beacon." Kip smiles at Brenda and waves shyly. Brenda's cheeks turn pink with pleasure.

And Mark says, "Well, fuck me." Eleanor gasps, "Mark!" And then everyone, including Brenda, laughs.

Brenda kept her jacket buttoned throughout her entire meeting with Mark Reynolds. She liked him from the moment they met. She especially liked his girlfriend, Eleanor, so smart and stylish with a warm smile and an easy laugh.

Brenda and Eleanor fell into an intimate conversation in the Ladies' Room later that morning, when Eleanor announced that she liked to imagine that she could suddenly see everything in its basic construction—"as naked atoms." She said, "Wouldn't that be trippy, Brenda? Like there would be no separation between you and me. Or us and the air we are breathing. Or me and the sink or you and the paper towel dispenser. If we could only see atoms, my gosh—if we were all reduced to atoms—there would be world peace. We would all be One."

Brenda gasped in genuine amazement. "My goodness, Eleanor, I thought I was the only one who ever considered that. I find it reassuring to know that I have something in common with everyone I meet. Especially since I'm an immigrant." By the time, Brenda and Eleanor walked out of the loo and returned to their tables, they were soul sisters.

Over the next three hours, over a fabulous breakfast of cinnamon rolls, artichoke casserole, and fresh berries along with Bill's great coffee, the little company bonded. They took turns telling stories. Funny ones mostly. Kip and Eleanor excelled at funny stories. As did Mickey. Sandy was no slouch either and could mimic a riotously silly Minnesota accent. Even the usually reserved Brenda found it easy to relax in this company.

And so on that day, they all began the journey of knowing each other. And in the rosy lamp light of the Day by Day Café, they took those first steps towards building the deep trust among themselves that would fortify and protect them as they faced unprecedented evil in America.

I was there that day and every day going forward ... and backward ... for that is how stories unspool. Because I had long ago released myself from any ambition to make a personal impact on the world—I had embraced the French *être*-my role in all of this would be simply to watch. And to record. I would make every effort to refrain from inserting myself into the events that would unfold over the next two years. And I have tried not to editorialize. But I will add this caveat right at the outset. While I have never considered myself to be cynical, I would never have believed that a small group of people—let alone these people—would actually change the course of history. And yet, to my great surprise, that is exactly what they would do.

Chapter 6 – First Rehearsal

The first rehearsal of *The Baby Honey Show* began with a reading of the sparse script that Mark had labored over. Eleanor and Mickey had set up a long table at one end of the basement of the Dollar Store and the entire company gathered around it. Sandy introduced Roger, her sound technician friend from Duluth, to the Rowlands. There was no need to introduce his wife, Louise. She and the women of the *Baby Honey* company had quickly fallen into step when they were introduced by Sandy soon after she and Roger arrived one week ago. Louise had spent days scouring textile sources for fabrics to use on the set. And she and Mickey had scouted the best secondhand stores for lamps and bric-a-brac. Louise had used her personal stash of herbal dyes to color the cloth to surreal intensities. She finished the final stitching at six o'clock the morning of the first day of rehearsal.

I was invited to take notes for Mark as the company knew me through my association with Bill and the Day by Day. So I was there at the birth of the project, pencil and yellow pad in hand.

The reading of the script was flat and uninspired, but then Mark explained what he envisioned for the scene, and the improvisations began. The cast and crew moved to the other end of the basement, to the living room set of *The Baby Honey Show*, where one hundred percent of the action would take place.

This "living room" featured comfortable chairs upholstered by Louise in playful geometric patterns of cherry red, lime green, and warm beige. A large beige couch was covered in plump pillows in complementary tones. There were two standing lamps that looked like modern sculpture, and a vintage glass ashtray on the coffee table held brightly colored wrapped candies that seemed from a distance to glow like jewels. The two walls of the living room set were covered by a cheery print that Louise had hand-painted on the flats, mixing her own paints from her personal stash of dried roots. Finally there was a staircase on the set. And a gingerbread railing crafted by Eleanor that led to the upstairs bedroom. The effect was obviously Make-Believe. Like a fairy-tale cottage where happy endings abide. It was simply the perfect place for a perfect American family to reside. Just standing on the set transported one to a more innocent time.

Mark suggested that Kip and Brenda choose their own character's names. Kip chose Peter because he thought it was a cool name. And Brenda picked Julie—the name given to her by her parents. The baby was called Baby. So, it was established. They were Peter, Julie, and Baby Honey. The Honey family.

The relationship between the Peter character and the Julie character morphed quickly into a palpable fusion of lust and philia. Boy, could Kip and Brenda act! It was hard for the rest of the company to take their eyes off of the charismatic duo. First of all, they were both so beautiful.

With their perfect bodies and flawless faces, they had nothing to be self-conscious about. So, everything they did—the way they touched, the way they smiled and flirted with one another—seemed natural and private. They were unfazed by people staring at them; I guess when you're beautiful, you just get used to it.

As a result, a viewer would be given unspoken permission to stare at Peter and Julie Honey for thirty minutes every week and not feel the least bit icky about it. In fact, they would be relieved to get away from their own ordinary lives. They might even—at some point—find that they had projected themselves right into the scene ... actually taking the place, at least in their imaginations—of one or the other of the lovers. And boy, now they would find themselves experiencing the whole show as a rapturous daydream.

You the Viewer would now be the one who is beautiful and loved. And that feeling would stay with you for hours afterward. Even days. And you wouldn't resent Peter and Julie for being so perfect. You would be grateful that they were. You would love them all the more for their unblemished beauty and become addicted to seeing them every week at the same time. It would make you ignore the drabness, even the cruelty in the world, and eventually you'd find yourself feeling safe and happy whenever you thought of *The Baby Honey Show*.

Mark couldn't help but congratulate himself for casting Kip and Brenda. And he couldn't be faulted for anticipating big success for *The Baby Honey Show*. I mean seriously—who could look away from this? I know I couldn't.

Sandy started filming immediately, even while they were still just rehearsing, in order to capture this "lightning in a bottle." Sandy had pressed Mark to buy the latest innovations in cameras. They looked like Ring Video Doorbells—the kind that people attached to their own homes so that they could surveil the periphery of their property. Because these cameras were small and unobtrusive, they could be mounted right on the set of *The Baby Honey Show* and provide intimate views of the couple smiling and laughing and just looking at each other. Sandy controlled the cameras by moving her fingers over a computerized keyboard while sitting well apart from the action in a small glass booth that held several monitors on which she could track the scene. As a result, it was easy for Kip and Brenda to believe they were alone in their home. And that allowed them to respond to each other with sincerity. By the end of the first day, Peter and Julie were deeply in love. And soon Kip and Brenda would be, too. We all watched it happen.

Roger, for his part, started recording when we were still at the table. It was Roger's idea to put together a custom laugh soundtrack rather than buy something the other sit-coms used. Those laugh-tracks always sounded so forced and phony. Instead Roger gathered great tracks of the company laughing—at times convulsively—other times affectionately—always authentically. And he began to assemble loops of the recorded laughter that he could lay under episodes of *The Baby Honey Show* going forward. But Roger went one step further.

Roger took inspiration from the laugh-track of the all-time greatest sit-com, the 1950s classic, *I Love Lucy*. Which he had watched again and again and again with his grandmother who lived with his family when he was growing up. Roger loved the hilarity of Lucy's slapstick, but what really jumped out for him was the laugh-track on that show. Sure, every sit-com had a laugh-track back then—most still do—but *I Love Lucy* had a special ingredient that made their laugh-track stand apart from the rest.

At some point, in every episode, in the midst of uproarious laughter, there would be a pause, and then one would clearly hear a woman's voice say "uh-oh." The "uh-oh" was like foreshadowing, a heads up notice to the audience to pay attention—Lucy was in trouble again. Uh-oh! It was like a vocal exclamation point and it appeared in every episode. Roger would wait for it and clap his hands when it happened. He'd say, "Did you hear that, Nana? Did you hear the uh-oh?" And his Nana would say, "I sure did, Roger. I wonder what's gonna happen now." It was a brilliant device. It made it seem like the audience on the laugh-track was alive and in the room with you. It made you feel less isolated even when you were alone in your family room in the suburbs.

So, Roger decided to use the "uh-oh" for *The Baby Honey Show*, as homage to the greatest TV sitcom in history. He enlisted Susana Rowland to stand at the back of the basement during lunch break one day and say 'uh-oh." Over and over again. It was so cute how she did it with her Spanish accent. A little nod to Desi Arnaz. Roger put it on a separate track so he could amplify specific moments in each episode.

It was also Roger's idea to come up with a theme song for the show that would play at the beginning and end of each episode. Again, he reached back into the golden age of sitcoms in America. He was familiar with many of them, but *The Donna Reed Show* was hands-down his favorite rerun. He really loved the theme music. It was a pretty melody, optimistic and feminine.

Roger, as a white kid in a middle-class home in a suburb of Minneapolis in the 1970s, had won the childhood lottery in this life; that's for sure. His family was financially secure and his life consisted of school and baseball and steak every Friday night because that was his Dad's favorite meal. But his wife, Louise, close in age to Roger—they were both in their early forties now—had experienced the same time period quite differently. She grew up in a small town in Wisconsin—the child of a mixed-race couple, both intellectuals. Her family was tolerated but never fully accepted.

Not surprisingly, Louise was the smartest child in school—every year, every class. It further isolated her. Fortunately, she graduated from high school early which saved her from unending ennui. She was offered full scholarships at all of the Seven Sisters (Vassar, Bryn Mawr, Barnard, Radcliffe, Mount Holyoke, Smith, and Wellesley) but at the last minute decided on a small women's learning collective in a remote corner of northern Vermont. There, surrounded by fresh air and happy women, she studied textile art and midwifery. She outed herself before her family that Christmas as a Witch. They were happy to see her happy.

The following summer, she interned at an organic fruit-and-herb farm in Vermont, where she met a wonderful older woman named Vivian who taught her to make magic potions and infuse them into dyes for her textiles. And she introduced Louise to an affable and self-possessed young man named Roger. He was recording the daily sounds of the plants growing on the farm which he would someday gather into an album called *Earth Tones*.

Within the year, Roger and Louise married and moved first to New York. They hung out at the Day by Day Café for several months before meeting a man who offered Roger a job on a small TV station in Duluth, Minnesota. Roger became the sound man and, in his free time, recorded the storms in Northern Minnesota. Louise inventoried wildflowers and herbs along the shore of Lake Superior and set about inventing dyes that captured the iridescence of the blue jay's wings. As it happens, they were wrapping up their individual projects when their old friend Sandy called and beckoned them back to New York City and a job on a TV show. Not just any TV show, she assured them. "This one has potential."

So, Roger decided to option the theme song from *The Donna Reed Show* for *The Baby Honey Show*. He conferred with Louise first. "You think it's too Caucasian?" he asked her.

Louise laughed. "Oh Roger, who do you think is going to watch this show? Not Black people. Black people aren't going to buy these baby clothes. Black people aren't nostalgic for the 1950s."

Chapter 7 — The Baby Honey Show

*I*t was mid-September now and there were six episodes already "in the can." The company had worked tirelessly through the summer. Mark and Eleanor along with the Rowlands had met with network executives and offered to pay for network time for the first six episodes in order to give the show a chance to find its audience at no risk to anyone except the producers. One of the execs had said, "So this is like an infomercial?"

And Mark had adamantly responded. "No," he said. "This is a wonderful story about a beautiful, young family. America is going to fall in love with *The Baby Honey Show.*"

Since there was no risk for the network, the executives offered Mark a primetime family viewing slot on Friday evenings. The entire country would see *The Baby Honey Show* for the first time on Friday, October 7, 2016.

Three days before the show made its national debut, Mark arranged a preview at 5 a.m. at the Day by Day Café. Bill brought in some extra chairs to accommodate the overflow crowd, and a big, flat video screen was set up on top of the counter by the baked goods. I tucked myself into my usual window seat, and Bill distributed beverages and individual bags of popcorn to the assembled audience, mostly regulars, who had looked forward to this day all summer. Some had been in the Café that day back in the spring when Mark first pitched *The Baby Honey Show* to Susanna and Bob.

The café quieted as the lamplights were turned off and the big screen on the counter lit up. The sky, visible through the picture window, was still dark, and this block of 75th street was empty. It was 3:30 in the morning. The patrons inside the Day by Day applauded politely when the theme music began and the words *The Baby Honey Show* appeared on the screen. Then Julie (Brenda) walked through the front door. And the audience went nuts—clapping, whistling, cheering. The sounds in the room matched the recorded soundtrack on the show itself much to Roger's gratification.

```
The Baby Honey Show—Episode #1
         "Happy Days"

(JULIE enters and calls up the stairs.
Soundtrack: Cheers. Applause.)


             JULIE

"Darling, I'm home!"

(She carries three shopping bags that
feature the Baby Honey logo—a tiny
pink dress, flipped coyly on one side
to reveal tiny white ruffled panties.
JULIE puts the bags down on the coffee
table and turns toward the stairs just
as PETER appears. There is an audible
sigh of appreciation in the café and
on the soundtrack. PETER descends the
stairs. He is bare chested, in a pair
of designer jeans. He smiles at JULIE.
```

*She smiles at PETER. The camera lingers
on their eyes.)*

                    PETER

Wow, Julie ... I missed you.

                    JULIE

(Drops her eyes and smiles.)
I can tell.

*(The audience softly moans at their ob-
vious love for one another.)*

                    PETER

Hey, where's our Baby?

*(Delighted laughter on the soundtrack
is matched by the laughter in the café.)*

                    JULIE

Mother and Daddy asked if she could
stay with them for the night and I said
'oh, sure.' You know, Peter, how much
they adore Baby Honey.

                    PETER

So then ... we have the house to ourselves for the evening?

*(PETER arches one eyebrow like a car-
toon villain. JULIE giggles and blushes. Delighted laughter. Soundtrack: Uh-
Oh! More laughter. PETER walks towards
JULIE and takes her in his arms. They
start to kiss. Catcalls in the house and*

*on the soundtrack. Then JULIE holds up
a perfect hand, presses it against his
chest.)*

JULIE

But wait, Peter—I went shopping after
I dropped Baby Honey off at my parents.
And I have to show you what I bought
for our precious child.

*(PETER sighs. Laughter. Then he smiles
at her. She smiles at him. She reaches
into the first shopping bag and pulls
up a tiny eyelet pinafore. Soundtrack:
Murmurs of appreciation. The live audience follows the cue. Then JULIE
retrieves another in a different col-
or. Soundtrack: Excited gasps. JULIE
reaches into the other bags and keeps
pulling up the same eyelet pinafore
in yellow, white, pink, etc. The audience on the soundtrack is ecstatic
with surprise. Applause.)*

JULIE

Aren't these adorable, Peter? Can you
picture our baby in any one of these?
And they are on sale now for only
$34.99 each! *(Audible wows are heard in
the café and soundtrack.)* And, as you
can see, Peter, this dainty pinafore
comes in five colors. *(More applause.)*
Lavender, aqua, pale lemon, tea rose
pink, and white. I just couldn't make a
choice. You will have to choose, Sweet-

heart. Which one would you like to see
on Baby Honey?

*(JULIE drapes the tiny dresses over the
back of the couch, creating a pastel
rainbow display. She looks at her husband flirtatiously.)*

JULIE

Well?

*(Laughter. UH-Oh. PETER shakes his head
and rubs his chin.)*

PETER

Oh heck, I can't choose either. I guess
we have to keep them all.

*(JULIE squeals happily and twirls show-
ing her perfect thighs under a silky
skirt. A couple of wolf whistles, applause.)*

JULIE

Oh my gosh, Baby Honey will be the belle
of the family reunion picnic tomorrow!

PETER

"Come here, Darling."

*(They fall into each other's arms and
start making out. Their kissing is
lusty but natural—a healthy extension of
their joy at being the parents of Baby
Honey. They just kiss but the kissing
goes on for the next twenty minutes. No*

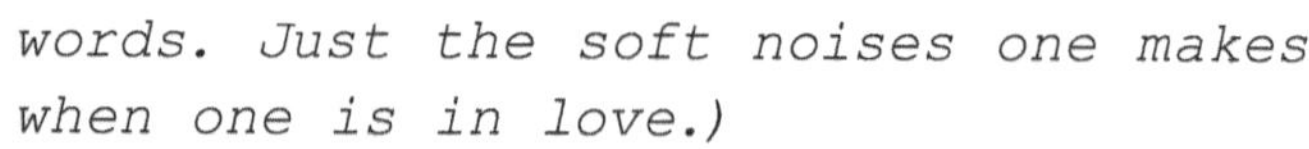

words. Just the soft noises one makes when one is in love.)

The patrons in the café are motionless; we watch the kissing in silence and seem to breathe in sync with one another. We are unaware of our surroundings. We are unself-conscious voyeurs. We are lost in daydreams of our own making. *For the entire twenty minutes.*

When the scene finally fades, and the *Donna Reed* music comes up, we look around sheepishly as we regain our sense of reality and realize where we are. Then we stand, as one, and applaud and stomp the floor and yell *Bravo!* Mark gathers the cast and crew and producers together at the front of the room. They take a deep group bow.

I have tears in my eyes. I have never been a part of anything like this. I feel like I have been accepted into a club and we have a shared primal experience. I am so exhilarated that when Bill begins pouring champagne and passing the glasses to everyone in the café, I accept one. I raise my glass and I down it in one long swallow. Yes, I broke my vow of sobriety. But I reason I was already intoxicated with *Baby Honey.*

Mark found a private moment with Eleanor. He nuzzled her cheek and whispered, "So … do you really think these people noticed let alone cared that Baby Honey never appears in the episode?"

Weeks before, at the end of an especially intense day of filming, Eleanor and Mark were lying in bed together, just settling into a much needed First Sleep, when suddenly she turned to Mark and said, "So you're never going to cast a real live baby to play Baby Honey?"

Mark said, "I didn't say never."

Eleanor rolled onto her side and looked him in the eyes. "Mark, don't you think the audience is going to think it's peculiar that there is no Baby Honey in *The Baby Honey Show?* We have several episodes in the can already and she hasn't appeared in any of them. Don't you think people are going to notice that?"

"No, I don't, Eleanor. To be honest, I don't think we need a real baby." Mark sat up now and said, "See I think the clothes suggest the baby. So, people will understand that the baby lives in the house, but has a busy social life. I think the audience will accept that the baby is wherever Peter and Julie tell us she is. At her gramma's or at the baby gym or at the movies with the babysitter. See Eleanor, this is right out of Advertising Copywriting 101—you just suggest and the audience does the rest. I'm letting them fill in the gaps. It helps the audience personalize the experience so it is reflective of their own lives and specific to their personal desires. Besides kid actors are awful—stiff and unnatural … fake sweet...."

Eleanor shook her head. "That's not true, but it doesn't matter. Our baby would be a real baby. She wouldn't have lines. She'd just act naturally."

"Yeah, well, that's a separate problem. Real babies are too real. They would make everything else in the show look fake."

Eleanor raised an eyebrow. "Mark, the show does look fake. That's the idea. It's a fairy tale."

Mark put his arms around her and held her. "Let's do it my way, El. Trust me. I know this is going to work. But if it doesn't, we can always cast the baby later. Like maybe in Season Two."

"I want a baby, Mark."

"I know, El."

On Friday evening, October 7, 2016, *The Baby Honey Show* debuted on NBC. A strange event had occurred that morning, an event that had absolutely nothing to do with Mark, Eleanor, Kip, Brenda, Susana, Bob, Mickey, Sandy, Roger, or Louise. This event furthermore had no connection whatsoever to the first episode of the show or *The Donna Reed* theme song. But this event would cause *The Baby Honey Show* to have the biggest national audience for a sit-com debut in the history of American television.

Chapter 8 – Uh-Oh

As dawn broke over the city of New York on Friday, October 7, 2016, the waxing crescent of the Hunter's Moon was six days into its monthly journey. It hung like a platinum scimitar in the still dark western heaven, then calmly ceded the sky to the rising autumn sun. Everything was hushed. It was 6:30 a.m. Mark and Eleanor had been awake since 3 and now, after an early breakfast at the Day by Day Café—of steel cut oats with cinnamon-dusted raisins—they strolled arm in arm toward their apartment on W. 77th Street. They talked softly in phrases, as they were too anxious to form whole sentences. There was something strange about the day and it was just getting started.

When they arrived back at their apartment, Mark turned on the TV and settled into the couch to wait for the *Today Show* to begin. Eleanor sprayed the room with her karma air freshener—Catasophistry—the one she bought last spring at the Dollar Store. She was on her second can. She insisted that it was bringing them luck.

Normally Mark and Eleanor didn't watch TV during the daytime, but that morning Brenda and Kip were being interviewed by

Matt Lauer on the *Today Show*. *The Baby Honey Show* would have its national debut that night.

Outside of the Day by Day Café, there had been little publicity about the show, almost no buzz at all. Over the summer, Mark had tried to engage a reporter at *The New York Times* to do a story, but he never returned Mark's calls. Neither did the reporters at *Rolling Stone*, *New York* magazine, or *Vanity Fair*. Mark had one connection at NBC, but he sold airtime for commercials and couldn't help them with publicity.

But the Rowlands knew an executive in the Creative Division at the network and pressed him to provide a promotional opportunity for the new show. Bob Rowland met with the fellow and successfully argued that despite the fact that NBC wasn't producing the show at that point, it had an interest in helping *The Baby Honey Show* succeed. The show was after all in a key position to help the rest of the Friday night NBC lineup. So, at the last minute, Kip and Brenda were offered a brief interview with Matt Lauer, one of the hosts on the venerable *Today Show*.

Eleanor joined Mark on the couch and squeezed his hand as Matt Lauer introduced the stars of *The Baby Honey Show*. The camera pulled back and there they were—Kip and Brenda, sitting beside him. Lauer visibly struggled to keep his eyes off the stunning Brenda, but feigned excitement about the sit-com and turned to Kip to ask what viewers could expect when they tuned into the debut of *The Baby Honey Show* that evening. Kip furrowed his brows and leaned forward on his stool. Looking every inch the Ralph Lauren model, he had been, he focused his sapphire blue eyes on the camera and said, "Well, Matt, I guess I'd have to say that it's mainly about a family with a mom, a dad, and a baby who visits her gramma a lot, and they all love each other a ton." There was a pause as Lauer waited for Kip to continue. Kip didn't.

Lauer turned to Brenda who laughed and shrugged, and said breathily, almost seductively, although I don't think that was her intention, "Yeah ... it's about love." Lauer's eyes widened. He said, "Wow, that sounds great!" The *Today Show* broke for a commercial and Lauer followed Brenda to her dressing room. He asked her if she'd like to have dinner with him that evening and she said no.

Back in the apartment, Eleanor sighed. "Well, that was ... okay." Mark turned off the TV and kissed her cheek. "I'm going back to bed," Eleanor stretched and said, "I'm going to take a nice long soak in a bubble bath and then I will join you." It was 7:45 a.m.

At 11:10 am, Eleanor and Mark were awakened by the phone. It was Mickey. He was screaming. "HOLY SHIT! PULL UP THE WASHINGTON POST! LOOK AT THE HEADLINE! THAT DUMB SON-OF-A-BITCH TRUMP? HE'S FINALLY MET HIS WATERLOO!"

There had been a continuous stream of news about Donald J. Trump over the past year and a half, beginning the day in June 2015 when he rode down his golden escalator at Trump Tower accompanied by his snake-eyed wife and announced he was running for President of the United States because Mexicans were drug dealers and rapists and they were overrunning America. From that moment on, this carnival barker dominated the airwaves, social media in every form, and everyday discourse between people all over the planet. There had never been such a figure in American politics. For one thing, he was a moron.

Of course, Trump would always insist that he wasn't a moron. He would insist that he was a genius, despite the fact that everything he touched went bankrupt sooner or later. Mostly sooner. Trump Steaks. Trump Water. Trump University. Trump Vodka. Trump Casino.

Etc. Etc. Etc.

He also insisted that he was a great dancer. He liked to show off for his fans at campaign rallies. He would stand stiffly on the stage and swing his arms side to side trying to keep the beat to *Rockin' in the Free World*. That sight had provoked Neil Young to insist that Trump stop using his music, but Trump ignored Neil Young's demand along with the complaints of every other artist whose music he used without permission. "So, sue me," Trump would sneer. And when they did, he'd sue them back *for suing him*. And he got away with it, because in the end, sane people would rather cross the street than deal with him. So Trump used *Love Train* by the O'Jays, in spite of their protests, and introduced some new moves that became his signature dance at rallies. He punched the air in front of him with his little fists, alternating a robotic thrust. He threw his head back, closed his eyes, and bit his bottom lip. Trump thought it made him look sexy.

Here are the facts: Trump was a fattish guy in a poorly tailored suit, ridiculous shoulder pads, an overlong necktie, and face makeup the color of egg yolk. His eyes were reptilian and his hair, a Crayola yellow comb-over, started at his neck on one side and floated over his crown. On a windy day it stood straight up and stiffly cha-cha-ed. He cheated at golf, he cheated on his taxes, he cheated on his three wives and he enjoyed fantasizing on Howard Stern's radio show about sex with his adult daughter. He was famously cheap, famously litigious. He made fun of the disabled and was dismissive of the country's fallen heroes. He had faked a bad foot to get out of being drafted during Vietnam and didn't deny it. He was suspiciously infatuated with Putin, and he was a fabulist who lied with the steady regularity of a metronome. Oh, and he had terrible body odor.

New Yorkers loathed him—they'd had him around for years and were tired of his act. But the rest of the country was just getting a load of this guy, having been introduced to him on an insipid television show, wherein Trump interviewed wannabe celebrities and then gleefully fired them. This amused a certain class of Americans who had built up a reservoir of resentment for successful people who worked hard and played by the rules. Twitter and Facebook fed these fans a steady stream of Trump stories. Flattering, not flattering—it never seemed to matter. What would soon become apparent was that half of the country wanted to elect a president who was a vain, mean-spirited, insecure bully, looking to settle old scores.

It was hard to fight back against Trump's crass cruelty. Nothing seemed to shame him. Until the morning of October 7, 2016. A story appeared on the front page of the *Washington Post* newspaper, complete with a link to an audiotape that had been created eleven years earlier in 2005. It featured Donald J Trump on a private bus accompanied by the co-host of *Access Hollywood* at that time—Billy Bush—who coincidentally was related to two former Republican presidents. The men were sitting in an NBC parking lot waiting for a soap opera actress, who would escort Trump to the set of *The Days of Our Lives*. Trump was scheduled to make a guest appearance that day, playing himself.

The camera crew and sound technicians had exited the bus and were setting up to capture Trump's meeting with the beautiful actress. Inside the bus, Trump entertained Billy by bragging about how much he enjoyed sex with married women—not to include Melania, of course. Billy giggled like a twelve-year-old. The entire conversation was recorded because both men were wearing microphones and the mics were hot. The tape was so shocking, it was immediately buried by *Access Hollywood* as well as by NBC—but it was never destroyed.

They say that in the years that followed, pirated copies of the tape passed among sound technicians throughout the city of New York. They say that every Christmas, the Sound Technicians Union in New York City hauled one out and played it as part of the entertainment at their annual holiday party. So, it might have been a sound technician who dug a copy out of his own sock drawer eleven years later and handed it to *the Washington Post*.

There was no doubt a fevered debate among the editors at the *Post* as to whether it should be made public. But times being what they were, they soon agreed to "run with the story." A transcript with a link to the full audiotape was the lead story of the *Washington Post* on Friday, October 7, 2016. Just one month before the election. And as they say, the story took wing.

It shoved every other news story off the radar of America. It broke into the daytime cooking shows on TV and saturated social media. It was picked up by every news source in the world. There was no escaping it. By noon, all of America was fixated on the *Access Hollywood* Tape, as it would be called. Millions of people listened to the tape on computers at work, on cell phones while standing in line at the grocery store, on televisions in their living rooms, and on large screens in airports around the world. Republican congressmen, senators and governors wrung their hands. American diplomats were mortified for their country as the news spread to our allies and enemies around the globe. This is what everyone heard the 2016 Republican candidate for President of the United States say:

I moved on her actually …

I did try and fuck her, she was married …

I moved on her very heavily … I moved on her like a bitch …

Then all of a sudden, I see her; she's now got the big phony tits …

I better use some tic-tacs just in case I start kissing her. You know I'm automatically attracted to beautiful … I just start kissing them. It's like a magnet. Just kiss. I don't wait. And when you are a star, they let you do it.

You can do anything.

Grab them by the pussy.

You can do anything …

And so it was that so many American TVs were still tuned to NBC that evening of October 7, 2016. Maybe shell-shocked Americans were too stunned to turn off their sets or maybe they were relieved to hear the sweet opening trill of *The Donna Reed Show* theme music. Whatever the reason, a record-breaking number of Americans watched *The Baby Honey Show* that night in its entirety. And as they did, they relaxed. They smiled as the beautiful young man and his exquisite wife flirted with each other, and spoke so thoughtfully to each other, with such respect and regard, and held one another with genuine affection and kindness. Americans forgot about the awfulness of the day. They told themselves—this is the way we really are. We are good and moral and loving. And decent. And if we aren't as perfect right now as we know we can be, this half-hour TV show offers a reminder of what American men and women always were and could be again. Because we are exceptional, and now is the time to make America great again.

Maybe that is why the audience for the first episode of *The Baby Honey Show* was the largest audience for any show in the history of television programming. It even exceeded the audience that tuned in to watch the *Apollo 11* Moon landing in 1969. Approximately 150 million people had watched Neil Armstrong bounce on the moon, but *The Baby Honey Show* drew an audience of 200 million. More or less accidentally. Maybe that is why Trump's political career survived. We were all distracted.

Act Two

Chapter 9 — Susana Rowland

Monday's Child is fair of face.
Tuesday's Child is full of grace.
Wednesday's Child is full of woe.
Thursday's Child has far to go....

Susana Rowland, longtime resident of New York City's swanky Upper West Side and adored wife of Bob Rowland, was born on a Thursday in 1955 in Buenos Aires, Argentina. Her mother, Noeme, was likewise born on a Thursday but took her first breath in Rome, Italy, in 1930. Noeme's mother, Susana's grandmother, Amandine, was born in Madrid, Spain. On a Thursday in 1910. And Susana's great grandmother, the mother of Amandine—Eugenie was her name—was born in Paris, France, in 1878—also on a Thursday.

I would not be surprised to discover that every woman in Susana's direct line going back a millennium at least—maybe longer—was born on a Thursday. For this was a family that was uprooted often and traveled far. They were Jews and the hatred toward Jews is as old as Christianity itself. Through no fault of her own, Susana was born to be a refugee.

Susana, however, had the extreme good luck to be born *the day of a Full Moon* which is well known to endow a human with superior endurance. So, she, unlike the other women in her family, had survived into old age. She was sixty-one now in this year 2016. She was in excellent health, still beautiful by any standard, a successful businesswoman, beloved by her husband and friends. There had been terrible trauma in Susana's younger life and pain so delirious that for years she refused to let herself sleep for fear she would re-experience it if she didn't remain vigilant. But time, while not actually healing, did eventually harden a part of her heart. At least she no longer cried. And she no longer bargained with God. Truth to tell, she pitied Him.

She read somewhere that God, having lost His way, was looking for a pristine human soul to teach Him how to be godly. Susana would, in time, consider the possibility that such a soul might exist. And that it could be the best hope for the world if a person lived who was unscarred by the coarseness and cruelty that proliferated throughout the human race. It was a long shot, but Susana wouldn't rule it out. She likened herself to Robinson Crusoe, who, having been swept ashore on an island—and thinking himself forever alone in the world—sees a human footprint in the sand and sets off in search of the subtle impressions its soul may have left in other creatures. In this way, Susana kept herself open to hope.

Now, with your indulgence, dear Reader, I will provide a short survey of the history of Jewish persecution in Europe since the Middle Ages. It is absolutely necessary to confront the savage cruelty of which human beings are capable, when they believe themselves to be acting in the service of their Cult, if we are to truly understand America in 2016.

Susana's family had ancient French roots, so that is as good a country as any in which to begin the story of their odyssey. There is no record to indicate how long they had been living in France, but it is known that during The First Crusade, around the year 1096, the Holy Knights in their unholy zeal unleashed a storm of hate-filled violence against the Jews in cities along the eastern border of France. Jews were accused of "Blood Libel"—a conspiracy theory that has popped up repeatedly through the ages, recently reemerging on YouTube in time for the 2016 presidential election in the United States. It asserts that Jews kidnap Christian children and ritually murder them to use their blood in their Passover rituals. Anyway, Susana's ancestors were forced to leave France sometime around the beginning of the twelfth century. They ended up in England.

During periods of calm, the Jews, who were diligent in their studies, and industrious in the application of their skills, contributed significantly to the economic, intellectual, and artistic life of Europe's great nations. But during times of scarcity—inflation, drought, the mismanagement of city budgets, the overextension of the treasury by a war-happy king, whatever the reason—when the cash in the coffers ran short, the Jews were always blamed.

Even in the best of times there were spasms of inexplicable violence against Jewish communities. The carefully cultivated Otherness of the Jews in Christian Europe made them a convenient target for any latent barbarism in the local populace. A way to let off steam from time to time. And in the twelfth century, the quaint custom of having Jews wear a six pointed yellow star—by which they could be identified and shunned—gained popularity in certain countries. And was never completely abandoned.

Susanna's family was expelled from England in the Jewish purge of 1290. They settled in what is now Belgium and, in 1347, were blamed for the Black Death that was engulfing Europe. In 1370, six Jews were burned at the stake and most of the rest of the Jewish community was massacred. The few survivors threw in the towel. One of them was a female ancestor of Susana. She fled to Portugal and gave birth to a daughter—undoubtedly born on a Thursday—who then had to flee again in the 1400s and ultimately ended up in

Spain where a diverse population of Christians, Moors, and Jews lived in relative harmony until....

In 1478, King Ferdinand and Queen Isabella demanded that all Jews and Moors convert to Christianity. The monarchs were especially apprehensive about the increasing prosperity of the Jewish population. Their majesties issued a proclamation: any Jew who refused to be baptized would be subjected to brutal torture and death. Many Jews immediately cooperated, but even those who voluntarily converted to Christianity were tortured to death just in case they were faking their love of Jesus. In 1492, as Christopher Columbus embarked on his journey to a brand new world, a sad caravan of frightened Jewish refugees—men, women, and children, Susana's ancestors among them—fled Spain and dispersed throughout the Continent looking for a home.

Susana's ancestor headed to Florence, Italy—where it was understood that a Renaissance Enlightenment overseen by the powerful and cultured Medici family protected the Jews in that fair town. It was true that many Jews flourished in Florence at that time, enjoying special privileges and protections not available to Jews in other cities in Europe. But in 1569, the Roman Pope got involved and the Jews were refugees again. They fled Italy and settled in the Netherlands. They were soon expelled. They fled to Scotland and were driven out of there. They fled to Paris, a homecoming of sorts after almost 900 years of exile.

And that is where Susana's Great Grandmother Eugenie was born on a Thursday in 1898. Right in the middle of the Dreyfus Affair. Dreyfus was an officer in the military, a Jew, who was falsely accused of being a traitor. He was eventually absolved, but the long-simmering anti-Semitism—which had always been a feature of French life—had been brought back to boil. France was not safe for a Jew. So young Eugenie and her parents were once again on the run.

They retraced their ancient steps now, returning to Spain where they found peace and prosperity in beautiful Andalusia. Eugenie grew up, married, and, on a Thursday, gave birth to a daughter that she named Amandine. Alas, the peace didn't last. When Amandine was ten years old, she witnessed the slaughter of her family by a

Christian businessman who suspected that the Jews were stealing his clients. His rampage spared only Amandine, who was ferried to safety in Italy by a sympathetic priest and deposited into a Jewish ghetto in Rome. There, she came to adulthood.

World War II. Hitler in Germany. And in Italy—Benito Mussolini. Mussolini's long-time mistress was a Jewish woman so the Jews assumed that they could ride out the rising wave of anti-Semitism in Europe by keeping their heads down and their feet firmly planted in their Roman ghetto. But four years later, in 1938, Mussolini dumped his Jewish lover of twenty-seven years, and, in short order, passed his infamous racial laws. The persecution of the Jews in Italy began.

Amandine had grown into a woman by this time and was now a mother herself. Her teenaged daughter, Noeme, had been portentously born on a Thursday, so they kept a packed bag under the bed at all times. Amandine considered seeking refuge for herself and her daughter in the United States but heard the story of the 900 German Jews who were refused exile in America in 1939 after sailing across the Atlantic to escape Hitler's reach. Many on that boat were children. Nevertheless, President Roosevelt refused to respond to their desperate cables and the ship was turned back to Europe. The passengers were turned over to the Nazis. I'm sure you can imagine their fate.

So Amandine and Noeme returned to France, hoping to find safe harbor among a few old, Christian friends who still lived there. But by this time, Nazi sympathizers among the French were openly collaborating with the German occupation forces in Paris. These traitors would serve as catspaws to the soldiers of the Reich until the end of the war. Even in the final days, when Germany was already defeated and the German army was retreating back behind its own border, these French collaborators forced 30,000 French Jews onto trains that carried them to Auschwitz, the infamous Death Camp, where they were murdered before they could be rescued by the approaching American troops. Amandine and Noeme escaped that fate but were afraid to stay in France. This time they headed to Poland and watched with relief as the American GIs finally arrived with their smiles, cigarettes, and chocolate.

Not surprisingly, the end of the war in Europe created mass confusion as millions of uprooted people attempted to find their way back to their home countries. Curiously, one group of refugees were the "ethnic Germans" who, with the encouragement of Hitler, had moved into Poland after it was conquered by German troops early in the war. Their mission was to colonize, actually "Germanize," Poland so that it could be quickly assimilated into Deutschland.

Now the war was over and Hitler was dead. The Poles rounded up these German nationals living among them and forced them out of Poland. But, for reasons that aren't clear, Germany refused to take them back. So these Hitler-loving people had to find a new home far away from Europe. They made their way to Lisbon, Portugal—a port town on the Atlantic Ocean—where they boarded ships that would take them to Buenos Aires across the sea in the South American country called Argentina.

Noeme was now twenty years old. She was a passenger on one of those ships. A refugee Jew, surrounded by refugee Nazis, who treated her with unexpected kindness. Perhaps they had tired of war and the ecstasy of white supremacy, their bloodlust sated for the time being. Noeme traveled alone; her mother had kissed her goodbye at the dock but refused to accompany her on this trip. Amandine could not bring herself to start over again. She was fifty years old now. She returned to Italy and died a year later. She was Noeme's last remaining relative.

Noeme settled in Buenos Aires and soon after met a native-born Argentine, a handsome Jewish man named Abraham León who was a professor of business law at a local university. She married him and, on a Thursday in 1955, during a full moon, gave birth to a little girl, their only child. They named her Susana Eliana Fermoza Viva León. Yes, she would one day be Susana Rowland.

There is much more to her story. However we don't want to lose sight of the events unfolding in 2016. Not the least of which is the election of Donald J. Trump as America's 45th president. Oh, and *The Baby Honey Show* is about to receive its first fan letter.

Chapter 10 – A Fan Letter

I t's December 10, 2016. Eleanor and Mark are having dinner at a little Italian place on West 81st Street. Nothing fancy. Candles and wine and good cacio e pepe. They like the owner, a heavy-set young man named Cassius, who was born and raised in Rome, Italy. He knows what he is doing when it comes to cacio e pepe, that's for sure. It blows Eleanor's mind that mere water, grated Romano, and black pepper can make a sauce that creamy. She always orders it and, after the first bite, inevitably announces that she "still can't believe that water and Romano and black pepper can make a sauce this creamy!" Tonight, she hugs herself and adds, "It's like alchemy, Mark—like turning metal into gold was to the ancient people. Except that Cassius is successful in *his* endeavor. This stuff *is* gold!"

Mark laughs. "You are your mother's daughter, Eleanor. Always going for the most immoderate metaphor." Mark orders his usual—the pork medallions. He notes that he and Eleanor seem to be settling into predictable patterns of behavior. Dinner at six. It's nice. He welcomes routine. He is going to ask Eleanor to marry him. He will surprise her with a diamond ring on Christmas Eve if he can keep from spilling the beans earlier.

As already noted, the food was good at Cassius's place, but the real appeal of eating in the little restaurant—at least for Mark—was that a patron could order dinner at dinner time. Dinner was Mark's favorite meal. Interestingly, the Day by Day Café had recently added a new chef named Jacques who expanded the menu to include a daily dinner plat du jour, but it was served between the hours of three and eight in the morning.

Bill, the owner of the Day by Day, had met Jacques, a handsome African man from Senegal, through a mutual foodie friend. Jacques had studied cooking in Paris and had come to America just eighteen months before. He had been hired to work at a high-end French brasserie on West 59th Street. But within a month of arriving, Jacques discovered American comfort food and became totally infatuated with recreating the recipes. He left the brasserie, got employed at a diner on Broadway and gained forty-six pounds over the next year. Soon after that, he met Bill. It was love at first sight for each of them. Bill thought Jacques looked like a Black Pavarotti. And Jacques thought Bill looked like Clint Eastwood in his prime. Just before Thanksgiving, Jacques moved into Bill's apartment and, soon after that, he became the co-chef at the Day by Day Café.

Jacques expanded the menu, adding hearty fare. Meatloaf and mashed potatoes with a side of steamed broccoli. Macaroni and cheese with a side of southwestern chili. Shepherd's Pie and Tater Tots. All served between three and eight in the morning. Word spread. Jacque's offerings were an immediate hit; the café was filling up every morning. It seemed now that everything the *Baby Honey* Family touched was successful.

But I digress. Let's return to the evening of December 10, 2016. Cassius Restaurant, West 81st Street. New York City. The tables are all occupied but the place has a breathless quiet about it. Mark and Eleanor face one another across a checkered tablecloth. Mark looks deeply into her luminous eyes. If he squints he can see his own eyes reflected in the pools of her irises. Mark is feeling a serenity he has never known. He is now a man with an extravagantly successful TV show, the woman of his dreams by his side, good friends. Every dream has come true. He turns his head to look out the window. Plump snowflakes land gently on the moon-colored sidewalk. First snow of the new winter. Two weeks until Christmas.

Eleanor interrupts his reverie. "Speaking of my mother, she told me on the phone this morning that she saw a kid at the mall last weekend that looks just like Baby Honey. Seriously, Mark. That's what she said. And she emphasized, 'Spittin' image!' That's what she said, Mark! Baby Honey is 'the spittin' image' of some little girl at the Eastwood Towne Center shopping mall in Lansing, Michigan." Eleanor purses her lips.

Mark laughs. "Oh wow! That's amazing, Eleanor! It means my theory is working!"

Eleanor continues, "I said, 'Mom! We haven't cast the baby yet. You can't know what she looks like. *We* don't know what she looks like.' And Mom says, 'Oh you're such a know-it-all, aren't you, Miss Hollywood Elite.' And I said, 'I'm in New York, Mom. Not Hollywood.' And Mom said, 'I rest my case. You think you know everything.'"

It was a fact. *The Baby Honey Show* was a phenomenon right out of the gate. It had dominated the ratings since its debut nine weeks ago. Furthermore, sales of *Baby Honey* products were off the chart. Media critics fell all over themselves trying to explain the appeal of a show about baby clothes and two people kissing. Mark claimed to understand and he once again laid out his theory. "Look Eleanor, it's simple. It's Copywriting 101. You provide the viewers with a blank canvas with just a few details and that allows them to paint any scene they want. They watch Kip and Brenda—excuse me, I mean Peter and Julie...."

Eleanor whispers conspiratorially. "They've moved in together. Did you know that?"

Mark looks momentarily crestfallen, but quickly recovers. "Anyway ... the viewers watch Peter and Julie kiss for twenty minutes and their minds just naturally wander. It becomes their fantasy. The viewers can put themselves right into the scene if they like. You know—pretend they are Peter or Julie. Or they can substitute a girlfriend or a boyfriend. Or husband, wife, co-worker, teacher, stranger they saw on the bus. And they can imagine they are kissing or scuba diving. Or dancing in the moonlight. Whatever." Mark blushes and looks down at his hands. "I'm just saying that viewers don't have to stick to my script. It's just a vehicle for everyone to dream freely."

It wasn't obvious to most people. In fact it even took me a few months to recognize that Mark was a Romantic. He was a quiet, self-contained, self-conscious, thirty-six year old man. Not poetic by nature, but there is no doubt—he exalted love. Ironically, it was his insecurity that led to the success of *The Baby Honey Show*. Yes, he was an average Advertising Copywriter who had accepted the job of selling a line of baby clothing for the Rowlands. That was his intention. But something had happened that first morning in the Day by Day Café. Mark let go of his inhibitions. Writing the show became a sensual thrill. He would see himself as Peter and imagine kissing Brenda. But just as often, he would substitute Eleanor for Julie. Or Sandy or Louise. Once he substituted Mrs. Roland. And he didn't feel guilty. Because no one but him would ever know.

What soon became apparent was that viewers across America were doing the same thing. That was the magic of *The Baby Honey Show*. It encouraged average people to create their own fantasies once a week, every week. You might liken it to a guided meditation. Twenty minutes of uninterrupted silence, submerged in romantic love. Just kissing, but you, the Viewer, were in control. You could cast it to your liking. No one would laugh at you. It would all remain private.

Furthermore, because *The Baby Honey Show* was Mark's sincere labor of love, the overt marketing pitches he wrote for the baby clothes didn't feel like hard-sell tactics. They felt like foreplay.

The following Tuesday, the *Baby Honey* company was having breakfast at the Day by Day Café. Mr. Rowland, who typically said very little, suddenly stood and announced, 'We have received our first official fan letter." He held up a piece of feminine-looking stationery, cleared his throat, and read the following:

Dear The Baby Honey Show,

I am 43 years old and, you know, I have never written a fan letter before in my whole life, but I have to tell you all how much I love your TV program. I quit my bowling team because it was on Friday night and I want to watch the show. And I don't want to record it on my DVR because I want to see it with everyone else in the country at the same time so that no one accidentally tells me the plot on Facebook and ruins it for me. You know? Anyways, the other girls started watching the show too, and they loved it too, so we rescheduled bowling to Tuesday nights. Anyways, we all love the show so much. We buy clothes like the ones that Julie wears and dress up and pretend we're Julie. Ha ha! And we pretend our husbands are Peter. Ha ha! Anyways, it makes us feel so relaxed. Oh and we are so crazy about Baby Honey. She looks so much like my best friend's granddaughter. Emily? Shoot! You wouldn't believe it. They could be, you know, twins. All the girls agree. And Emily wears all the Baby Honey clothes, too. When I have a granddaughter, you can be sure that she's going to wear them, too! So, keep up the good work. Thanks so much.

Yours forever and always,

Marjorie Taylor Greene
Christian, Mom, Small Business Owner.
100 Percent All American

P.S. I formed a Baby Honey Fan Club here in Dalton, Georgia, and I am the president, you know.

Eleanor tossed a look in Mark's direction but he pretended not to notice. In the weeks that followed, the fan mail increased exponentially and now every letter mentioned the baby. It seemed everyone by now had seen a Baby Honey look-a-like in their community—which meant that everyone by now was "seeing" Baby Honey on the show. This only served to confirm Mark's conviction that it was completely unnecessary to cast a real baby in the role.

In another development, Mrs. Rowland decided to produce a line of Mother-Daughter clothes for fans of Julie and Baby Honey. Mark introduced the new line immediately on the next episode.

The Baby Honey Show—Episode #10
Friday, December 16, 2016

(The Baby Honey Show theme plays and *fades as the camera finds PETER sitting on the couch with his hands over his eyes. Soundtrack: enthusiastic squeals. Immediately JULIE appears, descending the stairs. Soundtrack: Wolf whistles, cheering, applause. She wears a kimono-like bathrobe. She is carrying a*

*Baby Honey shopping bag. She crosses to
the couch and smiles at PETER.)*

JULIE

Okay, Sweetheart. You can open your
eyes now.

*(PETER does. Long close-up on his beau-
tiful blue eyes. He smiles adoringly at
JULIE and starts to pull her close. She
gently presses him away. PETER sighs.
Soundtrack: Laughter.)*

PETER

So which color pajamas did you put on
Baby Honey tonight? You were upstairs
forever getting her ready for bed.

(Soundtrack: Laughter. Uh-oh.)

JULIE *(Coyly)*

Oh, listen to you, Mr. Peter Honey! Are
you jealous of Baby Honey's bath and
story time with me?

PETER

No! Never! I love both my girls. Cross
my heart. It makes me so happy to know
that this family is so full of love.

*(Camera closes in on PETER's eyes. Then
on JULIE's eyes. Soundtrack: Audible
sighs.)*

JULIE

Well, Peter, the Baby Honey pajamas—sizes newborn through two years—come in five colors.

So, there's a lot to choose from. I had a hard time deciding between Yellow, Pink, Blue, Lavender, and White. (*She removes the pjs from the bag and lays them across the back of the couch. Enthusiastic squeals.*) But I chose the yellow one for tonight. She looks like a little buttercup! (*Soundtrack: Wild applause.*)

PETER (reaching for her)

Oh Julie ... You have the best taste.

(*JULIE steps back from him. Soundtrack: uh-oh.*)

JULIE

But Peter, there's more!

(*JULIE reaches into the bag and pulls out a tiny, two-piece bathing suit.*

Soundtrack: gasps and giggles.) Look at this little bathing suit! Could you die?

(*Applause.*)

PETER

Oh, I'm dying, Julie. I'm dying.

*(Soundtrack: Huge laughter. JULIE un-
ties her robe and drops it to the floor
to reveal that she is wearing a two-
piece bathing suit underneath. It is
the adult version of the one she bought
for Baby Honey. Soundtrack: Gasps and
applause.)*

JULIE

Look, Darling! Baby Honey now has a
line of Mother-Daughter clothing! Baby
and I have matching bathing suits!!! I
can't wait to take her to the pool at
the Club!

*(Soundtrack: Catcalls, whistles, manic
applause. PETER and JULIE fall into one
another's arms. The Kiss. The kissing
goes on and on. Silence—no soundtrack.
After twenty minutes, the theme song
softly begins and then swells as the
credits roll. Fade out.)*

Among the audience for *The Baby Honey Show* that night were Eleanor and Mark. Cuddled on the couch in their own living room
watching their own big screen, they remained silent through the
twenty minutes of kissing and through the theme music and credits.
Finally, Eleanor stirred.

She turned to Mark and said, "So what did you fantasize about?"

Mark blushed. "You know about that?"

Eleanor unfolded her legs and stood up. She grinned at Mark
and took his hand. "I'll show you mine if you show me yours." He
followed her into their bedroom.

Mark proposed that night. He just couldn't wait 'til Christmas Eve. He gave her the ring and Eleanor said YES and they opened champagne and called the Rowlands who by this time were like parents to them. The Rowlands were thrilled to hear the news. They insisted on having a dinner party in their honor. But it would have to wait until they returned from Washington, D.C. They were invited to Trump's Inauguration. They had seats on the grandstand right behind the new president.

Eleanor said to Mark. "I thought the Rowlands hated Trump."

Mark nodded. "They do."

Eleanor made a face. "Then why are they showing up at the In-auguration?"

"Mrs. Rowland said she's going to assassinate Trump. So, Mr. Rowland got them tickets."

Eleanor laughed. "She's so wacky."

Mark shrugged. "I don't know, El. I think she means it."

Chapter 11 – The Inauguration

On Friday, January 20, 2017, Donald Trump is sworn in as the forty-fifth president of the United States at a lackluster celebration on the capitol steps. His speech, written by his advisors—Stephen Miller and Steve Bannon—depicts America in a condition that could be likened to the landscape of a Mad Max movie. Pure carnage. Hopeless. As the speech ends, Former President George Bush is overheard saying to Former First Lady Michelle Obama, "Man, that was some weird shit."

Things would get weirder.

Trump was stung by a bee during his inaugural address to the nation. On a cold and rainy January day in Washington, DC., President Trump was stung in the back of the neck by a bee. He inhaled sharply halfway through his speech but resumed immediately, reading the teleprompter in his signature sing-song drone. So anyone watching probably attributed the quick sniff to Trump's cocaine habit. Even Melania seemed not to take notice. Or maybe she simply didn't care. She was in a sour mood.

Trump, however, was upbeat throughout the evening festivities, congratulating himself repeatedly and dancing badly with Melania to the music of 3 Doors Down, a Post-Grunge Band from Escatawpa, Mississippi. Trump had personally asked Beyoncé to perform for him—as she had performed for President Obama at his inauguration—but she laughed at the suggestion as did every other A-list performer. Trump made a mental note to instruct the IRS to go after all of them.

When the evening celebrations had ended and President Trump had retired alone to his White House bedroom, he tucked himself under the sheets, wolfed down a Big Mac as was his habit, followed that with a Big Fart, also part of his nighttime routine, and then fell into a dreamless sleep. He slept fitfully until 2 a.m. at which time, he sat up and started tweeting about what a bitch Beyoncé was. He felt completely normal.

Susana Rowland would lament that night that she and her hat pin had missed their mark. She had unfortunately accepted as truth the quack doctor's report that Trump's weight was a "perfect 210 pounds distributed over an athletic six foot frame." Of course, seeing him in person she realized that was fake news. But it was too late. She made the following entry in her journal.

> *January 20, 2017—I stung him with my small, bejeweled hat pin and hoped for the best. Alas, I had underestimated his corpulence and the amount of strychnine it would take to bring the monster down. Oh well … least said soonest mended. I'll try again. And again, if necessary.*

Trump's first act as president was to establish that he had the biggest crowd at his Inauguration, larger than that of any president in the history of the country. The press had provided the world with video of empty bleachers along the parade route to the Capitol that morning and compared the final numbers in Trump's audience with the throngs that showed up for President Obama's swearing in. Obama's inauguration was the best attended in history, a fact that would make Trump increasingly nuts. Because Obama, among other things, was Black. And Trump, among other things, was a Bigot.

Trump watched these news reports on the three TVs he had set up in the President's private dining room. He threw his lunch against the wall. Then he dispatched his press secretary—Sean Spicer, a flush-faced young man in an ill-fitting suit—to scold the press and repeat Trump's lie about the inaugural numbers. Spicer tried to overcome the resistance of the press by pounding the podium and screaming louder, "THIS WAS THE LARGEST AUDIENCE TO EVER WITNESS AN INAUGURATION—PERIOD!—BOTH IN PERSON AND AROUND THE GLOBE." The press countered with more facts—51.2 million viewers tuned in to watch Obama's swearing-in whereas 38.3 million watched Trump take the Oath of Office. No contest.

Trump threw an eighteenth-century candlestick at one of the TVs and shattered the screen. Trump then threw that TV itself into the hall and demanded a replacement. His closest adviser—Stephen Miller, a rabidly racist, self-hating Jewish man from California who never left Trump's side—gushed approvingly as he watched the new president rage. "I must observe, sir, that never before has there been a president of the United States who could lift—let alone throw—a TV set that far."

Trump flushed. "Not even Obama?"

Miller snorted, "He'd never even try."

Trump smiled, "Weak ass."

Miller nodded. "For sure."

Next Trump insisted that the official photographs of the Inauguration, taken by the National Park Service, be altered to reflect the "new reality" that the event "had no empty seats" and that "there were no open spaces on the mall." The photos of Trump's Inauguration were cropped and photoshopped in keeping with Trump's wishes. They were framed and hung in the Oval Office where Trump could look at them and show them off to visiting ambassadors, to sycophantic Republican Senators, to his vapid daughter, Ivanka—a Senior Adviser in the White House now who dropped by every morning to announce, "I'm having a party tomorrow night, Daddy. Tell Melania I've got first dibs on the Blue Room."

Trump showed his phony photos to former Secretary of State Henry Kissinger, who was in constant touch with Trump during the campaign, and now claimed an office in the West Wing. Kissinger and several Russian agents visited the Oval Office daily now—private meetings during which they would relay Putin's instructions. But that first day, all Trump wanted was for them to see his doctored photos and agree that Trump had the biggest inauguration crowds ever. Kissinger and the Russians looked at the pathetic man holding the photoshopped pictures, sweat streaming down his red cheeks, an anxious smile emphasizing his overbite. They said, "Довольно дерьмовая явка." Trump hadn't allowed a translator to be in the room so he simply assumed that their words were a lavish compliment.

Regardless, the argument over the *size* of Trump's Inauguration wouldn't die. It spilled over into a meeting a couple of days later at CIA Headquarters where the new president was expected to honor agents who had died protecting the nation's security. There Trump stood in front of a wall of stars, each representing a fallen hero—an agent who had given his life in service to this country. Trump ignored the tribute, launching instead into his repeated assertion that the crowds at his inauguration were the largest in history. Much bigger than Obama's who, by the way, "wasn't born in this country."

Once again, the press in attendance pushed back with evidence. Trump called all journalists "scum" and "fake." The press responded by reading excerpts from Trump's personal Twitter account in which just two weeks before the Inauguration, President-Elect Trump had disparaged the CIA for investigating Russian interference in his election. Trump had tweeted: "Yeah—the CIA ... these are the guys who said Sadam Hussein had weapons of mass destruction. Like the CIA could find their own ass with both hands."

Trump's schoolyard taunt shocked the men and women of the CIA and the room fell stone silent. Trump seemed to sense that he was losing the crowd. He immediately pivoted and decided to show his bonafides as Commander in Chief. He squared his shoulders and, ignoring the carefully written teleprompter speech, said, "A lot of people don't know this but we actually dropped TWO bombs on Japan during World War II. One on Hiroshima and the other on Nag-a-saki." Trump pulled his eyelids in a disgraceful caricature of a Japanese person. "NAG-a-SAKEEEE! NAAAG-a-SAKEEE!"

Trump farted and continued, "It's a true fact. People never heard about this and they say, Sir? How do you know this? And I say my uncle was a professor at MIT. So, you know, the egg doesn't roll far from the goose. Yes, People, I know things. And here's the amazing part of the story. It's kind of funny actually ... you'll get a kick out of this. That SECOND BOMB? It was an ACCIDENT. They didn't mean to drop it. True story." Trump chuckled. "What can I say ... it happens ... our armed forces fuck up a lot."

Trump shrugged. "But no more because I will lead strongly. As your commander in chief—I will keep us strong. And speaking of strong ... have you ever had a day where you catch a whiff of yourself and think Jesus, I stink?" Trump nodded to Stephen Miller who began walking around the perimeter of the room holding up a package of Trump Deodorant. Trump smiled and said, "Yes, I, Donald J. Trump, President of the United States of America, have produced the strongest deodorant in the history of the world. Just $133.99 for one long-lasting roll-on. This beautiful deodorant not only stops you from sweating like a pig, but you can also use it as a room freshener. It's that strong. It smells like ... well, what would you say, Stevie?"

Stephen Miller obediently removed the lid and sniffed. "Like the Grand Canyon, sir."

Trump beamed. "And it's attractively packaged in red, white and blue. Make America Smell Strong Like Your President! TRUMP DEODORANT. $133.99. At Walmarts and gas station counters all around the country. Get yours today!"

The officers remained silent, unsmiling, as the realization sunk in that the Leader of the Free World was an idiot. Trump turned to leave and they offered tepid applause—an insult that did not go unnoticed by Trump. He turned to Stephen Miller and whispered, "Take down their names and addresses and send them to Putin. That should stop this whole collusion investigation in its tracks."

Stephen Miller clicked his heels and saluted. "Got it, sir."

The following day, President Trump's obsession with the crowds at his inauguration continued. He woke up at two in the morning and Rage-Tweeted for four hours so Kellyanne Conway, a political pollster and Senior Counselor to President Trump, met with the press on the White House lawn. She settled the issue by saying that Trump *did* have the biggest crowd ever but conceded that the White House had "alternative facts." The press was stunned into silence. It was only the first week of the Trump presidency and the country was already exhausted. But Trump, energized by his anger, set about putting together his team.

Chapter 12 — Heil Trump!

"Nazism is no ideology but a magic formula that attracts a definite type of men. It is a form of characterology."
Sebastian Haffner, historian.

It's important to understand that Trump wasn't looking for experienced or even competent individuals to work in his administration. Trump—at heart—wasn't an ideologue. He was a nihilist. And a sadist. But first and foremost, he was a narcissist. Trump was looking for adulation and blind loyalty. Even when it meant breaking the law. Trump would assure the hesitant that they'd never pay any price. "Just do what I tell you to do and don't worry. I'll pardon you."

Naturally, his quest led him to seek out American Nazis. They were in vast supply in 2017. Having hidden in basements and gun shops for much of the decades since the collapse of Germany in World War II—they were now crawling out from the shadows—encouraged first by Candidate Trump during his campaign and now clamoring to abase themselves before the 45th President of the United States.

For a certain kind of man, there is something seductive about submission. Show me a Cult Leader—no matter how malevolent—and I will show you the ring of fanboys who encircle him, each experiencing a sensual thrill out of prostrating himself in the presence of not only the thuggish leader, but the rest of the tribe as well.

Many young men get their first taste of the delight of submission in the hazing rituals of a university fraternity. Even Trump was rumored to enjoy a good spanking from time to time. And so it is that many of our most prominent American Nazis have been nurtured on elite Ivy League campuses. Harvard alumni, Steve Bannon and Jared Kushner, come to mind. They of course found immediate positions as advisers to the new president.

The rank and file of Trump's followers, however, were not well educated. Trump let them know he appreciated them all the more for that. At a rally in Nebraska during the campaign, Trump made his philosophy clear when he announced: "I love the poorly educated. They are the most loyal. They don't read."

One particularly loyal group christened themselves The Proud Boys. Certainly, a more accurate handle than The Proud *Men* despite the fact that the tyro adults in this fraternity were all well into their forties, fifties, even sixties. A similar club formed and called themselves the Oath Keepers. A Christian Family Values collective, it was joined by millions of men and women who reveled in the fact that, with Trump's tacit approval, they would FINALLY be allowed to openly hate Black people, Latinos, and Jews—all in the name of the Lord. They felt they owed this liberation to Trump and pledged fealty in return.

Even in the midst of so many competing loyalists, Stephen Miller stood out. He had fallen hard for Donald Trump. Not sexually; Miller appeared to be heterosexual despite his lack of success with women. No—Stephen distinguished himself by exhibiting an aptitude for cruelty that amused Donald Trump in a way that few things did. And Stephen Miller quickly became one of the new president's closest advisers.

A mere week after the inauguration, on January 27, 2017, Trump signed an executive order—fashioned by Stephen Miller—that banned travel from all Muslim countries except ones where Trump was trying to build hotels. The ban went into immediate effect without time to plan or even to alert the affected countries, throwing airports and the Department of Homeland into chaos. They say Trump actually laughed that day, something he was rarely seen to do.

That same week, Stephen Miller coached the president through a series of introductory and congratulatory phone calls with world leaders. They started with Mexico's President Enrique Peña Nieto.

The Oval Office—January 27, 2017
Official Transcript

Trump sits at the Resolute Desk dialing the phone. Stephen Miller kneels next to him watching attentively.

"How many countries are in the world, Stevie?"

"Oh, I would have to say...."

"Thirty? I bet there are thirty."

"Yes, you're right, sir."

"I'm not getting a dial tone, Stevie."

"Mr. President. I believe he expects to phone you."

"I don't want to sit around waiting on these guys to call me, Stevie. I want to show them that I'm a take control kind of guy. That I'm in charge now."

Stephen says, "Of course. Uh ... sir ... you have to dial a 1 before all the other digits in that number."

"Fuck." Trump slams the phone down and starts again. Finally, a phone rings in Mexico City.

"Hello?"

Trump says, "Hello, President Peeny?"

Stephen whispers, "It's pronounced pen-ya ... President PEN-ya Nee-AY—toe."

Trump sighs and says under his breath, "Jesus, these spic names...." Then to the President of Mexico, he says, "This is Donald J. Trump president of the greatest country in the history of the world. The country of America in the United States."

"Ah, yes ... Congratulations, President Trump, on your election. I and my country wish you all the best...."

"Listen, President Neeto, you were on TV in your country last night and my main guy, Eagle-Eyes Stephen Miller here, caught your act...."

Miller blushes. "Thank you, sir, for the acknowledgment. That means a lot."

Trump continues, "So Stephen tells me you told your people that you won't pay for the Wall."

"Yes. That is true, Mr. President. It is completely unacceptable to Mexico that you have asked us to fund this wall along your southern border."

"Look, I already told everybody that you're going to do it. So, you have to."

"You should have talked to me before you told everyone. I have no intention of funding your wall."

"You're going to look like an asshole, Peeny. I'm telling you ... Everyone in America is going to say, Who is this douche bag Mexican guy?"

"I understand, President Trump, the small political margin that you have now in terms of everything you said you would do during your campaign. But I would also like to make you understand the lack of margin I have as President of Mexico to accept the situation. And this has been, unfortunately, the critical point that has not allowed us to move forward in the building of the relationship between our countries."

"You don't understand, Peppy. I have to have you pay for the Wall. I have to. I have been saying this for a year and a half on the campaign trail. The millions of people who show up at my rallies have heard me promise.... Boy, do they show up for Trump! People say it's incredible.

People say no one has ever drawn crowds like this in the history of the world except Hitler, and I say—with all due respect to Hitler—I have bigger crowds."

"Excuse me, President Trump? Excuse me...."

"They say 'No one has ever seen anything like it, sir. How do you do it, sir?'" Trump shoves the phone into Miller's hand. "Tell him, Stephen."

"President Nieta, Stephen Miller here. You have to understand that a person in President Trump's shoes cannot afford to look ridiculous. The whole world needs a strong American leader."

Trump takes the phone back. "And my inauguration was bigger than Obama's. You know it and I know it."

Presidente Enrique Peña Nieto calmly responds, "It makes no difference. Mexico will not pay for the wall. It is out of the question."

"I HAVE TO HAVE MEXICO PAY FOR THE WALL. I HAVE TO!!!"

"No."

Pause.

"Okay, Pedro ... Listen ... hear me out. Here's how we'll handle this. You don't say that you are going to pay for the wall. And you don't say you aren't going to pay for the wall. You just say nada. Zip it. Then I go and tell everyone here in America that you have agreed to pay for the wall BUT, hold on … let me finish. I will cover the cost of it by taking money out of the Social Security fund. And here's the beauty part—it won't cost you a peso. Old Americans will cover the bill."

"No, President Trump."

"No one will be any wiser. It will be a win-win."

"I will not be complicit in one of your lies."

"C'mon, I need you to do me this favor."

"No, I will stand my ground, President Trump. I will insist publicly that Mexico will not pay for this Wall."

"I HATE YOU!"

"Now I must return to my meeting. Good luck, Mr. President."

"I'M NEVER SPEAKING TO YOU AGAIN."

President Trump slams the phone back in its cradle. Later that morning, Trump hangs up on the Australian Prime Minister as well. He looks at Stephen Miller, his face red with rage, and Miller assures him that there are foreign leaders who love him.

"Sir, think about Crown Prince Mohammed bin Salman. He's invited you to visit Saudi Arabia to dance the sword dance with him. That's a big deal. He never did that with Obama. And what about Vladimir Putin? My gosh—Putin hates everybody, but he adores you. He will do anything for you."

"That's true. He already has." Trump still looks sad.

Miller says, "Hey, I have some gossip that will cheer you up, sir. Guess who's gay?"

Trump pouts, "Lindsay Graham. Duh. I already knew that."

Miller smiles. "Yes, but there's another...."

Trump sighs, "Mitch McConnell. Everybody knows that, too."

"Okay. But there's someone else, too. Guess again."

"Jim Jordan. C'mon, Stephen, this is boring. Guessing fags in the GOP is like shooting elephants on a safari. You can't miss."

"But would you have guessed Mike Pence?"

Trump sighs. "He calls his wife 'mother.' What do you think?'"

Miller looks dejected. Trump says, "But this is good work, Stevie. You've done a great job. Start a list of homos and add these names. I may use it someday. Leave off Jared for the time being. But keep him on the Jewish list."

"Will do, sir."

Trump looks reflective for a moment. "You know Pence stares at me like Nancy Reagan used to stare at Ronny—like she was madly in love with him? Of course, she was faking it. That woman was a terrible actress. But you know—I think Mike is really sincere. I think he's actually in love with me."

Miller says, "So should I put his name on the homo list?"

Trump nods. "Definitely."

Stephen Miller appears on CBS *Face The Nation*. February 2017:
"Our opponents, the media, and the whole world will soon see as we begin to take further actions, that the powers of the president to protect our country are very substantial and will not be questioned."

Chapter 13 — The Stars Align

Brenda Beacon and Kip Barrett were now television stars on a level never seen before. They were written about in all the major media. They became fashion influencers and routinely appeared on the covers of *Vogue* and *Elle*. *Time Magazine* christened them "the power couple of the year." And because they were never seen apart, the paparazzi took to calling the couple BRENKI, a fusion of their names which underscored the marriage of their souls.

They were offered countless opportunities to hawk products from cologne to cell phones, but Brenda replied, "No, thank you. We're already in a commercial." And they never set up a page in Facebook or any other social media although their fans routinely discussed them on those forums as well. BRENKI did accept invitations to appear as guests on popular TV talk shows. Kip was transitioning into being a public intellectual and, of course, Brenda was already one in private, so their TV appearances were unusual.

Brenda's background as a public defender became known to America the day BRENKI appeared on Ellen DeGeneres' daily talk show. Brenda spoke at length of her parents' complicity in supporting a violent dictatorship in Argentina. She attributed her shame over that to giving her the impetus to champion the rights of the downtrodden in society. Her compassion gave her a populist sheen that only enhanced her classic, movie-star beauty. She became even more beloved by Americans that day, particularly among the disadvantaged, many of whom were Trump supporters.

When Ellen turned her attention to Kip, he offered an intimate narrative of his own life story beginning with his birth in a suburb of Denver, Colorado, and his high school awards which included *Best Looking* and *Most Nice*. Kip added, "You will find this incredible, Ellen, but I was also voted *Most Likely to be an Influencer*. So you could say my classmates were prescient." The audience sighed approvingly. "But I felt isolated and empty. I didn't want to be a pretty face."

Ellen tucked her legs under her on the couch and took a swig of bottled water. Kip continued, "So I went to the University of Colorado for three semesters. And I dual-majored in Physical Education and Philosophy, and I would have graduated on time but I got noticed by a modeling agency rep who saw me trying on sneakers at a large mall in Denver and rushed to sign me and then I moved to New York and then I was a Ralph Lauren model with a hot shot agent. Yes, I was seduced by glamour. But I felt empty inside. "

Ellen nodded and rearranged her legs into a cross-legged yoga position. She looked at Brenda. "So how did you guys meet?"

Brenda smiled and said, "Well, Kip and I believe it was divine intervention. I had never had a boyfriend before."

The audience gasped. Ellen's round eyes got rounder. "Say what???"

Brenda laughed. "I guess I was waiting for the right person and I found him." The audience sighed again.

Kip nodded. "I didn't even realize Brenda was pretty the first time we met because she was so interesting—so our connection was totally metaphysical—but I took her to dinner and that's when I realized she was beautiful and not just outside, you know. She's a thoughtful person. And a great conversationalist. And at the end of the date, she said to me, 'Kip, you are educatable. Go back to college.' No one had ever recognized that in me before." Kip paused and wiped a tear from his eye. The audience was so silent, they appeared to be holding their breath.

"So, we fell in love." The audience exhaled in relief.

Kip resumed his story. "So I took classes at City College all last year and completed my Philosophy degree in December and now I'm hooked on reading and learning ... especially history. I love history. Everything keeps repeating itself which is so totally surreal. Like Life is a Wheel. And we are all hamsters." The audience nodded their heads.

"You know you can almost predict the next revolution? Brenda and I lie in bed some nights and, after we've made love, we talk about the self-defeating attraction humans feel for tyrants, and the need for strong institutions to ensure that we survive the seduction of autocratic monsters. Because without structure, things can go to hell quickly. And that's when dictators take over. Which–for sure—you don't want."

The audience was wide-eyed. "Nooooooooo," they said.

Kip looked at Brenda now and smiled. Brenda smiled back at him with her whole heart. The audience sighed. Ellen looked impatient. As Kip was about to launch into a recitation of his recent thesis that American Black people absolutely deserve financial restitution because of Slavery and the generations that were robbed of inherited wealth, Ellen cut him off. She said that they had to move on now because there was a kid waiting to come on the show next who had trained her dog to dance. And Ellen was going to dance with them. The audience roused themselves now and applauded.

BRENKI wasn't invited to appear on Ellen DeGeneres' show again but they did show up on *The View* where they were interviewed as experts, not just on law, world history, philosophy, finance, and fashion, but on child-rearing as well. Brenda and Kip were, of course, prepared. They had enrolled in an online course in Child Psychology together to bone up on the basics. During the interview, Kip referred to the book *Pink and Blue: Telling the Boys from the Girls in America* by Jo B. Paoletti. Kip said, "I wrote my paper on the social manipulation of gender in babies in the twentieth century." Then Kip spoke at length about gender dysphoria and how it was a real thing and how Americans needed to be more like the ancient Greeks who had the class to let people be themselves.

BRENKI's appearances were of course being noticed by the powerful American Christian Taliban Society (ACTS) who monitored all Wokeness in public media, but BRENKI had a strong fan base among MAGA. So the leaders of ACTS chose to keep their powder dry. For now.

BRENKI's appearance on The View generated controversy but it also allowed the country to finally discuss gender openly. Mark and Eleanor, being die-hard Humanists, thought there was an opportunity to use *The Baby Honey Show* as a platform on which they could keep this conversation alive. Mark therefore asked Kip to write the next episode of *The Baby Honey Show* based on what he had learned in his studies. Kip's lack of skill at writing a sit-com was more than compensated by his passion.

The Baby Honey Show—Episode # 14

(Opening music ... JULIE enters with shopping bags. Soundtrack: applause and catcalls.)

JULIE

Hi Honey! I'm home.

(PETER comes down the stairs. Soundtrack: applause and catcalls.)

PETER

Hi, Julie. I just put Baby down for her nap.

                    JULIE

Oh darn. I wanted to play with her a
few minutes.

                    PETER

YOU CAN PLAY WITH ME! *(He grins. JULIE
laughs. They kiss. Soundtrack: Uh-oh,
laughter.)* Let me see what you have
there. *(He opens a shopping bag.)*

                    JULIE

I bought Baby a sweet little cardigan sweater. *(She pulls a pink one out
of the bag and holds it up. The camera zooms in.)* Isn't this the yummiest
pink?

                    PETER

(Looking pensive. He strokes his chin.)
Didn't it come in other colors?

                    JULIE

Well, yes—it came in lots of colors. The
blue is attractive, but the pink....

                    PETER

Then I think you should exchange it for
the blue one.

                    JULIE

(Laughs) But Peter, she's a little
girl.

PETER

Do you hear what you're saying, Julie? Human beings aren't color-coded. And we shouldn't raise our child to think that there is only one way to be a girl. We don't want to fall into that trap.

(The audience applauds.)

JULIE

Oh gosh—I hadn't thought of it that way.

PETER

I want our Baby to discover her sense of herself by living and growing in a healthy and nurturing and diverse environment. Not by being labeled.

JULIE

I want that for her, too.

PETER

Of course, you do, darling. *(Peter touches her arm lovingly. Soundtrack: The audience sighs audibly.)* We want her to have lots of friends. Every race, creed, and sexual orientation. Just like our own friends. Just like America! We want her to accept the natural differences that occur in people. Just like we do. And that all people deserve love and respect. We want her to grow up to be as smart and accomplished. And nice.

(Soundtrack: Audience applauds wildly.)

JULIE

Oh Peter ... You're right! Blue for boys and Pink for girls—that can be so limiting if we associate certain behaviors with colors. How utterly silly I was to think she had to wear pink!

PETER

In the olden days, Julie, boys and girls—dressed alike in little dresses. Look at the old photos. The boys wore dresses. I'm not lying. That's because they didn't have diapers then and this way—kids could just pee on the ground without removing anything. Our forefathers were practical! And Scotsman wore kilts for the same reason. So they could pee even if they were marching or fighting in a war. Like Mel Gibson in *Braveheart*. *(Soundtrack: Audience cheers.)*

JULIE

You are fascinating, Peter. You know so many facts.

PETER

That's because I read a lot. It is a very fulfilling pastime. The point is wearing dresses never made anyone gay. And even if they were gay it wasn't because of their clothes. Children grew up to be exactly who they were meant to be. *(Soundtrack: Audience cheers.)* Even if they played with dolls or painted their fingernails. By the way, little kids in the olden days all had long hair, too. You couldn't tell the boys and girls apart. And no one cared.

JULIE

So the whole idea of pink for girls and blue for boys is a modern perversion?

PETER

Exactly!

JULIE

Well, our little Baby Honey would look fabulous in the blue cardigan.

PETER

She can wear any color she likes. That's the point. Let her choose.

JULIE

You're right. Peter. You are so naturally wise but best of all, you're kind. And tolerant. I wish all Americans were like you. You make me so proud. *(Soundtrack: Audience coos.)*

PETER

Well, there are some people who say I'm
too woke.

(Soundtrack: Uh-oh. Laughter.)

JULIE

Woke turns me on.

*(JULIE winks at Peter and grins.
Soundtrack: applause, gentle laughter.)*

PETER

Well, I think I will sit down now and
read Huckleberry Finn by Mark Twain.
I am reading my way through nineteenth-century American literature at
the moment. It is helping me see the
development of the American character.
For better and worse.

JULIE

And I am reading *The Handmaid's Tale*
by Margaret Atwood. I am interested in
how subversive ideas find their way into
commercial literature. But let's read
later, Darling. Right now, I just want
to make love.

*(JULIE looks at PETER with rapt admi-
ration. PETER smiles and takes JULIE's
hand. He looks deeply into her eyes.
They move to the couch and they kiss
and kiss and kiss and kiss.... For twenty
minutes. Then credits roll. Fade Out.)*

The morning after this episode aired, *The Baby Honey Show* got its first bomb threat. But, in the weeks that followed, copies of *Huckleberry Finn* and *The Handmaid's Tale* flew off the shelves at local libraries and bookstores. And on playgrounds in cities and towns all over America, little boys were wearing pink and little girls were wearing blue.

Chapter 14 – The DREAMER Has a Dream

Two days later, Sandy had a dream about Trump. She sat motionless on the bed and stared past Mickey into space. Finally she spoke. "I think I just witnessed a crime."

Mickey said, "Where were you?"

"Here. In bed. I was sleeping. But this dream ... this dream was so real. Something bad is brewing at the White House, Mickey. I was there. I watched them."

Mickey studied her anxious face. "Tell me your dream."

Sandy closed her eyes and began to recount her vision.

President Trump is having dinner at Mar-a-Lago. His single guest is Henry Kissinger. Their table is surrounded by white billionaires who make no attempt to hide the fact that they are eavesdropping on the president and his esteemed guest. The secret service officers sit at the next table, enjoying fine wine and thick steak. Trump, for his part, is red-faced with excitement, almost giddy. "I did it, Henry!

I fired the son of a bitch! I fired James Comey! I fired the Director of the FBI! Now their investigation is over! I got away with it! I stole the 2016 election and they can't do a thing about it!"

Kissinger half chuckles, "Well, give credit where credit is due, Donald."

"Oh yes. Thank Vlad for me."

"He knows you are grateful. He says he loves you."

Trump gasps. "Holy Fuck! Vladimir Putin loves me?????"

Kissinger snorts. "Perhaps not love...."

Trump sighs, "Oh...."

"But he is very impressed with you. He says you are almost demonic."

"Really? He said that?"

"Ice in your veins. No feelings. No empathy. No patriotism. No loyalty to country. You are the perfect man for this job."

"Wow." Trump snaps his fingers at a waiter. "GARÇON!"

The waiter approaches. "Yes, Mr. President? Have you gentlemen made a choice?"

Trump turns to Kissinger. "Have the meatloaf, Henry. It's the best. They say ... people who have this meatloaf ... they say that they have never had meatloaf like this. They say it is the best meatloaf in the history of the world. Never seen anything like it."

Kissinger hands his menu to the waiter. "I'll have the pork chops. And another one of these." He lifts his cocktail glass.

"What are you doing, Henry? You can't eat pork. You're a Jew!" Trump turns to the waiter. "Get him the meatloaf."

Kissinger says firmly, "I vant the pork."

Trump shrugs and nods to the waiter. "I'll have my usual, Dimitri." He turns back to Kissinger. "You're going to hell, Henry. They say Jews who eat pork go to Hell."

"I'm going to hell anyway. Might as well eat what I like." Kissinger laughs.

"I'm going to convert to being a Catholic when I start to die. They all get into Heaven."

Kissinger changes the subject. "Listen, Donald, there's something you need to do next."

"Name it, Henry."

Everyone in the room adjusts their chairs to hear what Kissinger will say. Dmitri stops to listen.

"You must pull the United States out of NATO, Donald. To weaken Europe so Russia can incorporate Ukraine and then attack Czechoslovakia and Poland. So he can put the Soviet Union back together again. This is a special request from President Putin himself. In honor of his birthday this week."

Trump looks confused. "But it's May. Putin's birthday is the seventh of October. I know it by heart. I have it marked on my wall calendar and circled with my Sharpie. I always send him nylon stockings and chocolate on his birthday and a note that says, "from an admirer in America." Trump's face gets even redder. "It's sort of a joke...."

Kissinger patiently replies, "In Russia, you get two birthdays, Donald. You did not know this? Putin celebrates one of his birthdays in May. And the other one on the seventh of October."

"Lucky bum! I wonder why Melania never told me that. She was my birthday gift from Vladimir in 1998! But I only get one birthday a year." Trump pouts. "I hate America."

"So, Donald, can I tell Vladimir Putin, the President of Russia, that Donald John Trump, the President of the United States, has agreed to the power sharing plan?"

"Sure. We'll pull out of NATO tomorrow."

Kissinger makes a satisfied grunt. "Yes. Good. It will make things simpler in the world. Just two supreme leaders. You and Putin will then be able to divide the planet and command obedience to the New Stability. You'll see. People will love you for it. No more war."

Trump gulps his Diet Coke and burps. "So, Henry, who gets the shit-ass countries?"

"You guys can work that out later."

"What about China?"

"I'll handle them."

Stephen Miller enters the restaurant. Trump waves to him. "C'mere, Stevie. Join us. Join us. I want you to meet Dr. Henry Kissinger. Stevie here is our Angel of Darkness at the White House. He talked me into putting all those people at the border in cages. He said it would make a point."

Kissinger shakes Miller's hand. "I hear great things about you, young man."

Miller gushes. "What an honor to meet you, Dr. Kissinger. I am your biggest fan."

"Thank you. Thank you."

Miller's face is bright red. "May I add something, sir?"

"Please...."

"Well, I just want you to know that my guiding principle in life ... my mantra, if you will, is something you said in an interview before I was even born. Cover your own ass."

Kissinger nods. "Ah yes. Make sure that you have the President's Chief of Staff put in writing that you warned the president that what you were advising and what he was acquiescing to might be illegal or even a war crime. And keep that written memo in your back pocket at all times. Always Cover Your Own Ass."

Stephen nods. "I'm writing that down, too, sir."

Kissinger continues, "In 1971, I encouraged the military dictator in Pakistan to slaughter millions of innocent men, woman, and children in neighboring Bangladesh. They were becoming progressive. Like Democrats. You know?"

Stephen says, "Yes, sir. I heard about that."

"Did you? I'm surprised. Most Americans don't pay attention to anything outside their own border. They might never have learned about this genocide—but for the fact that George Harrison of the Beatles wrote a fucking song about it. Bangladesh."

Stephen nodded. "Yes. I know the song. Disgusting. Popular culture must be censored."

Kissinger continues, "Well, the word got out that I had caused a genocide. And I was nearly indicted by the World Court! But I had a memo blaming Nixon in my back pocket. You see?"

Stephen laughs. "Okay, I see."

"And now you, Stephen, are separating these brown children from their mothers and sending them out to work as indentured servants for wealthy white families across the country. Never to be heard from again." Kissinger wags his finger. "I'm just saying that I hope you have covered your own ass." Kissinger winks and points to Trump.

Trump explodes, "HEY! HEY! I'M THE CENTER OF ATTENTION HERE! I'M THE FUCKING PRESIDENT OF THE US OF A! TALK TO ME!!!

Miller bows and says, "Oh God ... I apologize, sir. I'm so very sorry....

Trump looks at him coldly, then turns his attention to Kissinger. With a cruel smile, he says, "Henry—I think you should know that Stevie here had an ulterior motive for putting all those women and children in cages at the border. Didn't you, Stevie? The real reason you wanted to break the hearts of all those Latin American gals down at the border—ripping their families apart like that, sending their babies away forever—that had nothing to do with your so-called White Nationalism. No—it was simply because YOU CAN'T GET A DATE. CAN YOU? And you REALLY HATE girls!" Trump laughs dryly. "Oh Jesus! Look at his face, Henry. Is he the Jewiest guy you've ever seen? He makes you look like an Irish Catholic out of Boston. Oh by the way, I'm keeping a list of Jews just so you know." Trump smirks.

Kissinger calmly sips his drink. "You're a jerk, Donald."

Trump quickly backtracks. "Oh, you're safe with me ... I'm the president. And so long as I stay in office, no one is going to come after my Jew friends. Understood?"

Kissinger eyes him coldly. "You are a pimple, Donald, on an ass's ass. You can't do anything without the permission of the Illuminati. You know it. And I know it."

Sandy opens her eyes, shrugs and looks at Mickey. "Then Mrs. Rowland entered the scene carrying a gun. And I woke up."

Mickey responds, "Holy Shit! That's not a dream. You are channeling Trump! You have an inside line to Trump! Holy Shit!"

"So, what should I do? I can't tell the FBI. I don't want the government to know I even exist. They'll have me deported, Mickey."

"I won't let that happen, Sandy. Never! I love you. More than my own life."

"And I love you, Mickey. From the moment we met."

"Let's elope today."

"Okay. And then we will tell the Family my dream. They will know what needs to be done."

<hr>

For the record, it appears that Sandy's dream *was* a prophecy. A prophecy that came true two months later when on May 9, 2017, Trump fired FBI Director James Comey. Meanwhile, Stephen Miller began to lay the groundwork to ensure that Trump remained in office after his first term. In an interview with *Face the Nation*, Miller asserted a new conspiracy theory—that "thousands of illegal voters were bussed into New Hampshire" for the 2016 election. Miller offered no evidence of this voter fraud, but insisted that these illegal votes contributed to the fact that Trump lost the popular vote in that election by three million. Miller announced that the Trump Administration would be hyper-vigilant in the next election. They were already training election watchers in every state.

Chapter 15 – Buenos Aires 1951

And now the rest of Susana Rowland's story....

As noted earlier, Susana Rowland's mother Noeme arrived in Buenos Aires, Argentina, in 1951 aboard a ship out of Lisbon, Portugal, a ship that was transporting hundreds of World War II German Nazis. The passengers disembarked into a country that was experiencing a vibrant cultural revolution under the progressive leadership of President Juan Perón. He and his beautiful wife and governing partner—who was known as Evita—were champions of workers' rights and women's suffrage. They built schools and affordable housing in poor neighborhoods. They established migrants' rights. Trade unions multiplied under Perón's leadership and Evita founded the first female political party in Argentina.

Naturally, the success of the Peróns' policies created powerful enemies—especially among the more conservative political forces in the country—notably the military. Sensing the enemies around him, Perón tightened his control of the press and became increasingly intolerant of political dissent which angered the activists at both ends of the political spectrum. In the midst of all these tensions came rumors that Perón was secretly consenting to provide refuge to some of the most infamous Nazis of the Third Reich.

To be honest, the average Argentine hadn't paid much attention to the recent "World War." It ravaged Europe and the Pacific, but Argentina—situated out of the way at the bottom of the world (some would argue that it is at the top, but that it is a matter of perspective)—anyway, the point is that the world mostly ignored Argentina. And Argentinians were content to be ignored. They followed the example of Switzerland and declared themselves neutral. And like Switzerland, they profited handsomely by keeping themselves open to cooperation with the Nazis.

Switzerland agreed to hide the gold and the valuable art that Nazi officers had pillaged from the homes of dead, wealthy Jews. And Argentina, under President Perón's watch, hid the most notorious of the Nazi war criminals who were frantically searching for safe haven outside Europe as the Third Reich was collapsing. In return for that protection, these Nazis moved the profits from their war industries to Argentina before the victorious Americans could track them down and confiscate the money.

Adolf Eichmann, who facilitated the "Final Solution" for Hitler and was personally instrumental in overseeing the extermination of millions of Jews, managed to get a BMW factory dismantled and relocated from Deutschland to a suburb of Buenos Aires in the chaotic days that followed Germany's surrender. Eichmann then slipped out of Europe with his family and settled into an upper-middle-class life in Buenos Aires where he gave himself a nice job as Senior Manager at the BMW factory. It was all pretty sweet for about ten years and then the Israeli intelligence agency tracked him down and abducted him and turned him over to the Israeli Supreme Court where he was tried for war crimes and hanged. But we're getting ahead of the story.

Another infamous Nazi, Dr. Josef Mengele, the Angel of Death, who tortured young Jewish children with excruciating medical experiments, was able to live out the rest of his days in a pretty village on the outskirts of Buenos Aires where he sheltered under an assumed name. And there were others, of course, many others. The Perón family, and their friends in the power centers of the country, got kickbacks from these monsters and ultimately became very rich.

There were credible rumors circulating in the country about all of this, but if Argentines felt in the least queasy about their country's complicity in protecting these sadists, they could always turn to the Roman Catholic Church for a bromide. The venerated St. Augustine wrote in his *Confessions* that as a young man he had sinned by trespassing into an orchard of pear trees with his friends and stealing fruit. He admitted that he didn't do it because he was hungry. He wasn't hungry. He wrote, "I had no motive for wickedness except wickedness itself. It was foul and I loved it."

I suppose all of us have our Augustinian impulses. In any event, I imagine the Roman Catholic Church leaders in Buenos Aires put their hand out to the wealthy exiled Nazis and got their cut, too.

> Note: For Americans who are just learning that South America exists—one can introduce oneself to the nation of Argentina, as a start, by watching the movie *Evita* about the Peróns. Released in Hollywood in 1996, it is, of course, a musical. Madonna plays the title role.

Back to 1951....

Noeme—the future mother of Susana Rowland—twenty years old now and living alone in Buenos Aires, found a job as a secretary at the University of Buenos Aires where she immediately met an older professor of Business Law named Abraham León. He was Jewish, childless, and a widower. They fell in love and married the following year.

That same year, the beloved First Lady of Argentina, Evita Perón, died of cancer. Perhaps it was his grief that made President Perón suddenly vulnerable. The military began to organize against him and three years later staged a brief but violent coup—dropping 100 bombs on the center of the city near the Presidential Palace. Three hundred citizens were killed but Perón escaped the assassination attempt and fled the country. Ironically, he found safe haven in Spain where for the next eighteen years, he lived in relative comfort under the military dictatorship of General Francisco Franco, a Fascist whose sympathies during World War II were with Hitler and Mussolini.

Meanwhile, back in Argentina, the Military elite established a dictatorship that was fairly impotent. The Military leaders forbade the mention of Perón's name and removed all statues in his memory. Union workers, however, continued to lionize the living memory of Perón in private gatherings at each other's homes and yearn for the day that he would return. Political dissent was not tolerated by the new Military leaders and all newspapers were censored. But university students demonstrated anyway and wrote manifestos which they handed out in the streets of Buenos Aires. Their parents, for the most part, ignored politics and focused on their growing families and the rate of inflation; and dreamed of one day buying a house and a BMW. Life went on. In the end, this military coup was merely a dry run. A rehearsal for the real thing which would come later.

Noeme and Abraham became parents. The baby, Susana Eliana Fermoza Viva León—future wife of wealthy American Bob Rowland—was born on a freakishly sultry autumn day. Noeme would one day tell her daughter that the temperature that afternoon was close to that of human blood. It was of course a Thursday.

Susana came of age in a home of privilege and taste as well as love. She went to the best schools. She wore the nicest clothes. She was pretty and popular. She attended the University of Buenos Aires where she majored in history and returned after graduation for an additional degree in education.

When former President Perón returned from exile in 1973, eighteen-year-old Susana and a young man named Ethan Duran found themselves standing side by side amid a raucous rally of university students at the airport. The young people had gathered to welcome the return of their progressive hero. Ethan and Susana left the rally together early that day. They would later admit that they had each fallen in love at first sight, which was so distracting they barely noticed when Perón's plane landed. But then they weren't animated by politics or even history at that point. Ethan was studying family medicine. He would be a doctor. Susana would teach in a public high school. Their future as a couple looked promisingly secure.

Perón won his election later that year and was returned to the office of President of Argentina, but political violence continued and when Perón unexpectedly died a year later, chaos erupted. A group of senior military officers battled with Perón's successor who was deposed and on March 29, 1976, the coup d'état was complete. General Jorge Rafael Videla became President of Argentina and immediately ushered in The National Reorganization Process or El Proceso as it was called in the press.

Upon taking the reins of power, General Videla fortified his position with fiery speeches at public rallies promising the people an end to the guerilla violence in the streets of Buenos Aires. He offered stability and prosperity, and a return to conservative values, "to the way things were."

The public, for the most part, acquiesced. The new government began cracking down hard on any remaining critics. They broke up student demonstrations, dismantled trade unions, and censored all publications. They oversaw school curriculums and banned books. The government hired and assembled a state police force that monitored all public events as well as workplaces. And because General Videla's government tolerated zero dissent, people soon became reluctant to express their criticism of his policies even among friends and family, even in their own homes.

By the end of the first year, the government had created Death Squads. Detention Centers were established within Buenos Aires and on the immediate outskirts. Now the military ushered in a period of absolute rule maintained by state terrorism. It would last from 1976 to 1983 and claim 30,000 lives. History would remember this time as The Dirty War.

Chapter 16 — The Dirty War: Argentina 1976–1983

*I*t began with a campaign to inflame the resentments of those who had been left out of the prosperity of the Perón years. To turn neighbor against neighbor. To create a national paranoia and a class of men and women consumed with unappeasable hatred. Reality was concealed or outright altered by lies. There was a steady drumbeat of assurances that the nation would finally attain its unfinished destiny and emerge as the utopia that never was but existed in the collective mythology of the Fascists now running the country. They promised to Make Argentina Great Again.

The newspapers hailed General Videla's ascension to leadership as "a reasonable solution to runaway inflation and chronic unrest." The majority of Argentines were willing to sacrifice their liberty in the short term if it resulted in cheaper bread and quiet streets. Even the United State of America gave its tacit approval to the military dictatorship in Argentina. American Secretary of State Henry Kissinger was in frequent contact with the generals in the new government. He offered this menacing advice. "If there are things that must be done, you should do them quickly."

Then people started disappearing.

Lists were created. The names of labor union leaders and leaders of the Resistance. The names of poets and painters, of writers and journalists. The names of suspected homosexuals, left-leaning teachers, outspoken students. The names of clergy and the socially conscious who served the poor. And the names of Jews. The government made the lists and uniformed men carried out searches, going door to door. Questioning neighbors, co-workers, family, bystanders. Returning again months later for additional sweeps. Neighbors turned on neighbors.

People were taken from their homes, from their workplaces, from their schools and synagogues. Ripped from their communities like weeds. Detention centers sprung up around the country and those who were seen being escorted into them never returned. Those who were not threatened by the purge would shrug and say, *algo habrán hecho.* "They must have done something."

Susanna and Ethan Duran began dating soon after their meeting at the airport rally for Perón's return from exile. A year later, just weeks after the death of President Perón—Susanna and Ethan became engaged. Ethan graduated from the School of Medicine at the University of Buenos Aires and was immediately given a position at the esteemed Hospital Posada in the city. Susana accepted a position at a local high school, teaching a freshman survey course on Egyptian history. Even though Susana and Ethan were both Jewish, General Videla's henchman seemed uninterested in them. Perhaps it was because their parents had raised them as secular Jews.

Ethan's father was the highly respected author of several books on the history of South America. His mother was an anthropologist and adviser for the Pio Pablo Museum in Cachi, Salta Province. Ethan had a younger brother named Mateo. The family had for generations paid mere lip service to Judaism. By the mid-twentieth century, there were family members who had never set foot in a synagogue. Ethan was of one of them.

Susana's parents were also Jews and they too were not observant. Susana's mother, Noeme, had been raised in the Jewish Ghetto in Rome but had long ago given up on God. Susana's father had been given a traditional education in the faith and privately missed attending synagogue, but he understood his wife's atheism. And so it seemed that the León family, like the Duran family, were unlikely to draw attention from the antisemitic General Videla and his Death Squads. Unbeknownst to them all, Ethan's younger brother Mateo, now in his third year at the University of Buenos Aires, had recently experienced a religious conversion. Not only was he now a devout Jew, an observant Jew, but he was openly attending synagogue on a regular basis.

Ethan and Susana married in early 1975. They moved into an apartment near the Hospital Posada so that Ethan could walk to work. They agreed that they would postpone starting a family until the political climate seemed less unstable. In the evenings, Susana and Ethan talked about current events. Ethan had worshipped the late president of Chile, Salvador Allende, a popular socialist and physician himself, who had advocated the global distribution of resources as a means to end the grinding poverty in his country. Ethan blamed Allende's recent assassination on Nixon, the president of the United States, and on Nixon's adviser, Secretary of State Henry Kissinger.

It was a credible accusation. Kissinger had complained for months in the American press about Allende's socialist policies—in particular, the increases in Chilean workers' wages which had made President Allende a hero to working people around the world. Kissinger disparaged the young people in Chile who, in his opinion, had been "indoctrinated with socialist humanist values." In an interview with the press in the late summer of 1973, Kissinger said, "I don't see why we have to stand by and watch a country go Communist because of the irresponsibility of its own people." Soon after that interview was published, on September 11, 1973, President Allende was assassinated and a military dictatorship began a reign of terror in Chile.

Then the following year—on July 1, 1974—President Perón, the democratically elected president of Argentina, was found dead in his office. Ethan blamed the United States Secretary of State for his murder as well.

Susana countered, "Perón died of a heart attack."

"They made it look that way, Susana. I'm sure it was the American CIA again."

"Shhhh, keep your voice down, Ethan. The walls have ears."

"It was murder! I assure you—this has all the Kissinger hallmarks. He is having democratic leaders removed one by one."

"Don't talk so loudly. That nosy woman next door … I think she's an informer."

Ethan dropped his voice. "Think about it. Allende and Perón–both elected leaders, both known for their championship of civil rights, both popular with the workers and students. Both murdered by the US government! The American people turn a blind eye. But rest assured, Susana, America is also seeing its final days as a democracy."

A Brief Sidebar that Further Illuminates How Henry Kissinger is an Asshole

On April 2, 1982, in the sixth year of The Dirty War, Argentine military forces invaded the Falkland Islands, a British colony about 300 miles east of Argentina in the South Atlantic Ocean. It made no sense. The Falkland Islands were in no way a threat to Argentina. But the Argentine dictator, General Videla, was wary of a growing restlessness among his people. The economy was collapsing. The regime needed a distraction. Videla decided that a small war would stir national pride and unify the citizens behind his "strong man" leadership.

Britain had long claimed the Falkland Islands and was loathe to let the Queen's English-speaking subjects fall under the rule of a vicious South American dictator. So Britain, of course, fought back. Argentina was over-matched from the start, but received moral support and a small number of troops from Bangladesh, a country with whom they had no political relationship, but one that had obsessive fan support for Argentina's football team.

It should be noted that football engenders political alliances among fanatical followers in many countries around the world. Football is, after all, a simulation of warfare contained in a stadium. Like a really violent video game—only live. In Argentina, the leading cause of death among young men under the age of thirty-two is being crushed on the field of a football game by a stampede of fans from the other team. So, the risks of being a football fan are higher than one might initially imagine, but oh, the excitement. So it seems possible that Bangladesh might join a war just for the kicks.

But I offer an alternate theory as to why a little country like Bangladesh would take this risk and go to war against Great Britain on behalf of a country—Argentina—with which they had no particular alliance except a shared passion for sport. I assert that Bangladesh was motivated instead by its decades-old hatred of the United States, an ally of Great Britain. I will explain.

It goes back to 1971 when the nation of Bangladesh declared its independence from Pakistan after a bloody Liberation War. Pakistan's ruthless military dictatorship, at the time, headed by President Yahya Khan was loathe to let go of what had been the former country of East Pakistan. Khan was encouraged to punish the small, newly formed DEMOCRACY of Bangladesh by none other than United States Secretary of State, Henry Kissinger. And his sidekick, President Richard Nixon.

Soon after getting the green light from Kissinger, Pakistan's military invaded Bangladesh and slaughtered its citizens by the millions. It was reported by international journalists, that the streets actually ran red with the blood of innocents. Even the United States' own Special Envoy to Pakistan (appointed by Nixon) begged Nixon to put pressure on the military junta to let up. Nixon however followed the advice of Henry Kissinger just as he did in Vietnam and Chile. And Argentina. Once again America turned its back on a fledgling DEMOCRACY. America sided with a savage military dictatorship in Pakistan and was rightly blamed for the genocide that followed. That created a legacy of mistrust between Bangladesh and the United States that endures to this day.

So Bangladesh saw the Falkland War as an opportunity to finally throw a punch at the United States by throwing a punch at its proxy, Great Britain. They say that all politics is personal. They are right.

But as you might have already guessed, Bangladesh's involvement wasn't enough to turn things around. After seventy-four days and nearly 1,000 casualties—mostly on Argentina's side—the Falkland War ended. Britain had won decisively. The Argentine people were left humiliated on an international stage. They blamed General Videla's government for starting the war in the first place. And the military's grip on the nation began to loosen.

But in a final effort to maintain its autocratic rule, the government stepped up its terror campaign on its own citizens. Just as the Vichy French sent 30,000 French Jews to the Nazi Death Camps in the final days of World War II, Videla's Death Squads now rounded up the remaining Jews in Buenos Aires that they had missed in earlier sweeps. The United States government, fully aware of the dire situation in Argentina, refused to intervene.

And that returns us to Susana Rowland's story.

Chapter 17 — The Legacy

On October 1, 1982, Susana and her young Argentine husband, Ethan, hosted a dinner party at their home for their respective families and announced that they were expecting. The baby was due in March of 1983. There was much rejoicing. At the same party, Mateo announced that he was about to receive ordination as a rabbi at Templo Libertad.

His parents were aghast. "You are taking such a risk, Mateo," said his father. "Jews are on the List. I beg you to put this action off a while longer. The junta is struggling now. They are in their final days. Wait a bit. Perhaps help will still come. The United States will step in."

Ethan glowered, "No, the United States will not step in, Papa. They will side with the Dictatorship. As they always do."

"Isn't Kissinger a Jew? Surely, on that basis alone...." his father said.

Ethan scoffed. "He only allies with money and power, Papa. Principles? Morality? They mean nothing to Henry Kissinger—who was the son of immigrant Jewish refugees himself. Who escaped from Europe after World War II. How does he sleep at night?"

Senor León turned back to his younger son. "Why call attention to yourself now, Mateo? You are endangering all of us."

Mateo looked pious. "I am putting myself in God's hands, Papa."

Susana's mother, Noeme, ran to the bathroom and threw up in the toilet.

In January, 1983, Rabbi Mateo León was arrested by the secret police. He was taken to a detention center where he was tortured for weeks under a huge swastika painted on a windowless wall—by men who wore Christian crosses around their necks. Burned and methodically ripped limb from limb, Mateo begged God for strength but finally gave names. He turned in his brother and sister-in-law as radical Left Wing thinkers. And after more torture, he gave up the address of his parents. Mercifully, they finally let him die.

Incredibly one of the largest torture centers was located in the Hospital Posadas where Ethan, completely unaware, had been practicing medicine now for almost six years. The Torture Center took up an entire building known as the "Chalet" in the large hospital complex. It had been set up four days after the military coup in 1976. And was heavily guarded twenty-four hours a day by its own elite force.

The building was kept off limits to other hospital personnel. In fact, like Ethan, most of the employees at Hospital Posadas were completely unaware of its existence, let alone its proximity to healing services. But not all. Complicit doctors were enlisted to administer or at least monitor the torture. No detainee was allowed to die "too soon." Often the torturers weren't seeking information. It was simply torture for torture's sake. No sounds escaped the building but inside, the halls rang with the delirious screams of innocent men and women. None but a handful of detainees survived.

It will come as no surprise that Ethan and Susana were eventually taken from their homes and placed in adjacent locked rooms in the Hospital Posadas Detention Center. They never saw each other again. But Susana heard her young idealistic husband being tortured for days. She was placed in a room next to his, strapped to a bed, her hands tied. Nine months pregnant now and in labor. She struggled to breathe, to not cry out. She heard the rough laughter next door and the torturer's demands. She heard her husband crying. She would later learn that after days of electrical shock and merciless beatings, they finally raped him with a six foot metal rod that ruptured his organs. She heard his high pitched terrified scream and his final call to his mother. It was another thirty minutes before he was dead.

By that time, their baby was born. A girl. The nurse, in a moment of compassion, brought the infant close to Susana's face so she could kiss her once before she was taken away. Susana drank in her face. Her eyes so dark. Her skin the color of honey. Susana inhaled her scent and waited to die.

But, as you know, Susana lived. She was released from the Posadas Detention Center the following morning. She wandered the streets in a daze. A kindly woman approached her, as if by divine design, and took her arm and gently steered her to a car. She was taken far into the countryside and nursed at the private home of the woman and her husband, strangers who were not fellow travelers in any sense. Just good souls.

There were other women there, also in their mid-twenties like Susana. No one spoke, no one asked questions. The kindly couple cooked and brought food and aspirin and clean clothes to the women and listened when anyone of them was ready to talk. Susana never cried—not once while she was with the couple. But her sadness was profound. She knew she could not remain in Argentina. Ethan was dead. Mateo was dead. The Durans were dead. Her parents were dead. Only she and her honey-colored baby had survived. And God only knew where the baby had ended up.

After weeks of silence, Susana finally spoke to the couple. "I wish to go to Uruguay. To the beach at José Ignacio. Our beloved Argentine writer Jorge Luis Borges has reported that José Ignacio is the Elysian Fields for Argentines. Upon death, we will be turned into angels there and get to commune with other angels. I will find my Ethan there. And my mother and my father."

And so, Susana went to José Ignacio, as beautiful a place on earth as one can imagine, where a sugar-white beach stretches for miles and elegant hotels line the shore. She walked along the surf every morning, noon, and night, speaking to no one, thinking of nothing but death for months. But all the time, her resilient body and mind were being rejoined in muscle, blood, and spirit. Perhaps that was the legacy of her ancestors' endless struggle to survive trauma through the centuries. A year later Susana felt restored enough to determine a way forward. A reason to keep living. In 1984, she set out to find Henry Kissinger and kill him. That is how she ended up in New York City.

Chapter 18 – The Engagement Party

Mrs. Rowland, how did you and Mr. Rowland meet?"

Susana laughed. "I will tell you after dinner, Eleanor. But first, we must celebrate you and Mark. This is your day. Here, let me take your coat."

Mark and Eleanor had become engaged at Christmas, but, as you might recall, the Rolands were tied up with Trump's Inauguration in January. So the party was planned for a Sunday in March. A celebration delayed is still a celebration and the *Baby Honey* family arrived that day, tumbling through the door like children, always excited to be together in the wealthy couple's legendary apartment.

Several months before, Eleanor had come across an old issue of *Architectural Digest* magazine that featured a photo spread of three of the Rowlands' homes: a house in Connecticut, a house in San Diego, and their incredible New York condominium. She had shared the article with Mark over breakfast at the Day by Day.

"They are so rich, Mark," she whispered.

"We already knew that," he replied.

"But I'm still surprised. Aren't you surprised? They seem so … normal."

"I don't think they are."

———

Bill and Jacques arrived at the Rowlands' apartment early the morning of the Engagement Party. They promptly took over the kitchen. Susana had been diplomatic with Jacques about the menu; nevertheless she was firm. She had insisted over his initial objections that he forego the diner food that had infatuated him for months and instead reach back to his French training. She said, in her most conciliatory voice, "Yes, dear Jacques, comfort food is indeed soul-satisfying, but on this occasion, we are looking for beautiful food to make us feel rarefied and powerful. Our souls will have to wait for comfort."

Jacques acquiesced. The menu featured individual aspics of delicate crabmeat to be followed by beautifully dressed lamb chops and an airy soufflé of asparagus. To be followed by a filet of rare beef in an elegant wine and cognac sauce accompanied by roasted pommes de terre and the freshest spring peas imported from England. Finally for dessert, la pièce de résistance—a Charlotte Russe dripping with raspberries.

The Rowlands' apartment was massive. A private elevator opened into a spacious foyer which gave onto a window-lined living room, anchored in one corner by a grand piano. Despite the grandeur, the apartment felt welcoming, even cheery. Marmalade flames danced in the fireplace and Bob, sitting at the Steinway, played an upbeat medley of Cole Porter tunes as the guests arrived. It was one of those last days of winter. A seam of air ran down the center of each city avenue, separating cool gusts from warm breezes. As if Mother Nature were in a playful struggle with Herself and couldn't settle on the season. We all entered the apartment sweating and wrapped in scarves.

Susana greeted each of us with a warm smile and a kiss on the cheek. Then we immediately dispersed. We all knew our roles. Mickey and Brenda gathered the coats and headed to the master bedroom. Roger joined Bill in the large dining room where they set the table under Bill's meticulous direction. Sandy headed to the kitchen where Chef Jacques put her to work arranging a tray of canapés that featured Argentine delicacies including cold marinated octopus. Louise filled the crystal water glasses in the dining room. Kip sorted through the wine bottles that Mr. Rowland had selected and opened three to allow them to breathe before dinner. And I sat on the piano bench next to Mr. Rowland and made myself useful by turning the pages of his sheet music.

After laying the coats across the Rolands' large bed, Brenda went into the master bathroom and closed the door. Mickey returned to the party. Brenda listened to his footsteps retreat down the parquet floor back toward the living room. Then she slipped out of the bathroom and positioned herself in front of a large dressing table in one corner of the bedroom suite.

There were silver-framed photographs, seven of them, surrounding a mirrored tray that held various brushes, pots and tubes of makeup, and an elegant flacon of Susana's bespoke perfume. Brenda lifted the petite crystal bottle to her nose and inhaled. It smelled like Susana. Elegant and Mysterious. Brenda carefully replaced it on the tray. She leaned down and faced each of the photos. Family photos, obviously. Most in black-and-white. One of Susana looking so young and pretty holding the hand of a young man—dark haired, dark eyed. Maybe twenty-five? Suddenly Brenda was aware that Susana was standing in the doorway. Brenda startled and turned red.

"It's okay," said Susana, gently. She entered the room and walked to Brenda's side.

"He's very handsome."

"Yes, he was. My first husband. His name was Ethan."

"He died?"

"Yes. Too young."

"I'm sorry."

"Me, too." Susana slipped an arm around Brenda's waist. "I always mean to ask you, Brenda—what is your real name? The one you were given by your parents?"

"Julieta Christina Maria Raquel Elena Isabel Rosati Morales."

Susana laughed. "Oh my."

"I'm adopted."

"Yes. I know."

"And my mother said she had gone eight years trying to get pregnant without success. And every year a new baby would appear to her in a vision with a new name. So, she used them all. She gave me all the names. I was the culmination of all her dreams." Brenda laughed.

Susana's face fell.

"You never had children, Mrs. Rowland?"

"I lost my baby."

Brenda suddenly wrapped Susana in her arms. A gesture of intimacy, from the usually self-controlled Brenda, that surprised Susana. Susana inhaled deeply and tears ran down her cheeks. Brenda whispered, "You can tell me anything, Mrs. Rowland. I will understand." Susana stepped back now and touched Brenda's cheek. Then she turned and walked out of the bedroom. Brenda followed.

I suppose you are thinking that Brenda is Susana's long lost daughter. It might indeed be true; I never asked. Suffice it to say that Susana had, by this time, allowed herself to love the children of other women with a mother's heart. It made her protective of all women.

Meanwhile, in the kitchen, Louise was watching Jacques plate the aspics. Jacques, for his part, was watching Louise out of the corner of his eye. He was always struck by her beauty. Her face was perfectly proportioned with almond eyes and high cheekbones. He thought she strongly resembled his sister, still living in Senegal. He spoke softly. "Louise, you are especially quiet today."

"Roger and I have been arguing."

"Oh?"

"I want to move away from America. It's so dangerous now especially for Black people like us, Jacques. Roger is so naïve. He always assumes that everything will be fine. He thinks the racism in America is overstated. He doesn't understand. He's white."

Jacques nodded. His voice was a plummy contralto. "Where would you move to, Louise?"

"Well, I have thought about Senegal … where you're from. I would be in the majority there, wouldn't I? I mean being Black. I would love to experience that."

Jacques went to the sink and washed his hands. He grabbed a towel and dried them. "Do you know, Louise, that there is a slave class in Senegal? Yes, it's true. And they are Black—as Black as me. As Black as you. They are born into the class. They know who they are. It's not based on race. It's a caste. Although the government tries to deny it."

Louise's eyes rounded with genuine surprise. "Were you…?"

"No. But there was always a risk. Those who are not born to the slave class are often kidnapped and forced into slavery by their own people. Especially children. Children are so vulnerable in Senegal. Forced labor. Forced marriage. Many children are forced into begging. It is a poor country, Louise. And like everywhere else, there are immoral people in Senegal. I tell you the truth. I feel safer here."

Louise was quiet for a long moment. "But Roger and I want a baby. I'm forty. It may be too late. But even if it isn't, the last thing I want is to bring a child into this country where that monster Donald Trump calls the shots."

"America is a big country, Louise. Trump will find it impossible to control all of it. Even with his army. People will resist and even better—people will ignore him.

"The states that are most enamored of Trump will suffer most. Young people will leave. Businesses will move out. Hospitals will close. Schools will close, too. The Red States will quickly become a wasteland of poverty and ignorance. Meantime the wealthier states will work around Trump's attempts to isolate America from its allies. These Blue States will boldly negotiate their own treaties and trade deals with other countries. Form their own alliances. And there will be lots of small acts of defiance in towns and cities all across the country. That will confuse and exhaust Trump. He has a poor attention span to begin with, and his inner circle is inexperienced and unprepared. There will be revolution. People will realign in surprising ways. Don't quit before the battle even begins, Louise."

Louise put her arms around Jacques and rested her head on his broad shoulder. She said, "You have been doing a lot of thinking about all of this."

He patted her back and then said, "Yes. When the dust settles, I intend to be on the winning side."

Act Three

Chapter 19 – Crazy Love

The meal was a hit. When every delectable morsel had been cleared from every elegant plate, and every murmured thank you had been expressed, Eleanor turned to Susana and said, "Now I want to hear your love story. Tell us how you and Bob met."

Susana smoothed the tablecloth with her fingers and said, "Actually, it was Mickey who put us together."

Eleanor gasped, "You're kidding!" All of us looked at Mickey who kept his head down.

Susana nodded, "Mickey and I go way back. I met Mickey at the Day by Day. Oh my gosh, this was in late 1986. I had just arrived in New York and found myself one early morning in front of the Day by Day Café. The lights inside ... the little table lamps were so welcoming. Well, you all know how it beckons." Susana took a sip of wine and resumed her story. "I had found the place quite by accident on my nightly journey through the upper west side. I had terrible insomnia during those years. So I wandered. And one morning, around three, much as you did, Mark—I entered the Day by Day. And that very first morning, I met Mickey. "

Eleanor turned to Mickey and said, "Mickey! You stinker! You never told me." Mickey shrugged and stood. He moved around the table refilling wine and water glasses, avoiding his friends' curious eyes.

Susana laughed softly. "Oh, my goodness—he was in his twenties then. Sitting alone at a table working on a movie screenplay that he was writing. He offered me the seat across from him. Of course, I wasn't so much older myself. I felt older but ... Anyway, I poured out my heart to Mickey. There is something about him that makes you want to confide. He makes you feel safe."

Eleanor smiled and said, "That's true, Mickey."

Mickey returned to his seat. Sandy, sitting next to him, kissed him impulsively on the cheek. "Had you bought the Dollar Store yet?" she asked.

Mickey shook his head. "No. I was living paycheck to paycheck in those days. I worked for a caterer."

Susana added, "Oh, but what a caterer! The finest in New York City at that time. So good, in fact, that when the billionaire founder of the Forbes empire, Malcolm Forbes, turned seventy and held a birthday bash for himself in Morocco a couple of years later, it was Mickey's caterer that was selected to provide the food. That caterer sent its very best cooks, of course. And that included Mickey who was a superb sous chef at the time."

Sandy punched him gently in the arm. "You never said a thing...."

Mickey shrugged again and looked at Susana. "I can keep a secret," he said softly.

Susana smiled at him. "We are family, Mickey. It's time to tell the story." Susana took another sip of wine and went on, "Of course, the caterer also sent their most efficient and discreet wait staff to the Forbes party and that included me."

There were gasps of genuine surprise. Susana laughed. "You see Mickey had gotten me a job soon after we met and I had refined my skills first working in the kitchen and eventually serving at some of the most lavish parties in New York City. It was exciting and I was actually pretty good, wasn't I, Mickey?"

"You were so disciplined, Susana."

"Yes, I worked hard to be good at the job. You see I had big plans for myself. At one of those Manhattan parties I met a handsome man named Bob Rowland. We exchanged a few words and I guess we each made an impression on the other, because when we ran into each other again at the Forbes party in Morocco a year later, we remembered each other."

Bob smiled. "You're unforgettable, Susana."

Eleanor said, "Oh wow—I want to hear about the Malcolm Forbes' party."

Susana took a sip of water now and began. "It was August in 1989. Malcolm Forbes owned a palace in Marrakesh–his own private palace. Can you imagine? The Palais Mendoub. Of course, we, the catering staff, arrived days before the party on a private chartered airplane. Paid for by Mr. Forbes. We would be cooking and serving eight hundred people for three days once the party began."

Sandy looked at Mickey, her eyes glowing. "And you were there?" she said. Mickey nodded. "Yep. I was there."

Susana continued, "The guest list included movie stars—Elizabeth Taylor among them. And businessmen. Bob Rowland was there. And politicians and statesmen. Henry Kissinger was a guest." Susana paused, seeming lost in her memory.

Eleanor said, "Go on, Mrs. Rowland. Go on. This is so cool!"

Susana smiled. "Well, let's see ... The Forbes party ... The eighties were a period of ostentatious wealth as you may have heard. The Reagan Years. There were many huge parties in those days but this one topped them all. It cost millions, but the mantra of these people was 'If you got it, flaunt it.' And at this party, these wealthy people were in a mood to celebrate. They let their guards down. Literally. Their bodyguards took their plates down to the garden every evening and refilled their glasses repeatedly with good wine and Berber whiskey. Oh, they had a jolly party among themselves.

"The serving of the main course on the third and final night had been carefully choreographed to resemble a ballet. There were a hundred wait staff circling in and out of the kitchen so that each guest would receive their food while it was still hot. We had begun rehearsals back in New York weeks before. It was literally a dance. We were like ballerinas moving lightly, silently through the room. We didn't just serve an assigned row of guests. We came in contact with them all. All 800! It was part of our performance. An orchestra played—Tchaikovsky's *Swan Lake*—and we swirled in and among the guests. Always in motion. We were beautiful, but we were indistinguishable. All dressed identically in short black uniforms with high necks and white organdy collars and aprons. Our hair arranged identically—pulled tightly back from the face and smoothed into a top knot wrapped in black velvet ribbon. You see, we had no individuality. You couldn't tell us apart. Not that the guests were looking at us. They only had eyes for each other. They talked to one another. And they laughed. They flirted. And they bragged. They looked deeply into each other's eyes. They were all intoxicated well before the end of the meal. I've forgotten how many bottles of wine were served.

"Former Secretary of State Henry Kissinger was in his element. He never denied himself anything. So, he was feeling no pain. He barely noticed the knife blade that entered his back. He burped as I recall. And looked sick and then pushed back his chair and burped again and then there was blood.

"By this time, I was back in the kitchen. I handed the knife to Mickey who placed it into a dishwasher that had been loaded with prep bowls, and knives and chopping utensils, and was ready to run. Mickey closed the dishwasher door and turned it on. It was nearly ten minutes more before Kissinger fell sideways out of his chair and the blood began to spread, finally drawing attention to his situation.

"No one ever suspected me. No one. Except Bob Rowland. You see, while the other 799 guests kept their eyes on each other, Bob hadn't taken his eyes off me—not once during the three days of the party. He had developed a little crush on me. To tell you the truth, I always found that to be a nice quality in Bob. He's not a snob at all. Imagine. Bob, with his wealth, fell in love with a poor waitress in spite of her social status. Why, it's almost a Cinderella story."

Here Susana paused and allowed her stunned guests—with the exception of Mickey—to absorb her astonishing confession. There was silence until she spoke again.

"Bob soon found me in the kitchen arranging dishes of Baked Alaska on the dessert trays. He whispered, 'Do you smoke?' I said no, but I was willing to take it up that night. We walked outside and crossed the garden to a grove of old oak trees. A dense canopy of leaves created deep shade wherein we could hide from the other guests who were now emerging from the palace for an evening stroll. No one seemed in the least alarmed by Kissinger's accident. Bob lit two cigarettes and handed one to me. I puffed without inhaling, and then I asked, 'Is he dead?'

'I don't believe so. He has been taken to a local hospital. I suppose we will find out soon enough.'

'I hope he is dead. Are the police....'

'Yes, but there are no reliable witnesses. Everyone is drunk. No one remembers....'

'I have good reason.'

'I'm sure you do. He's a war criminal. He deserves assassination.'

'You know this?'

'Oh yes. I have known Henry Kissinger for years.'

'He encouraged the monsters who killed my family, who tortured my young husband to death, who took my baby. He gave the military junta the green light. He directed the CIA to help destroy the democracy in my country.'

'Let me take care of you forever, Susana. You will be my purpose in life. My reason for being. I love you, Susana.'

Susana paused now and looked around the table. "They call it *l'amour fou*." She turned to her husband, "Did I say it right, darling?"

Bob nodded. "Yes. *L'amour fou*. Crazy love."

"Crazy. It sounds better in French, doesn't it?"

"I never thought you were crazy, Susana. You were brave and principled. And you still are. The world has so few heroes willing to take on the monsters. You've given my life purpose. I would die for you, Susana."

Susana blew a soft kiss in her husband's direction. Then she returned her attention to Eleanor who had asked the question in the first place. She patted her hand. "He lived. Kissinger survived. The bastard is still alive. I'm afraid I'm not a very good assassin. But that doesn't make the endeavor any less worthy of the risk. If at first you don't succeed...." Susana now rose from her chair and said, "I'll get dessert. And then I will tell you why I did this."

No one left the party until the early hours of the following morning. They stayed and listened to the story of the Dirty War. Just as I relayed it to you in Chapter 16. And later that evening, Susana confessed to her ill-fated attempt to poison President Trump on the day of his Inauguration. She looked around the table and announced, "But Trump is a puppet. The real villain is Kissinger. And whoever else is pulling his strings. We will be turned into a military dictatorship if we don't organize quickly."

As the shock settled in, someone said, "In a democracy, the people get the government they deserve."

And Mrs. Rowland said, "Well I don't deserve this government and neither do you! Resist. Pick your fight. Pick your weapon. Go to battle."

Chapter 20 – Make America Smart Again

Two thousand and nineteen was certainly a challenging year to embark on a literacy campaign in America. Books were being banned and history, repressed or reinterpreted. Librarians were being threatened and teachers black-balled, often in the name of Jesus. Americans were overwhelmed by a daily tsunami of misinformation. No one knew whom they should trust. The Republicans blamed the Democrats. The Democrats blamed the Republicans. They were both wrong, of course. The problem was the Billionaires. But too many Americans were in awe of Billionaires. The Billionaires owned everything in America, including Trump and all three branches of the government. They controlled the military, Wall Street, and the Press. And all Social Media. They determined who could speak publicly, and what they could say. When Trump lied, they amplified his lies by broadcasting them on their domains.

Kip and Brenda had managed to stay impervious to Untruth because they were both voracious readers. In the books they read—

history, science, anthropology, art, philosophy, even mathematics—
Truth was always evident. And once you accustom yourself to seeing
what Truth looks like, you are unlikely to believe lies no matter who
speaks them. Because you acquire critical thinking skills.

So Kip and Brenda, in an effort to save America, embarked on a
mission to restore a love of books among Americans. It was a race
to stay ahead of the Billionaires' nefarious plans for the country to
become totally illiterate. Fortunately, none of the Billionaires read
books themselves. And Trump was already illiterate. And they were
all arrogant so it hadn't occurred to any of these men that there
were Americans who still liked to read. So they didn't worry that
bookstores were still in business. That gave Brenda and Kip a bit
of a head start. The first step was to refamiliarize Americans with
written words so they *could* read books. Kip and Brenda called their
plan—Make America Smart Again.

They appeared on *The Late Show with Stephen Colbert*, a popular
late night program on network television, wearing T-shirts of their
own design. Brenda's read: I AM PULCHRITUDINOUS. Kip's
read: I AM NOT JEJUNE. They brought one along as a gift for
Colbert. It read: I AM PUISSANT. Colbert immediately stripped
down to his bare chest and put it on. The audience cheered.

Kip said, "We call these our Fancy Word Shirts. Aren't they
cool?" The audience clapped enthusiastically. "American kids are
falling behind the rest of the world in every category of education.
You know this is true. Right, Stephen?"

Colbert nodded. "Yeah. That's what they say."

Kip continued. "This is happening here in the USA, Stephen!
Where every kid can get twelve years of education for free! It's
damn embarrassing. Where's our national pride? We are becoming
the dumbest nation on earth. And the sick part is that it's all being
encouraged by the President."

Brenda added, "Voters are easier to dominate when they're
dull-witted. Which explains why Pro-Trump governors and state
legislators are banning books and attacking public libraries."

Colbert produced a wan smile and said, "Hmmmm ... where has that happened before?" The audience groaned.

Kip nodded. "Here's a tip, folks. Start buying up books while you can. Real books are going to be worth a fortune!"

Brenda nodded "Kip's right. Books are a great investment. Especially now as they become rare."

Kip added, "So get in on the action today! Buy Books!"

Brenda added, "And while you're at it, read them."

The audience cheered wildly. Stephen Colbert sat back and smiled. He knew that this interview would be talked about tomorrow. He looked at Kip and said, "So tell me about the shirts."

"Well, if we want people to buy books and actually read them, they have to be reintroduced to words. There are no emoticons in books." The audience laughed.

Brenda smiled, "Our written language is being reduced to hieroglyphics, Stephen. Which would be neat if we didn't have a better alternative."

Kip picked up the thread. "But we do! Words are super fun when you get used to them. And they can be sexy. Right, Brenda?"

Brenda's eyes widened. She clasped her hands over her breasts and huskily pronounced the following: "LUCENT. LUMINOUS. ASTUTE. RADIANT. FULGENT...."

Colbert looked at her rapturously. "Wow ... when you put it that way...."

Brenda cooed, "Emoticons can't begin to express the subtle variations, let alone the rapture, which can be found in our language. Words can be voluptuous. Words can be salacious."

The audience squealed.

Kip patted his T-shirt. "These shirts are like flash cards. You can learn a new word every day. Impress your friends!"

Brenda smiled. "So that is our mission, Stephen. We are giving these shirts away. They're free. Just go to *The Baby Honey Show* website and pick one out. Or two. You can have one for each day of the week if you like. Wear them everywhere. Learn lots of new words.

Exchange words with your friends. Be part of the movement to Make America Smart Again!"

The audience cheered.

Colbert mused, "I remember a time when Education and Literacy would be pet projects of a First Lady."

Brenda nodded. "Melania Trump has been in the country many years longer than I have, and she still speaks English poorly. It's a wonder some of President Trump's followers haven't beaten her up. As we have seen, they are hostile to people with accents."

Colbert raised a finger. "Let's be fair, Brenda—Trump's followers only beat up *brown* people with accents." The audience groaned.

Kip threw his hands up in the air. "Be Best? Be Best?? Will someone tell me what the hell that means?"

Brenda shook her head, sadly. "Mrs. Trump doesn't understand basic English sentence construction. It's an especially bad look for the wife of a xenophobe."

Colbert looked innocently at the audience and said, sweetly. "Maybe Melania really doesn't care. Do you?"

The audience howled with derisive laughter. Colbert's eyes danced.

Brenda added, "Oh and I forgot to mention, Stephen—each Fancy Word T-shirt order comes with a free dictionary. Signed by Kip."

Kip nodded, "Remember—if I'm educatable, you're educatable." The audience applauded.

Colbert patted his shirt and sighed, "Well. Now that we've broken the ice. I have a question for America's Sweethearts." He turned to Brenda and Kip and asked, "What else would you two say is wrong with Americans today? I mean other than the fact that we are illiterate."

Kip turned to Colbert and said, "I think the most dangerous thing is that Americans don't find the same things funny anymore. Really! That's a sign that we are coming apart as a culture."

Brenda sighed, "The most benign cartoonists are getting hate mail."

Colbert nodded. "You know, that's true. Used to be only the really great comics got hate mail. Used to be a badge of honor. Now every second-rate clown gets doxed."

Brenda added, "Even our Baby Honey gets threatening letters. Can you imagine? Threatening a baby?" The audience booed.

Kip leaned back in his chair and crossed his legs. "The great nineteenth-century historian, de Tocqueville? You all should read his book, by the way. He predicted that humor would eventually be bred out of Americans because of the sheer diversity of the population. He said the country was so big it could physically accommodate more people than it could assimilate. So eventually anything funny was guaranteed to offend someone. I think the same thing brought down the Roman Empire."

Brenda nodded. "Yes, I believe that was a factor."

Colbert leaned forward and smirked, "Speaking of the immigration crisis ... as you all know, President Trump is terrorizing refugees who cross the southern border by separating babies from their mothers and putting all of them in cages. So the question on the table now is this—Will torturing refugees bring humor back to America?"

The audience half-laughed, then groaned. Then laughed again.

Brenda responded, "Men with autocratic ambitions—which Trump clearly has—know that they must control women, if they are to successfully control the culture. Because women create the culture. They carry the future in their bodies. The Trump regime is starting with immigrant women, but American women are their real target. Trust me—Trump and his Party Leaders are very afraid of women."

Kip added, "Women vote in larger numbers than men. The Trump agenda relies on controlling American women."

Brenda said, "They will start by controlling women's bodies."

The audience fell silent. Colbert leaned toward Brenda. "Please, go on."

Kip said, "Read the history! Women got the vote in 1920 and what followed was an era of progressive policies like there had never been before. Civil rights, Integration. Worker's rights. Unions. Environmental protections. Expanded healthcare. And reproductive rights."

Colbert interjected, "The GOP has made no secret of the fact that they want to outlaw all of those things. And you're right. They do seem to be aiming first at reproductive rights. They want to ban abortions nationally. They have also announced that they will make birth control illegal." The audience jeered.

Kip interjected. "Don't you see? They want to drive women back into the home so they can't influence public policy in the public sphere. But they insist these are pro-family actions."

Brenda nodded. "The irony is that many young women would love to have children. And *would* have babies if abortion and birth control remained safe and legal. But women are afraid to take the risk of getting pregnant knowing that doctors will be forced to let them die if something goes wrong. Many young women are actually being voluntarily sterilized to avoid that possibility. As a result, the birth rate in America is dropping like a stone."

Colbert mockingly exclaimed, "Damn! Foiled again!"

Brenda continued, " Of course, a falling population will affect all of us. Fewer workers to keep our economy thriving. Products will become scarce and more expensive. Inflation will rise. Fewer doctors and teachers. Even the billionaires will eventually see their bottom line affected."

Kip looked directly at the camera now and said, "History tells us that a society that is cruel to women is ultimately doomed."

Colbert said, "Now that should be on a T-shirt."

In the next week, a campaign to disparage *The Baby Honey Show* emerged on social media. The attacks were vicious but they failed. The show continued to gain new viewers. Furthermore, in that first month following Kip's and Brenda's appearance with Colbert, orders for the Fancy Word T-Shirts topped forty million. The Rowlands now turned half of their *Baby Honey* clothing factories over to creating the shirts. Every member of the Family contributed words. Including me. RESIST. CONFRONT. REFUTE. THWART. DEFY.

Each shirt displayed a single "fancy word" on the front side. And on the back side of the shirt, the following was printed: ***Don't Trust Social Media.***

Chapter 21 – The War on Women

Moderator: "Do you believe in punishment for abortion—yes or no—as a principle?"

Trump: "The answer is that there has to be some form of punishment."

Moderator: "For the woman?"

Trump: "Yeah, there has to be some form."

Candidate Donald Trump at a Town Hall in 2016

*T*he following morning, the Family gathered at the Day by Day to hear Sandy relay her latest dream. Every seat in the restaurant was taken. Sandy was becoming famous as an Oracle. We all—patrons and family alike—trusted her power to see what was coming, and thereby prepare us for the worst. Sandy took her seat in front of the wall of bookshelves and began her colorful recitation.

182

Trump is sitting behind the Resolute Desk in the Oval Office. He is alone except for his most trusted adviser, Stephen Miller. Trump takes a long pull on his Diet Coke, burps and says, "So, I'm in Bergdorf Goodman one afternoon farting around ... no, wait ... I was looking for a birthday present for Marla. Yeah. That's right. This was years ago, when I was married to Marla. God, I remember that afternoon so clearly. Anyway, I run into this woman. Gorgeous woman. Blonde, tall. Big tits. She looked a lot like Marla. But she had a funny name ... like A.J? E. J.? Anyway, I say to myself, 'I should fuck her. Yeah, seriously. Fuck her right here in Bergdorf's. Why not? Right?'"

"You are the man, Mr. President," Stephen Miller says, his bald head turning bright pink.

"Well, Stephen ... the next thing I know she is entering a dressing room and I just follow her right into the room. And she goes, 'What are you doing?' And I said, 'I'll show you what I'm doing, Darling."

Stephen giggles and accidentally drools on his slacks.

"So, I slam her up against the wall and I take my pecker out and she's trying to push me away and I'm just getting more...."

There's a knock at the Oval Office door. Trump growls, "WHAT NOW?"

A female voice on the other side of the door says, "Mr. President, Ginny Thomas is here to see you."

Trump slumps. "Oh, Christ."

Stephen comes to the president's side. "Sir, she is bringing you the name of the next Supreme Court Justice. The one you have to put on the bench. He is hand selected by the American Christian Taliban Society. You owe them."

"Ugh, but why do I always have to spend time with Ginny Thomas? Can't they send someone else? I can't stand

to look at her. A body like a linebacker. And that dopey, little girl voice. And she's certifiable, Stephen. I swear she's nuts."

Stephen crosses to the door and opens it a crack. He addresses the woman in the hall.

"Give us five minutes more, Kellyanne. Just stall her a bit longer. The president is working on an important Executive Order."

Stephen returns and stands before the Resolute Desk. "So, finish your story, sir."

"That's basically it. I fucked her. And she got all upset. But that's an act, Stephen. They always do that so they don't feel like a whore. But she loved it. I know she loved it. And she knows she loved it."

Stephen nods. "Okay. I'll have Kellyanne bring Mrs. Thomas in now."

"You know I don't get it, Stevie. Clarence Thomas is an ugly fucker, but he's got tons of money. The American Christian Taliban Society has been very, very good to that Darkie. He didn't have to settle for a dumpy white woman. He could have had a beautiful Black wife. I mean there are a lot of beautiful Black women out there who would have married him for his money even if he is repulsive. For Christ's sake, he sold himself short. He didn't have to settle for Ginny...."

The door opens. Ginny Thomas steps into the room and freezes awkwardly as Kellyanne retreats, closing the door. "Hi," says Ginny in her baby voice. "I couldn't wait any longer."

Trump rises and crosses to her, his hand extended. "Ginny! Darling, how are you? You look amazing in that ... what is that? Aqua? A lovely aqua caftan. So flattering with that tangerine lipstick. You know I'm partial myself to orange makeup. Come sit here. Let's be comfortable in these extra-large chairs. You know my advisor, Stephen Miller."

"Yes. Hi." Ginny whispers.

Stephen steps forward and offers his hand. "Nice to see you again, Mrs. Thomas."

Ginny sits and pulls a piece of paper out of her handbag. "Before we get to the business at hand, here is my latest list of disloyal people in your White House, Mr. President. You need to dismiss all of them immediately."

Trump takes the paper from her hand and studies it. "Steve Bannon? He's on this list?"

Ginny nods. "He is the worst. A blabbermouth! My spies tell me he talks to every person who is writing a book about you, Donald. None of us can afford that."

"But I fired him a year ago."

Stephen Miller says, "He's back, Sir. He has an office in the West Wing. Peter Navarro let him in again."

Trump shakes his head. "Oh, Peter. My Peter. He's cuck-oo, you know. But he's my China Trade guru."

Ginny and Stephen answer together. "We know."

Trump smiles. "Chi-Na ... Chiiii-Nah. I love saying Chi-Na. It makes me feel like I'm Chew-ing. Can-dee. Chewy Candy. Cheweeeeeee."

Ginny and Stephen answer together. "Uh huh."

Trump eyes the two of them coldly. "You know all my other advisers told me not to hire Peter. They said he's a loon. A Fuck-up. A Nutjob. But My Peter loves me. And that's the price of admission, kids. Love me or get out." Trump pauses to let that sink in. Then he says, "Stephen, tell Bannon to pack up his desk. I want him thrown out imme-diately. Again." Stephen clicks his heels and turns sharply. He exits the Oval Office.

Trump turns back to Ginny. "Okay, that's done. So, do you have the name for the Supreme Court?"

"His name is Brett Kavanaugh. He is an anti-abortion Christian. Just like Gorsuch."

"Gorsuch?"

"Justice Gorsuch? The one you appointed last year. Remember? The vacancy came up while Obama was in office but Mitch McConnell blocked Obama from appointing anyone until we had you in place? Remember?" Ginny pauses and notes that Trump looks blank. "When was your last cognitive test, Donald?"

"No, no ... I'm fine. I was just thinking ... Gorsuch. I know that guy ... Gorsuch. He's kind of a stiff, isn't he? He never takes my calls."

"Nevertheless Gorsuch is a fighter for the Cause, Donald. He's anti-abortion to the extreme—he is willing to allow a mother to die in agony. Anything to save a White baby. That's how Pro-Life he is."

"Wow, where do you find these guys?"

"Actually, we make them a deal they can't refuse." Ginny giggles, an insipid trickle of gasps, then resumes, "They will sell their souls for money. But as the Christian Taliban says, money is not sinful when it is used to coerce men toward the Light. Anyway, Kavanaugh is a superb pick for the Supreme Court. Very much in the mold of Gorsuch. Although he does have some baggage; he raped some girls in college."

Trump waves a hand. "Whatever...."

"Well, you know the Left will try to make something of that but we'll smear these women and threaten their children. They'll shut up." Ginny pauses and stifles another giggle. "The best part is that Kavanaugh is even younger than Gorsuch. He will be on the Court for a long time. And

he, like Gorsuch, is committed to getting the birth rate up again among American White people. The Dream is about to be fulfilled, Donald."

Trump takes a swig from his Diet Coke and nods. Ginny continues enthusiastically, "We simply cannot continue to allow the White population to be overwhelmed by people of color. We will never be able to win an election again. White women must be forced to give birth."

Trump nods. "Do you have any kids, Ginny?"

"No. I don't like children." Ginny smiles sweetly and shrugs her shoulders. "But they are necessary for the future of the country. We will need workers."

"Yeah, that's true ... especially if Stephen puts all the colored people in cages. Who's gonna pick oranges? Who's gonna pick lettuce? I mean think about it...."

Ginny gives him a cool stare. "White children can be taught to do those jobs, Donald."

"I don't know ... the ones I know are lazy as fu.... I mean lazy as all get out."

Ginny purses her lips. "I'm talking about POOR White children. Not YOUR sons."

Trump shrugs. "Oh...."

Ginny resumes, "Anyway, we are keeping our eye on Justice Ruth Ginsburg. Her seat will be the next vacancy. She's had cancer about eleven times now and we were all afraid that she would have stepped down when the Democrats were in full power at the start of Obama's term. That way Obama could have picked a Liberal like her and that would have kept the Court Liberal. But she didn't step down. And the GOP got back in power at the midterm. Democrats are so bad at this game." Ginny snorts. "Anyway Ruth is going to die on your watch, Donald. And the American Christian Taliban Society has already picked another justice for you to appoint. And then we will have a conservative majority on the court. And then we can eliminate abortion altogether and ban contraception, too. And White women will have to have babies. Except rich ones who will fly to Sweden for a safe abortion. But our Cause will be fulfilled. We will be a White Nation again!" Ginny closes her eyes and sways in her seat. She sings a gospel hymn. "Oh, happy days. Oh, happy days. When Jesus washed...."

Trump watches her with contempt. "What are you going to do with your husband, Ginny? He's Black."

Ginny freezes and her cold eyes meet Trump's cold eyes. "I am color-blind, Donald. I only see the White in Clarence."

Trump stands up. "Good for you. Well, I guess that concludes our business. Thank you for coming, Ginny. Always a delight." Trump walks her to the door and opens it. She walks through. "Tootle-loo," he says. Closing the door after her, he mutters, "And they say I'm a misogynist."

Trump returns to his desk. There's a sharp rap at the door of the Oval Office. Trump growls, "YEAH? WHAT NOW?"

The door opens and Trump's favorite Dirty Trickster—Roger Stone—peers into the office. His face is darkened with black charcoal. "HEY! WHERE DA WHITE WOMEN AT?"

Trump explodes with derisive laughter. Roger enters the office and flops in a chair. He grins viciously. "Now you can tell the fucking press that you finally hired one of them."

Trump wipes his eyes. "Do I have the Best People or what?"

"Then I woke up." Sandy shuddered and took a sip of her cold coffee.

Mark shook his head, "How do you remember all these details? I can't remember my dreams at all."

Eleanor said, "I don't think she's dreaming, Mark. I think you were having an out-of-body experience, Sandy. I think you were physically there."

Susana said, "I agree! Now we have a spy in the White House! You must take me the next time you dream, Sandy. I will assassinate Trump."

Louise said, "Is Trump aware that you are in the room, Sandy? Does he see you?"

Sandy said, "I'm not sure–but now that you mention it, I think Roger Stone saw me last night. And I think he suspects that I'm undocumented."

Mickey took her hand, "We are legally married now, Honey. You are safe."

Jacques said, "I understand that Stephen Miller has a plan to nullify that law."

Susana said, "Then I will kill him, too."

Kip's attention was suddenly pulled to the bookshelves covering the back wall of the Day by Day. Rows and rows of paperbacks that Kip could not recall having seen before that moment. As he watched, the entire collection of books suddenly shivered and shimmered. Kip closed his eyes in disbelief, and when he opened them, the light was gone but Kip found himself once again staring at the bookshelves.

He exclaimed, "A LIBRARY? THE DAY BY DAY HAS A LIBRARY?? HAS THIS BEEN HERE ALL LONG??!!!!!"

Bill laughed and said, "Yeah, Mr. Bookworm. It's been here forever. I'm surprised you haven't noticed it 'til now."

Chapter 22 – Kip Finds an Old Book

Actually, it's easy to understand how even Kip, with his love of books, might have missed this little library. Nothing changed in the Day by Day Café so it was easy to overlook the obvious. The mismatched chairs and tables, the individual table lamps with the soft pink shades. The *Philodendron* at the front window, its deathless, heart-shaped leaves now permitted to climb the walls and form a canopy at the apex of the ceiling. And, of course, the wonderful wall of bookshelves, crowded mostly with dog-eared paperbacks, a few hardcover volumes in the mix. All of them best sellers in their day. Many of them long forgotten. Those Americans who were still literate in 2019 preferred reading on a Kindle or listening to audiobooks. Many said that print was dead. But not Kip Barrett. Kip loved turning actual pages. He approached the wall of books with reverence.

During his young school years, Kip's academic acumen had been largely overlooked because he was so incredibly good-looking. Teachers gave him automatic As on quizzes and tests regardless of his errors. No one ever corrected him. And no one encouraged him to read and think and express his thoughts. It was assumed that he would become a model. So, Kip succumbed to an innate laziness and never picked up a book all through school. He became what everyone expected him to be, an inarticulate Adonis.

But water seeks its own level, as they say. Kip met Brenda Beacon. On their second date, Brenda accompanied him to the New York Library where he signed up for a library card, his first, and he started to browse. He devoured books on the biology of insects that first week. On the origins of the planet the next. On botany and astronomy and anthropology over the next few months. Then he turned to world history and American history. To Geography. His appetite for facts seemed insatiable. Kip, however, was not drawn to fiction. But Brenda encouraged him to "read promiscuously. Read every book and any book, my Love. You will see—reading story-books is important. It will make you a critical thinker."

So, Kip began at the top shelf of the Day by Day Library, climbing the ladder and drawing down a well-worn copy of *The Catcher in the Rye* by J.D. Salinger, published in 1951. He was immediately drawn to the young protagonist. Kip's own childhood could not have differed more from that of a prep school drop-out, estranged from his wealthy parents. But the boy's emotional life reawakened memories in Kip. Of his own sense of isolation among his peers, of his disillusionment with his parents' world and of a yearning to protect the vulnerable. Kip marveled at the writer's ability to create an emotional connection to a stranger living 66 years into the future.

The next book on the shelf—*My Friend Whitey*—was published in 1954, by Pete, the original owner of the Day by Day. Pete's story of an underground zoo in a peaceful 1950s America—"where everyone had plenty to eat and everyone lived in harmony regardless of their race, creed, or religion"—frankly annoyed Kip. He knew the history of the period. The Communist "witch hunts" of the '50s turned Americans against one another. Books and movies were banned. The powerful House Un-American Activities Committee in Congress was hauling in writers and intellectuals and accusing them publicly, without any evidence whatsoever, of being traitors to

America. Citizens were thrown in prison. Innocent lives were ruined. Kip said to Brenda, "Why would Pete whitewash that truth?"

And Brenda said, "Perhaps he was being sarcastic. Or maybe it comforted him to write his fantasy. We will never know, Kip. He's dead. But he had right to say whatever he wanted to say. Because we are all protected by the Constitution. Of course, you can reject his premise. You are protected, too."

Kip read on. *Peyton Place*, published in 1956. A soap opera set in a small New England town featuring extramarital affairs and shady business deals. *Mandingo*, a 1957 novel about inter-racial love on a Southern plantation. *Dr. No* (1954), and *Goldfinger* (1959)—Ian Fleming's thrillers about a suave British spy taking on international evil while wearing designer suits and drinking perfect martinis. *To Kill A Mockingbird* (1960)—a haunting story of racial violence and injustice. *Cat's Cradle* (1963), a brilliant satire of religion by Kurt Vonnegut. *The Group* (1963), by Mary McCarthy—about eight Vassar graduates—covered controversial topics like extramarital sex, contraception and lesbianism, and was banned for a time in Australia.

It was fair to say that the little library provided a survey course on the psyche of mid-twentieth-century America. Tales of optimism were followed by tales of woe which were followed by tales of liberation. Heroes were countered by villains who were tripped up by anti-heroes. Authors who tiptoed to avoid censorship one year would be replaced the next year by writers who would explore the same terrain with robust candor. Always—always—the country seemed to lurch wildly in every direction but somehow land on the same spot where it had embarked on its journey in the first place. And the odyssey would start anew. As the great eighteenth-century philosopher, Friedrich Hegel, so wisely observed: "We learn from history that we do not learn from history."

One morning, a few weeks later, a book on the bottom shelf caught Kip's eye. It was wedged between *Fear and Loathing in Las Vegas* (1971) and *The Stepford Wives* (1972.) It was not only out of place—it seemed out of time. A very old volume. *The American Instructor, or, Young Man's Best Companion* was written and published in

1748 by none other than Benjamin Franklin, America's beloved Founding Father. Kip, for the first time, ignored the order of the books and skipped to the center of that shelf. He pulled out the Franklin volume.

It took Kip a moment to realize that the book was a carefully handled original. It appeared, at first glance, to be a textbook guide to learning basic mathematics. Kip was intrigued. He placed the book in his backpack and began reading that night.

When Kip came upon the final chapter of the book, titled "The Poor Planter's Physician," the subject switched from mathematics to household tips. There was advice on such topics as caring for horses' hooves. There was instruction on how to write a proper letter. And there was this:

> *Now I am upon Female Infirmities, it will not be unreasonable to touch upon a common Complaint among unmarried women, namely The Suppression of the Courses. This don't only disparage their Complexions, but fills them besides with sundry Disorders. For this Misfortune, you must purge with Highland Flagg (commonly called Belly ach Root) a Week before you expect to be out of Order; and repeat the same two Days after: the next Morning drink a Quarter of a Pint of Pennyroyal Water or Decoction, with twelve drops of Harts Horn, and as much again at Night when you go to Bed. Continue this 9 Days running and after resting 3 Days, go on with it for 9 more. Ride out every fair Day, stir nimbly about your Affairs, and breathe as much as possible in the open Air.*

Kip read it twice. He put the book down and looked out at the pretty full moon in the southern sky. It appeared to wink at him. He shook his head vigorously; then focused his eyes on that passage again. This time, he took note of the admonition that followed. Regarding women in need of "suppressing their courses," Franklin had written " ... *nor must they long for pretty Fellows or any Trash whatsoever.*" Kip had no doubt now—this was an explicit recipe for abortion. An at-home, do-it-yourself abortion. In a math textbook. From 1748. Written by Ben Franklin.

Kip knew from his copious readings in primitive medicine that abortions had been done since the beginning of civilization. The ancient Greeks had their methods, as did the Romans. In the early Middle Ages, midwives passed down their best knowledge regarding bringing a baby safely into the world as well as ending a troublesome pregnancy that might threaten the mother's life. The women of the Native tribes of North America identified the abortifacients among the herbs and flowers of the prairies and were known to share the knowledge with the housewives of the New World. Slave women brought their knowledge of abortifacients from Africa and the West Indies. Those who were subjected to especially cruel treatment from their masters, routinely aborted their pregnancies in an act of love, to save a child from a life of unrelenting misery.

It should be added that abortions were done without fanfare. A simple decision made and executed by a woman in the privacy of her home. No questions asked. Women were trusted to know when the time was right to bring a new life into the world and they had methods to end an unwanted pregnancy at their disposal, long before there were Planned Parenthood clinics. Or medical doctors.

It became common practice in the early days of the nation to include such an instruction in a book of household tips. Even Cotton Mather, the Puritan preacher who participated in the Salem witch trials of 1693 in Massachusetts—and insisted that the colonies were established in the New World under God's approving eye—yes, even *that* Cotton Mather published a recipe for aborting a fetus. It wasn't regarded as a moral issue. It was considered Female Health and Hygiene.

Kip looked at the title again. The *Young Man's Best Companion.* Kip reasoned that Franklin might have anticipated that there would be young men who would find themselves in a situation where they needed to help a lady friend get rid of an out-of-wedlock pregnancy. Although it was just as likely that the book was always intended for women as well.

Franklin was reported to have often shared the story of a young widow who learned bookkeeping and was able to sustain her late husband's business after his untimely death, thereby saving her family from the Poor House. And Franklin had a daughter, his beloved Sally, who was a successful businesswoman in her own right.

Perhaps Franklin consulted Sally just before the mathematics and bookkeeping textbook went to print. Maybe she said, "You know what, Pop? You should put an abortion formula in the appendix along with tips for writing a decent business letter—thereby covering all the bases that an American female entrepreneur will ever need."

However, it happened—there it was. A Do-It-Yourself Guide to Abortion. Kip reviewed this stunning turn of events. Apparently, this book had sat on a bookshelf—in a field of old paperback novels—hidden in plain sight for decades. Perhaps it was a woman who tucked the book between two novels on a day in 1973 when, after a relentless, exhausting fight with the anti-abortion zealots, reproductive choice was finally made legal in America. Maybe that prescient woman had said to herself, "Just in case the dark forces of the Christian Right return to power." Kip half-laughed and said to himself, "And what better place is there to hide a subversive text from the vicious scrutiny of the American Christian Taliban Society than among old books in a café that is only open from three until eight in the morning?"

Kip carefully copied Franklin's prescription by hand in a notebook that he kept in his backpack. He would return *Young Man's Best Companion* to its place on the shelf that morning, but now he needed to wake Brenda.

She opened her eyes and, seeing how excited Kip was, sat up.

"Brenda.... Where do we find Highland Flagg, Pennyroyal and Harts Horn?"

Brenda blinked. "What are you talking about, my Love?"

Kip grabbed the book and showed her the recipe. She quickly deciphered its meaning and, like Kip, knew their challenge would be to find a way to distribute it without getting arrested.

"We will have to be discreet, Kip."

"That isn't my strong suit, Babe."

"I know that," said Brenda. She kissed him. "But it is mine." Brenda looked at the clock on the bedside table and noted that it was 3 a.m. She kicked off her blanket and stretched. "Oh boy! It's breakfast time. Let's go to the Day by Day and see if Jacques will make me Fried Chicken and Waffles again this morning. I'm famished."

The discovery of this abortion formula in an old book in the Day by Day Café wasn't the only miracle that occurred that week. In what might be called an ironic twist, Brenda had realized just the night before that she was pregnant. Brenda hadn't seen a doctor or taken a test, but, like many women, she knew her body. And it was telling her that she was carrying her heart's desire.

Brenda, however, knew that it was the wrong time to have a baby. America in 2019 was a dangerous place in which to be pregnant let alone in which to raise a child. It was, in fact, a bitter time. So Brenda decided to keep the baby within her body, where it would be safe— for as long as she felt it was necessary. The hidden baby would know when the moment was right to emerge.

Brenda told no one her secret. Not even Kip. And her body didn't betray her by changing shape in the months that followed. Brenda's baby slept quietly within her, giving her daily hope and strength for what was to come.

Chapter 23 – "The Good Ol' Days"

The Baby Honey Show–Episode #34

(JULIE enters through the front door. Carrying various shopping bags all labeled with the Baby Honey logo. She wears a shirtwaist dress in a pretty pink gingham pattern. It falls modestly to her mid-calves in what is known as a ballet length. Her small waist is accentuated by a slender belt. And a simple string of pearls hangs around her throat. Her hair is pulled back in a ponytail that swings from side to side when she moves. She epitomizes the 1950s ideal woman. Soundtrack: Audible coos of appreciation at JULIE's new style.

JULIE

Darling? Peter? I'm home!

(PETER emerges from off camera, wiping his hands on a dish towel. He goes to JULIE and embraces her. He kisses her. Soundtrack: Cheers.)

PETER

You are adorable, Julie.

(She blushes. Soundtrack: Audible sighs.)

JULIE

Thank you. What have you been up to today?

PETER

I dug a garden in the backyard. Just the size you requested.

JULIE

Oh, Peter! For my kitchen garden?! Oh, Peter, you are the most wonderful husband in the world!! Thank you, darling.

(Close up on PETER. He is smiling at JULIE ecstatically. Soundtrack: Clapping, sighing, warm laughter.)

PETER

You are so feminine, Julie. *Everything you touch grows.* Including me. You are such a good cook!

(He pats his stomach. Soundtrack: Laughter.)

JULIE

Oh, you're so silly! You are as handsome as ever. And just for the record, I will love you always even when you are old and gray and fat.

(Soundtrack: Laughter. Coos of approval. PETER kisses her.)

PETER

Sometimes I feel like we are living in the 1950s again. Everything is so perfect.

JULIE

I do like a lot of the clothes. But I'm glad we have vaccines now so our family isn't dying of polio. Or measles.

(Soundtrack: the audience applauds.)

PETER

That's true, Darling. I'm so thankful for that, too.

(PETER and JULIE kiss and remain cheek to cheek.)

JULIE

We can still wear the clothes from the '50s if we like.

PETER

Sometimes I like to wear bell bottoms from the '80s, too. I hear they are coming back in style.

(Soundtrack: Uh-oh.)

JULIE

Boy, I hope not.

(PETER and JULIE separate now. They smile at each other.)

PETER

So, did you find the seeds you wanted?

JULIE

I did. It was tricky but I found them.

(JULIE holds up packets of seeds.)

I learned today that these herbs were part of kitchen gardens back in the olden days during the time of the Founding Fathers. All of the wives had an herb and flower garden outside the door in addition to a vegetable gar-den. Of course, women have done that for centuries. But I wanted to rep-licate something completely authen-tic and all-American. (Soundtrack: Cheers and Enthusiastic Applause.) And

I found a woman who still grows these early American herbs. They are easy to grow and they're pretty. But first I need to show you what I bought for Baby Honey and me. *(Soundtrack: Applause and affectionate laughter.)*

(JULIE opens the bags and pulls out a gardening apron for the baby and a matching one for herself.)

JULIE

Aren't these the cutest things?! Look—we will match!!! And I can keep my dress clean while I'm planting my herbs.

(JULIE displays the baby apron on the back of the couch. She starts to tie the adult apron around her waist.)

PETER

Allow me.

(JULIE turns her back to him, and he takes the apron sashes and pulls her close with them. He kisses her neck as he ties them. She giggles. Soundtrack: Uh-oh. Laughter.)

JULIE

But wait! Look what else I found!

(JULIE pulls out toy gardening implements for Baby Honey, all made by the Baby Honey Corporation.)

JULIE

Baby-sized garden tools. To match mine. Aren't they precious? I also bought a Baby Honey sand box. It's still in the trunk. Could you bring it in later, Dear? It's kind of heavy for me to lift.

PETER

Your wish is my command, my lady.

JULIE

Baby can pretend that she's digging her own garden while I plant the real one. This will be such fun for us while you are at work.

PETER

When do you think your herbs will start flowering?

JULIE

Oh, almost immediately. These old fash-ioned herbs are very hardy and grow quickly.

PETER

Well, your garden plot is ready for your womanly touch. I wonder, Julie, can women who live in apartments have a kitchen garden like this?

JULIE

Of course they can. Clay pots can hold
individual herbs and they can be arranged on a windowsill or terrace or
even the fire escape. Every woman in
America should give this a try. We can
call them our Victory Gardens. Victory Gardens will make American families
self-sufficient just as they did during
World War II when women did their part
to defeat the Nazis.

*(Soundtrack: Enthusiastic Whistles and
Applause.)*

PETER

Gosh, that's right! There were Victory Gardens at that time. That's such
a cute name for your little project,
Julie.

JULIE

I have to pick up Baby in about forty minutes. My mother took her to her
swimming lesson today.

PETER

Your mother is such a fine woman. No
wonder you turned out so beautiful inside and out.

(Soundtrack: A soft ohhhhh.)

*(Soundtrack: clapping, Uh-oh! Laughter.
PETER and JULIE embrace and start kiss-*

Fan mail to *The Baby Honey Show* increased 400% during the following month. Everyone, it seemed, regardless of their political identities, loved Julie and Peter. The Left applauded Julie's self-sufficiency and the Right adored her femininity. Independents thought the couple was campy and sly. And everyone appreciated the generosity of the show which unfailingly allowed time every Friday evening for the Viewers' personal fantasies.

Fans continued to report that they had seen a child—a niece, a neighbor, a stranger—who looked exactly like Baby Honey. The *Baby Honey* Mother-Daughter clothing line was selling out as rapidly as it could be manufactured. The bomb threats had all but stopped. And now-predictably—everyone wanted to replicate Julie's Victory Garden. Fans wrote in and asked where they could purchase the "old-fashioned, all-American seeds."

In the meantime, Susana and Brenda located a farm that could produce and supply a large number of the herbs—Pennyroyal and Highland Flagg. Actually it was Louise who had said, "I know just the place" and introduced them to her old mentor, a midwife named Vivian, who owned Heritage Herb Farm in the vicinity of Bennington, Vermont. That was the farm Louise was working on when she met Roger. "It's a bewitching place," she said.

The Heritage Herb Farm had been operating for decades under Vivian's magical eye, and now Vivian, at the age of 85, was ready to hand the operation over to someone who would nurture and protect the precious herbs for future needs. Susana and Bob purchased the six-acre property in early spring and, shortly thereafter, moved into the lovingly restored eighteenth-century Farmhouse where they set up their new business. They invited Vivian to remain on the farm

as long as she wished. And she was happy to teach the new own-
ers and their Baby Honey Family how to identify and cultivate the
Pennyroyal and Highland Flagg that already covered one entire acre
of the property. Vivian also explained that Hartshorn was originally
acquired by grinding the antlers of red deer. But a modern equiva-
lent was ammonium bicarbonate found in baking soda and easily
accessed throughout America.

A call for volunteers went out through an underground alliance
of like-minded women—a network, composed chiefly of female
alumnae of Bennington College, that had been quietly expanding
for many years. They started arriving at the Farm bringing friends
and lovers to join in a movement to protect America's women from
the American Christian Taliban Society.

Under Vivian's cheerful tutelage, these young people were taught
to identify and harvest the hundreds of plants that were ready to
yield their bounty. By May, thousands of seeds were being separated
into two bins from which volunteers, under the direction of Bob
who was under the direction of Vivian, filled tiny brown envelopes
and affixed them with decorative labels that read—Victory Garden
Pennyroyal and Victory Garden Highland Flagg.

Louise put some of the volunteers to work immediately cutting
fabric to be used in replicas of the apron that she had designed for
the show. Julie now wore it in every episode.

The full skirt featured Franklin's abortion formula written in an
old fashioned font. Complete with the substitution of baking soda
for the hartshorn. The writing looked like innocent scribble. It was
surrounded by cheery illustrations of flowering herbs and tiny watering cans. But on close inspection, it was completely legible. A pocket
on the front of the apron, trimmed in red rickrack, held the two
packets of seeds along with instructions for planting, and a simple
caution that ingesting the herbs must be done with restraint, and
only as a last resort. Each apron was then carefully folded, packaged,
and readied for the U.S. Postal Service.

Meanwhile back in New York at the Day by Day Café, Sandy and
Eleanor read fan letters and separated those who requested Victory

Garden seeds, which was frankly most of them, into a pile labeled "orders." Hundreds of packages containing the apron and seeds were being sent out every day now.

To reach even more women, Kip and Brenda planned the immediate announcement of the latest *Baby Honey Show* Free Giveaway. They called their friends on *The View* and arranged to make an appearance on the popular daytime program. They also visited Stephen Colbert's Late Show. They had given away tens of thousands of their Fancy Word T-Shirts since their first appearance with Colbert when they launched the Baby Honey Make America Smart Again campaign. They would exceed that number with the apron giveaway.

Chapter 24 — Money Has No Smell

The Baby Honey Show, after a relentless two years in production, was now on hiatus. Episodes were rerunning weekly in every major market, delighting old fans and bringing in new. This allowed The Family to spend the summer months of 2019 together happily on the Heritage Farm in Vermont. I was invited to join them and, of course, I was put to work immediately harvesting herbs. I was unused to physical labor, but when the heart is at peace, the body grows strong.

I remember that summer as the summer that seemed to go on forever. Each day as lovely as the day before. Ribbons of frothy cloud-foam drifted lazily through the cornflower blue skies above. Sunshine toasted everyone's shoulders; birdsong harmonized with the laughter of new volunteers still arriving daily and fanning out over the surrounding fields to harvest the last crop of the season. A massive two-hundred-year-old oak provided warm shade for lunchtime picnics every day at noon. In the orchard, apples and pears ripened. In the kitchen gardens, late summer tomatoes lustily beckoned the hand of Susana Rowland who was turning them into jars of sauce for consumption over the dark winter months. Along a pathway between the farmhouse and the barn, blowsy-headed dahlias curtsied respectfully as Vivian's cat paraded her new kittens. And, at my feet, Pennyroyal and Highland Flagg danced confidently on their private patch in the sun.

The Vermont farm was not the only farm producing the abortion herbs now. Bob Rowland and Vivian had traveled the country all spring helping other like-minded women to secure their own acreage and plant seeds to add to the national supply. Bob Rowland bought a small farm for each woman willing to take on the work of the Victory Garden Project. By mid-July, there were Victory Farms even in deep red states. And countless private Victory Gardens were maturing in small backyards and on windowsills across America.

Bob Rowland became lean and muscular that summer. His face and arms, tanned, his hair an iridescent white, he seemed ageless. When he wasn't tilling the soil or planting the seeds or teaching others how to do so, he was ordering fabric for the aprons and writing down everything that Vivian shared by way of her midwife training and experience. Bob had it in mind to put together a book when he finally had the chance. Like Ben Franklin had. To share age-old knowledge and shield the women of the country from the aggressive ignorance of this Dark Age.

Susana watched her husband with reverence. She told him that she couldn't remember a time when he was more beautiful. The others were noticing Bob as well. Eleanor impulsively kissed him on the cheek one afternoon as they were wrapping up their work for the day. She said, "You're happy, Mr. Rowland. Aren't you?" He laughed, but his eyes welled with tears. "I will tell you, dear Girl. There is no greater feeling than having a purpose."

The Bob Rowland Story

Bob Rowland would seem to many Americans to embody the American Dream. He had grown up with enormous wealth that had increased exponentially every day now for two generations. But like so many

Americans, his family had roots in poverty. His grandfather had come to America in 1900 as a child, escaping the slums of London on a cargo ship bound for Baltimore. He had nothing in his carry-on sack but a spare set of underwear. His name was Leo Rowland.

Leo enrolled in the free public school and, being a bright boy with a sweet nature, received extra attention from the teachers. He excelled at math and, during high school, Leo secured a job as an accountant at a Burlesque Theater and Peep Show not far from the tenement apartment that he now shared with his pretty teenaged wife. Leo also had a practical imagination and, in his spare time, invented things for the convenience of the ordinary person. Like Idiot Mittens. He invented the first pair when his wife accidentally lost her favorite mittens one cold day. Word spread and people started requesting Idiot Mittens for their children. Leo's wife set up a small cottage industry in their apartment—knitting colorful mittens and braiding yarn into long strings, the ends of which attached to a left and right mitten. The string could then be draped around the neck, providing a safe conveyance for the mittens when they weren't on a kid's hands. Within two years, Woolworth's Five and Dime store offered a contract for the handy invention and Leo and his wife were on the way to their first million dollars.

Leo was a shy man; nevertheless, he befriended one of the strippers at the Burlesque Theater where he continued to work—a sweetheart named Myrtle who had a shy streak herself. She had confessed to him that while she enjoyed certain aspects of her job—the live music with the catchy tunes, and the chance to try out new dance steps—she wished she didn't have to remove *all* of her clothes. Because Leo was a modest man himself, he happily took on the challenge of creating a set of privacy pieces for Myrtle to wear on stage. Two nipple covers in gold lamé with a scarlet tassel attached to each. The tassels would swing in ecstatic circles when Myrtle danced. Leo also created the first ever G-string. Also, in gold lamé. He called the pieces The Modesty Set. The results were so snazzy that all the girls wanted them. And the men in the audience didn't complain. The fact was that some of the girls actually looked better with the Modesty Set on than with it off. As one of the guys said, "It leaves something to the imagination. Wowie!"

Within the following year, every stripper in the country, it seemed, had placed an order. Leo made deals with a fabric producer in Chinatown for the softest silks and satins in beautiful swirling patterns of gold, ruby, and blue—like the stained glass windows in the big Catholic church he and his wife attended on Sunday mornings. Leo always had good taste. Which is why he was approached in 1935 by a Hollywood mogul to create a line of women's lacy lingerie. The bras, panties, and slips sold like hot cakes from day one. Especially among the movie stars. They say Mae West was his biggest customer. In every sense.

Then in 1952, Leo's Modesty G-string went mainstream when it became the prototype for Brigitte Bardot's bikini bottom. And then business really exploded. Leo bought a building in the Garment District in New York City and hired dozens of women to cut and sew. By the time Leo was fifty-six, he was a billionaire many times over with a wife, a son, a daughter-in-law, and a toddler grandson named Bobby Rowland.

The Rowland family was generous. They built museums and symphony concert halls and ethical zoos—all free to anyone who knocked on the door. They built hospitals and playgrounds and set up scholarships for poor and middle-class kids to go to the colleges of their choice, all expenses covered. The Rowland name became associated with the best kind of noblesse oblige. The best kind of Billionaires.

When Leo's grandson, Bob Rowland, was twenty-one, his entire family—Grandfather Leo, Grandmother, Father, and Mother—died in a private plane crash. Bob was the sole heir to the family fortune. He was alone and bereft. For the next nine years, he suppressed his heartache by distracting himself with a lavish lifestyle. He became a Republican so that he wouldn't have to notice human suffering. Then he collected Rolex watches. He collected cars. He collected boats. He bought ridiculously priced scotch and joined aristocratic all-White men's clubs. He made it his hobby to know everyone who was anyone, but he never cultivated personal friends. He went to extravagant parties and had many lovers but never fell in love.

And then, in 1989, he met Susana. The most courageous woman he had ever known. He gave her his heart. She gave him hers. Everyone who knew them knew they were meant for each other. It was a happy marriage right from the start. But it isn't enough to just love one person. Not in the long run. A heart needs more exercise than that or it will lose its elasticity and eventually stop beating. Bob, however, had no way of knowing that then—he thought he had everything he wanted. He thought he was content. But what Bob actually was, was privileged which is a fancy way of saying he was numb.

Bob, like so many absurdly wealthy people, lacked a moral compass. He had simply never needed one. He had never agonized over a decision because he never had to live with the consequences. It isn't that he didn't recognize conviction when he saw it in others. He even admired it. He just didn't feel it himself. He wasn't immoral. He was amoral.

Bob spent hours every day studying his wife, trying to anticipate her every desire, trying to make her happy. He knew her life's work was to hold the wicked accountable and Bob was willing to assist Susana's assassination attempts. But he couldn't feel the disappointment that she experienced when they failed. "There will always be bad people, Honey," he would say to comfort her. He urged Susana to forget the past. He thought that was the kindest advice he could offer.

Then, in April of 2019, Bob accompanied Susana on the first trip to the farm in Vermont, prepared to open his wallet, as always, and cover the costs of anything Susana requested on behalf of the new Victory Garden Project. Bob had never regretted being wealthy. He remembered the words Grandfather Leo had often said to him. "Don't be afraid of wealth, Bobby. Money has no smell. Only men stink."

Bob had directed millions toward causes that Susana identified. The creation and launch of *The Baby Honey Show*; expensive tickets for Trump's inauguration. And now Bob had purchased the Heritage Farm along with a network of farms across America where abortifacients were being grown and privately distributed for the relief of American women. Some say that Bob was spending his life in the glow of Susana's reflected courage.

But something happened that summer in Vermont. It was an evening after volunteers had started arriving. A young woman shared the story of her sister's death as a consequence of an ectopic pregnancy. Bob Rowland sat among the women and listened to the entire story. The embryo had attached to the inside of a fallopian tube where, unbeknownst to the young woman, it had started to grow. As the zygote increased in size, it pressed against the inflexible Fallopian tube causing the young woman intense and unrelenting pain. Her husband raced her to the only hospital in their small town, thinking it was an appendix about to burst. The doctor on duty examined her and then told her that she was pregnant. He said, "Therefore I will do nothing for you. I am pro-life." Despite the young woman's agony, despite her husband's sobbing pleas for his help, the doctor refused to remove the fallopian tube and the clump of cells within, that under no circumstance would ever become a baby. Instead, he let the twenty-six-year-old woman suffer for the next twenty-hours and die of sepsis.

For the first time in his life, Bob Rowland felt moral outrage. It gathered in him like a storm, scooping up all the fury he had muzzled in his lifetime. A parade of horrific images passed slowly before his eyes. Newsreels of people suffering injustice, hate and, even worse, indifference—while those who could help, like him, looked the other way. Bob realized that he had always been aware of the pain around him, but he had always had the means to divert his attention. Now, at sixty-four years of age, Bob was at long last having a reckoning with his soul.

Bob thought of his "daughters—in spirit." Eleanor, Brenda, Sandy and Louise. What would become of them in this America? What would become of their children? And suddenly he found his fight. Women would be his cause. One cannot save the country unless one saves the women first. That isn't mere gallantry. That is a fact. Bob was now frantic with purpose.

Bob's first thought was to run for Congress in the upcoming mid-term election. But that was more than a year away and the likelihood of getting on the ballot through legitimate means, even with Bob's connections, was virtually nil. He was unknown. So, Bob decided to *buy* a seat in the U.S. Congress. He knew men who would trade theirs for the right price—and, frankly, who would even notice if Bob mangled the rules of so-called Fair Play in the current Trumpian age of corruption?

The important thing was that Bob Rowland would soon be on the floor of the House of Representatives, calling out the hypocrisy, the phony Christianity, the vicious misogyny of the GOP. And behind closed doors, he would be buying votes. He would be a champion of women's rights like no other man had ever been—undiplomatic, uncompromising, indefatigable, and relentless! And, armed with billions of his own dollars that he was willing to spend, he would be impervious to the pressure of American Christian Taliban Society. He would win every fight.

Within weeks of being seated, Bob was the most popular member of Congress. Everyone, regardless of their partisan affiliation, admired Bob. He was, after all, a billionaire. So when Bob bought himself the position of Speaker of the House a mere month later, not a single Congress member nor any of the Senators balked.

Chapter 25 – A Tête à Tête with Bannon

"If you really care about a serious cause or a deep subject, you may have to be prepared to be boring about it." Christopher Hitchens, *Letters to a Young Contrarian*

While the rest of the Family was finally putting the Heritage Farm to bed for the season, Brenda was in Washington, D.C., staying with Speaker Roland and his beautiful wife Susana in their recently acquired townhouse. The three of them were plotting the next move to trip up the Trump agenda. Brenda announced one evening that she wanted to meet Steve Bannon, a firebrand spokesperson in the MAGA organization, who had recently been thrown out of Trump's inner circle. He had nevertheless remained steadfastly loyal to the president. He was now launching a daily talk show.

Susana said, "We'll have him to dinner here. Then I will poison him." Bob Rowland chuckled.

Brenda replied, "Actually, I find him interesting. A worthy opponent. I want to meet him." So Brenda wrote a letter.

Dear Mr. Bannon—I understand that you are now producing a radio show in which you interview people of influence. I offer myself as a guest. I would love to go head to head with you. I have studied your background and feel that we could have a lively intellectual conversation that would be informative and entertaining for your listeners. My preferred date would be September 23, 2019, the Autumn Equinox. I have been working on a farm all summer and have profound appreciation now for the earth's coordination with the sun.

Respectfully,

Brenda Beacon

Steve Bannon responded immediately.

Dear Miss Beacon—I would be delighted to host a lady of your grace, beauty, and intelligence on my fledgling program. I record in a studio in Washington, D.C. You are welcome to bring a chaperon if that would make you more comfortable although I assure you I am a gentleman in every regard. I will send a car for you at 9:30 the morning of Monday, September 23, 2019. Where will you be staying on that date? Your humble servant, Steven.

On the morning of September 23, 2019, Brenda woke early in the Rowland's sun-filled guest bedroom. She peered out the window at the tree-lined street and marveled at the serenity of the neighborhood given the turmoil at the White House just a couple miles away. Still in her bathrobe, she wolfed down a huge breakfast of scrambled eggs, blueberry pancakes, spicy Philadelphia Scrapple, and baked beans, all lovingly prepared by Susana. After all, she was still eating for two. Then she lingered over her second cup of coffee as Mr. Rowland, freshly showered, joined them. He kissed the top of Brenda's head and gave his wife a peck on the cheek. "So how are we all this morning.?" He looked at Brenda. "Nervous?"

Brenda shook her head. "Not a bit. I have rehearsed everything on the phone with Kip. The objective is to be charming and undistracted by his arguments. I know what I have to do."

"I wish you would allow me to chaperon." Susana said.

"I'll be fine. Bannon's not a cad nor a fool. He's on a genuine crusade. He believes sincerely in the Rightness—in every respect—of his cause. And he hopes to persuade intellectuals on the Left with his arguments. I think he actually wants to find some acceptance outside the fringy goons in the Trump camp." Brenda excused herself now to shower and dress. She chose a sleeveless frock in a delicate periwinkle blue with a sash that tied in a bow at the center of her slim waist. It made her look innocent.

A private luxury car arrived at the Rowlands' and Brenda was spirited away to a Broadcasting Studio on R Street. She found Steve Bannon standing on the sidewalk. He opened her door and taking her hand, helped her to the pavement. He smiled graciously. "Welcome," he said.

Brenda surveyed him. A sloppy looking man with rheumy eyes wearing two dress shirts—one over the other—and a pair of baggy khaki trousers. Brenda frowned. "Have you been crying?" she asked. It sounded like a rebuke.

Bannon was momentarily stunned. "What?"

"Your eyes are red."

"Oh. Allergies."

Brenda nodded and said, "Well, Happy Equinox." She smiled. "Yes, you, too.

Another pause. Bannon seemed unable to move. He stared into her eyes and said, almost shyly, "You are very pretty."

"Thank you."

"I bet you hear that a lot."

"I do."

Another Pause.

Brenda said, "By the way, the root word of 'pretty' is 'crafty.' Did you know that?"

"No, I didn't." Bannon smiled at her and added, "So? Are you crafty?"

"Well, I don't knit or crochet...."

"Aw, c'mon...." He laughed.

"I don't do macrame plant holders...." Bannon laughed louder. Then Brenda smiled and said, "Yes, I am crafty."

Bannon winked at her. "I consider myself forewarned." He led the way to the door and opened it. She entered, still talking. "Why do you wear two dress shirts at the same time?"

"I think it makes me look like the guys on the beach in Malibu."

"I think it makes you look hot."

Bannon grinned. "I rest my case."

Brenda laughed. "Touché, Mr. Bannon."

Bannon opened a door marked STUDIO. "We're set up in here. You are, of course, familiar with cameras and sound equipment so ... unless you have questions."

"No, everything is quite familiar.

"This is Dietrich, our stellar engineer." A sullen young man nodded at Brenda.

Soon Bannon and Brenda were positioned across from one another at a table in the recording booth. Bannon said, "We will take breaks to plug in the commercial messages. Yes, I am actually making money from this endeavor. But I think it supports a noble purpose. "

"Which is...?"

"Dialog between the Left and Right. I think it is essential for the health of the country."

"I could not agree more, Mr. Bannon."

"Call me Steve."

"Brenda."

Bannon nodded. "I have to say, Brenda, that dress is very cute on you."

Brenda smiled. "The root of the word 'cute' is 'acute.'"

With that, it began. Bannon slated the episode and introduced Brenda Beacon. "She's more than beautiful. She is intelligent and thoughtful. Regal, I think you'd say. Thank you for being my guest today, Brenda. My goodness, I feel like a king in your company."

Brenda replied, "Speaking of kings, Steven…." She stared at Bannon's unshaven chin and pouted. "I just don't understand how a self-avowed Populist like you can support a wanna-be Billionaire-king like Trump."

Bannon grinned. "He is actually a very insightful man…."

Brenda shook her head. "No, he isn't. And you're too smart to say something like that, let alone believe it."

"I grant you, Brenda, he's an imperfect vessel," said Bannon patiently.

"He's vulgar, craven, and stupid," Brenda said pleasantly.

"A huggable monkey, playful and…."

"Narcissistic and dangerous…."

"Charismatic. He's doing good things for the country."

"He's petty. He fired you."

"He will grow into the role. He's just insecure."

"He's a sociopath. He will destroy the world."

Pause. Brenda noticed that phone lines were lighting up in front of the engineer. Bannon shook his head at Dietrich, indicating that he would not be taking calls. Bannon turned his attention back to Brenda. "I read that you were born and raised in Argentina. How did you end up in America?"

"The same way your family arrived here; I immigrated."

Bannon and Brenda spoke easily now. About Brenda's life in New York City. About Julliard. About Broadway. Bannon confessed that he had seen her debut performance in *Yawn* and had been impressed. She laughingly shared the details of the zombie commercial that led to her meeting with Mark Reynolds and Kip Barrett, the one that led to her fame on *The Baby Honey Show*. She talked about her status as an Influencer. "I take the responsibility very seriously," she said.

Bannon shared his experience as a Wall Street financier. As a Hollywood producer. "I own a piece of *Seinfeld*," he said. "And I made a film of my own. And I am Executive Chairman on Breitbart News. My political writing attracts millions of followers. And now I am starting this weekly talk show. I guess you could say I'm an Influencer, too."

They talked about their families. He, with affection, about growing up in a middle-class Irish clan in Norfolk, Virginia. And she, with honesty about her lonely adolescence in a wealthy household in Buenos Aires. Brenda said, "By the way, I was raised Roman Catholic like you. I am sentimental about the Latin Mass."

Bannon was suddenly animated. "The Second Vatican Council was grievously wrong when they translated the Mass from Latin into local languages. All in the interests of making the Mass modern. Modern!" Bannon slapped the tabletop. "It made the Sacred Mass pedestrian; that's what it did. Robbed it of all its mystery."

Brenda cocked her head to one side. "On the other hand, it allows people to know what they're worshipping. I think knowledge is a good thing."

Bannon grinned. "Spoken like Eve herself."

Brenda sipped her tea and kept her eyes on Bannon, noting his red face and the catch in his voice.

Bannon said, "And now a word from our sponsor, My Pillow. We'll be back in a minute."

Dietrich signaled that the mics were off and Bannon turned to Brenda. "This is nice. Brenda. Thank you for joining me. I'm enjoying myself."

"So am I," she said. "I mean it sincerely."

Dietrich signaled and Bannon said, "We're back with my guest today. Brenda Beacon, star of *The Baby Honey Show* and, as it turns out—she's so much more." He grinned at her. "So where were we when the Pillow Guy interrupted?"

Brenda said, "I have something I'd like to discuss. You attempted to insult the venerable Pope Francis by calling him a Perónist. I consider that a compliment. I am an admirer of the late President Perón. Why aren't you? He was a Populist."

Bannon now filled his audience in on the history of Juan Perón, the former president of Argentina, who died in 1974. He turned back to Brenda. "President Perón cheapened populism by placating the underclasses of your country with bribes."

Brenda countered. "Oh yes, all those bribes. Food, clean water, health care, education … what will the little people expect next?" She laughed airily. "You speak like the elite, Stephen. Are you an oligarch? I know you're very rich. But I thought you were a man of the people."

"I'm a capitalist, Brenda, but I am also a populist. I consider the welfare of the people to be the foundation of effective leadership. But we need to pay down the national debt and we can't do that if we coddle the lower classes."

"My goodness, every time the Republican Party gets power, they coddle the billionaires with tax breaks that they don't need. How does that reduce the debt?"

"I agree with you, Brenda. I think the tax break was a mistake. And I told Trump so. But we don't want to disincentivize hard work. We don't want the American middle-class to become dependent."

"Oh I think the middle-class is already working too much. Many need three jobs to cover just the basics of food and shelter. The rich control the means of production and the resources. And the distribution. So they set the wages. But you know when you think of it, the rich are completely dependent on the working class. The rich don't make anything at all—except money!"

"Ahhh.... You are a Marxist, Miss Beacon."

"Yes, I am. A true Populist. And let's just get this out of the way. Trump is not and never will be a Populist. Trump regards the Working People of America as just a mark for his overpriced Trump Vodka. Or whatever he is grifting this week."

"Really, Brenda ... you are just echoing Left Wing talking points."

"And Trump's family is just like him. It's amazing how brazen they are. One month into his term and Trump had already established a kleptocracy in the White House. The whole family is grifting and they don't even try to hide it. And now I understand that Ivanka intends to inherit the presidency from her father when he dies." Brenda laughed. "But as you yourself have said, 'Ivanka is dumb as a brick.' Was that the statement that got you fired?"

Bannon half-laughed. "Don't believe everything you read about me. I agree with you though. I tried to tell Trump that he made a huge mistake hiring Jared and Ivanka. Especially Jared. Apart from bad optics, Jared is an empty suit with excessive ambition. But Trump is a sentimental man at heart."

"So, Trump doesn't listen to you." Brenda looked at Bannon with sympathy. "I was born during the reign of a thin-skinned dictator, Steven. I know the territory. My parents actually championed that monstrous dictator, General Videla, in Argentina. He used to come to our home for dinner when I was a child. Oh, my mother would fuss over him and the minute he was gone, she'd stick out her tongue and make a face of disgust. Then hold her finger to her lips and say, 'Shhhh ... don't tell.'

"Videla's regime was responsible for the murder of 30,000 innocent people. Their only crime was that they didn't agree with General Videla. He put their names on enemy lists and sent his military out to round them up. Of course, it all finally caught up with him. Videla died in prison a few years ago. In a cold and lonely cell. They say during his long confinement, no one visited him and he turned as gray as the cement floor. I wish that would deter future tyrants. But I know it won't. Their lust for power and wealth is an addiction."

The show took another break to sell pillows.

When they were back on the air, Brenda said, "Your American Secretary of State, Henry Kissinger, conspired to put General Videla in power. He had the popularly elected president of Chile assassinated in 1973. It is accepted as a matter of record now that Kissinger and your President Nixon gave the CIA *orders* to kill President Allende of Chile so that a military dictator could take over in that country, too."

Bannon tried to control his anger; his voice sounded strangled. "Perón and Allende posed a great risk to the stability of the West."

"It is a shameful fact, Steven. America has consistently backed dictatorships over popularly elected governments in countries around the world. In Cuba. In Haiti. Iran. Zaire. Pakistan. Indonesia. Chile. Argentina. Bangladesh. Vietnam. And you know what I think? I think the Darkside of the Right Wing in America has been rehearsing in all these countries—becoming increasingly efficient at overthrowing democracies—all in preparation to do the same in America."

"Brenda, that's hysterical nonsense."

"And now—the Right Wing has its Strong Man in place. Trump makes no secret of his disdain for Congress, for the courts, for every institution in our government. For the rule of law. He wants no checks and balances on his power. He wants to be a dictator. He is open about it. And you support him as does your party. But I don't think this is what MAGA desires."

"Some countries become destabilized by democracy. The people aren't capable of governing themselves. They are poorly educated and easily distracted. They are seduced by communists!"

"These popular leaders whom you condemn, Steven, were pro-worker, pro-women. They built hospitals and decent roads. They built schools and democratized education. They modernized their countries, and the people loved them for it, voted for them. Yes, they were elected, Steven, and the United States encouraged the violence that replaced them with fascism."

Bannon leaned in. "And look at where we are now, Brenda. Every Western nation is now overrun by modernism. We have lost all that is sacred in our lives. We need to go back to a time of a strong central church."

"Tell me, Steven … would you go back to the seventeenth century and burn women as witches? Earlier? How about the sixteenth century? The Spanish Inquisition? Shall we torture Jews in a nostalgic nod to the days when the Roman Catholic Church oversaw the entire Western world? When was the world sacred enough for you, Steven?"

Bannon's voice rose, "Diversity, while well-intentioned, has made us all strangers to one another. We have nothing in common anymore. The nation has lost its identity."

Brenda eyed him coolly. "It is interesting that throughout the twentieth century and beyond, every wanna-be dictator offers the promise of returning to a sacred past that never was. Make America Great Again? Videla used the same slogan in Argentina long before Trump started his red hat campaign. Make Argentina Great Again! And inevitably that quest involved suppressing free thought and speech and stripping the civil rights of women and people of color. Suppressing the right to vote. Banning books. Rewriting history. Forcing everyone to be a Christian. And ultimately sending out Death Squads to eliminate anyone who resisted."

Bannon flushed and argued with intensity, "Human civilization goes in cycles and we are coming to the end of one cycle. *Strong men* are needed to prevent the complete collapse of civilization."

But at that moment, Dietrich cut in. "And now a word from My Pillow."

Mics off. The commercial came on. And Bannon leaned back in his chair. He smiled at Brenda and said, "Well, well, well...."

Her eyes sparkled. "I'm still having fun. Are you?"

"You know what? I am. You're putting me through my paces."

"And vice versa. I never get to have conversations like this." Brenda smiled warmly. "Except with Kip."

Bannon said, "I will yet win you over to my cause, Miss Beacon."

Brenda laughed. "I could never be a MAGA woman, Steven. Your women have such vulgar manners. Of course, they seem very much to Trump's taste."

"As I said, he's an imperfect vessel."

"You mean a useful idiot. "

They were back on the air. Brenda asked, " I have a question for you, Steven. You are strongly nationalist. You encouraged Britain to leave the European Union because you consider the EU to be an empire."

"I did. And I do. Empires are unsustainable—too many languages, too many cultures to assimilate. People feel a loss of identity. We need to return to our tribes. Let the Brits be Brits."

"You support Orban, an anti-immigrant fascist strong man in Hungary."

"He is serving the citizens of his nation. He is restoring the history and culture and creed of that historic nation. It is what the people of Hungary elected him to do."

"And yet, you and Trump and so many in the MAGA Movement are pro-Putin. Putin is threatening to invade Ukraine."

Bannon shrugged. "He wants to restore the old boundaries of his nation. He has that right."

Brenda shook her head. "No, he is attempting to rebuild the Soviet Union. The Soviet Union was an empire. The satellite countries are nations. Ukraine is a nation. Why are you not defending its sovereignty?"

Bannon said nothing but kept his eyes on Brenda who continued. "Doesn't Putin already have his nation? Isn't Russia a nation? You contradict your own argument, Steven."

Bannon shrugged. "Geopolitics is a complicated...."

Brenda interrupted. "And why is Trump so gung-ho on leaving NATO, a military and political alliance of the nations of Europe and North America that actually protects sovereign nations? Is it because Putin has insisted that Trump weaken the nations in Europe as payment for Russian interference on Trump's behalf during the 2016 election?"

"Okay, Brenda. Let's not get into conspiracy theories again."

Brenda pressed on. "Will you allow Americans to vote on whether they want to leave NATO?"

"No, that is the prerogative of the Executive Branch."

"But you say you want to dismantle the government and all its institutions. You want to make the government accountable to citizens. I would think, on that basis, you would agree to put every decision in the hands of the citizens."

"Now that's impractical and you know it."

"Let's get rid of the Electoral College while we are at it. Power to the People!"

Bannon was silent. He studied Brenda's perfect face.

After a moment, Brenda said, "I think you regard yourself as a populist, Steven. But you don't trust the people. And you fear that they won't vote the way you want them to unless you cheat. I know you worry about the country. And I know you have a personal stake in the future; you have children. I share your desire to save America from itself. But you rely on bullies and billionaires. I want to empower citizens."

Bannon nodded. "Brenda, this country can't sustain without a strong leader in place. We are too big. We have tried to have a democracy but citizens don't want the responsibility of governing themselves. They don't want to think. As I said, we have nothing in common anymore."

"But that is what a strong leader does, Steven! A strong leader articulates our common values and brings us together. Trump is deliberately stoking further division."

"He is a Father Figure. That's why they elected him."

"Well, maybe this time, the people will prefer a Mother." Brenda paused and then with her heart in her throat, made her final argument. "Pick me, Steven. You're right—the people want a strong and charismatic leader. But they want that leader to be kind and loving and just. Someone they can admire. Someone they will want to emulate. Pick me. They already love me, Steven. I can overthrow Trump. I'm the only one who can. Join me."

At this point, Bannon's mouth actually fell open. He glared at her; a flicker of fear animated his tired eyes. He finally composed his face and said, gently, "Are you serious, Brenda?"

"Pick me," she repeated, with a warm smile. "I want you on my side."

Bannon laughed indulgently. Then he signaled to the engineer and the mics went dead.

The car was paged and soon arrived at the curb outside the studio. Bannon walked Brenda to the car. He smiled warmly. "I truly can't remember a more exhilarating afternoon. You've certainly given me quite a lot to think about."

Brenda nodded, "In Mexico, they say *I am seeing you* rather than *I will see you.* They collapse time. Let us collapse time, Steven. Let's move quickly. I am seeing you." She winked at him, then slipped into the backseat.

Bannon returned to the studio and looked at Dietrich. He picked up a phone and called Roger Stone, a longtime political operative, known for his dirty tricks during the Nixon administration and now a regular visitor to the White House. Stone answered on the first *Boing*!—his signature ringtone. "Yeah? What did you think?"

Bannon replied, "She's as subversive as they come. And smart. Get someone to subpoena every episode of *The Baby Honey Show.* We need to find something—anything—we can use to turn her fans against her. She's got plans to take the White House. And she has her own cult. We need to take this seriously."

"I got just the girl for the job. She's the president of the fan club. A real up-and-comer. Name's Marjorie Taylor Greene."

Chapter 26 – At Home with Donald and Melania

From BBC News :

President Trump was scheduled to visit Denmark on 2 September, at the invitation of Queen Margrethe II. Last week, Mr. Trump suggested the U.S. was interested in buying Greenland, an autonomous Danish territory. Danish PM Mette Frederiksen described the suggestion as "absurd" and said she hoped Mr. Trump was not being serious. Trump immediately canceled the state visit.

---

*T*rump and Melania stand stiffly side by side in the Rose Garden outside the White House. Trump sniffs and addresses the gathering of reporters and other sycophants from his staff.

"As you know, Denmark is acting like a pussy about Greenland and we will get to that in a moment. But Melania happened to drop by Washington, D.C., for the first time in months, and I know you are all interested in the progress she is making on the Rose Garden redesign."

Everyone casts their eyes downward at the bare dirt and gnarled stumps. Trump continues, "As everyone knows, this very American garden was planted by the Puritans back in 1492."

A reporter interrupts. "Sir, the Puritans didn't land in Washington."

There is a hush. Trump turns his lizard eyes on the hapless man. "Get out," Trump growls. "Get out, you son of a bitch!"

Before the man can react, four of Trump's private bodyguards grab him, two under each arm, and drag him to the gate. They toss him out on the sidewalk. When they return, Trump addresses them. "Find out where his kids go to school." Silence.

Trump resumes, "So, as you can see, a bunch of roses are dead now because Melania hasn't been watering them." He looks at Melania. "But I'll let her lay out the details of her great plan herself."

Melania squints through dark sunglasses. Her well-documented annoyance at being the First Lady of the United States is only surpassed by her disgust at being married to Donald J. Trump. She had been working out the details of a divorce from him when he decided to run for president. She quickly negotiated the extension of her lucrative marriage contract and bought herself a condo in Miami. Nevertheless she is now trapped until her husband's term is over or he is assassinated. Today, she is wearing one of her smart ensembles. Skin-tight leopard print leggings and a white t-shirt on which the words *Je suis avec un Imbecile* are printed, in a metallic gold. The phrase is underlined with an arrow that points directly at Trump, standing there beside her.

A reporter breathlessly poses the first question. "Mrs. Trump—did you purchase your shirt in Paris?"

Melania rolls her snake eyes. "Oui," she says, dully. Reporters will write that Mrs. Trump opened the Press Conference by demonstrating her flawless French.

Trump looks at her and says, "Oh, very nice. You know how I hate that Frog, President Macron. I hate the French. I hate the French."

Melania lifts one shoulder in a Gallic shrug. "I know. I know."

Another reporter raises his hand. "Mrs. Trump, did your husband give you roses on your first date?" There are affectionate giggles throughout the crowd.

Melania is stone-faced. "No, Mr. Cheapskate here … he give me hundred dollar bill."

There is an awkward silence. Then Trump says, "Look, we agreed on the price beforehand."

Melania shrugs, "Besides, I don't like flowers to tell truth. They are ordinary. I prefer gold."

Another hand goes up. "So, Mrs. Trump, do you intend to tear down all the rose bushes that were put in by former first ladies?"

Melania pouts. "I am not doing anything. What you think? I am some dumb farmer? I don't dig in dirt. I dig gold. I am gold digger." She laughs dryly. She looks at Trump. "You get my joke?"

Trump laughs. The reporter scrambles, "Of course, Mrs. Trump. But do you have a plan to replace the roses."

Melania is now exasperated by the grilling of the Press. She hisses, "I don't care! Do you?"

Now Trump looks around and says, "Anybody got a question for me? Yeah, you." He points to a fresh face in the group.

"Thank you, Mr. President. The Danish government has called you disrespectful for your cancellation of the upcoming state visit."

"Well, they are disrespectfuller of me for not selling Greenland to me in the first place."

"But it is their territory, sir."

"I was willing to give them cash. Or Puerto Rico. Their choice. But now since they are being such shits about it, maybe we will just invade Greenland. How about that? We'll just take it. Like Argentina did to the Falklands."

"Excuse me, sir, Argentina lost that war." Members of the Press inhale and freeze.

Trump says icily. "That's a fake fact. Understand?" The young man nods. "And this won't be my last word on Greenland. You know it. And I know it."

Members of the Press exchange furtive glances. Trump suddenly adds, "Oh shit! I almost forgot to mention. Melania and I will be eating dinner together at Mar-a-Lago next Friday at 8 p.m. And we are offering Rich People a chance to not only watch us eat but listen to us discuss top secret stuff at our table with Russian, Syrian, Saudi, Korean, and Chinese agents. All you have to do is pay me $500,000 apiece to be seated at a table near me. That may sound like a lot, but you can sell the top secret stuff you hear that night for way more than that. So it's actually a smart investment. Oh, and one other thing—after dinner. I, Donald J. Trump, will be auctioning off my socks. The very socks your favorite president will be wearing that night. To the highest bidder."

Melania smiles, suddenly animated by the mention of money. "And I will be auctioning my brassiere. And my wedding band."

"So mark your calendar. Send me your check for $500,000. We'll get you on the list. And maybe you will be the lucky bidder and take home an incredible piece of Americana."

Melania speaks directly to the camera. "Yes, America, you heard right. If you have enough money, you, too, can take home true sentimental heirloom from House of Trump."

"That's right, Darling." Trump puts an arm around Melania. She shrugs him off. He continues, "Limited Addiction. That's what they call it. Edition. Limited Edition. Very valuable. My socks, her bra and ring. This will be your only chance until the next time Melania and I have dinner together."

Melania nods. "Not in near future, but maybe at Christmas." She turns sharply and walks back into the White House. Trump follows.

That evening. The Oval Office, from the Official Recording:

Trump stands in the middle of a circle of evangelical pastors. He is describing a recent faith experience. "So, I'm praying ... you know. I'm praying on my knees." He sniffs.

The gathered faith leaders say, as one, "Amen."

Trump throws his head back and stares at the ceiling chandelier and intones, "I'm praying and praying and praying and praying...."

"Amen. Amen. Amen. Amen."

"And then ... all of a sudden...." Trump's eyes widen in amazement. He looks at their pinched white faces. "All of a sudden ... mid-prayer ... I realize ... that ... I'm ... TALKING TO MYSELF!"

There is a gasp.

"Yes. It's a true fact! When I pray, I am praying to myself! Which can only mean one thing. I'm Jesus! I'm the Savior come back to life! I'M THE CHOSEN ONE!!! You know it. And I know it!"

Some of the preachers sob. Some cry out loud, "Hosanna in the highest!" One of the preachers—a woman—faints.

Trump looks at her with disgust. "Get her out of here."

Stephen Miller, who is standing in the corner of the room, leaps into action and drags the woman into the hall. Trump staggers to a chair and collapses dramatically. The preachers who remain attend him and gather at his feet.

"And it explains my suffering? Doesn't it?" Trump sniffs. "How many times has my beautiful wife Melania found me on my knees ... praying ... weeping.... Just a little bit. Not too much. I'm not gay. And she says, 'Why? Why did you give up our perfect life for this? For this crucifixion by CNN and the *Washington Post* and *The New York Times* and Comedy Central and Nancy Pelosi and MSNBC and the BBC and Saturday Night Live?' And oh, my Melania ... Saint Melania ... that's what I call her ... she has sacrificed, too. But not like me. I've had to live with her through all of this. And let me tell you that's no day at the beach. She's been a royal pill ever since we moved to Washington."

The preachers stand now and surround Trump, laying their hands on his shoulders. Trump shrugs. "But what are you gonna do? I'm Jesus. It's my burden to bear." Trump sniffs. "I want to take a moment now and reflect. On that great story from the Old Testament the one where Jesus goes to see the money loaners in the church. And they give him a ton of shekels. That's what they called their money back then. Shekels. They were all Jews. Like you, Stevie."

Trump tosses a look to Stephen Miller who reddens and retreats back into a corner as Trump resumes his speech. "And Jesus takes the shekels and puts them towards his campaign to help everybody become a Christian, and then he turns a loaf of bread into grape juice. And they have a party. But they all say grace first. Nobody's ever seen anything like it. It's a beautiful thing."

The preachers begin to squirm. Trump takes note and jumps ahead in his sermon. "Okay. Here's the point. My daughter-in-law, Lara—you know her—broad shoulders and a mouth like Gary Shandling? Oy! Remember him? He was a Jew like Stevie over there."

Stephen Miller winces.

Trump farts and continues, "So anyway, Lara counts the money that comes in from your congregations every week and she says some of you have been a little light. She says ... now I don't like to say this. I frankly don't care, but Lara says, 'Father, I think they are skimming from the collection plates.'"

The preachers look guilty. One says, "We have to give some of the money to the poor."

Trump's eyes are ice. "Hey, Buddy, you're looking at Poor! I got a family you wouldn't believe. They are always hitting me up ... especially the boys. And Melania is into online-shopping now. We get packages dropped off by Amazon three times a day."

The preachers look at their feet. Trump adds, "But just remember ... who is the Chosen One who's going to overthrow Roe once and for all? And make women have to swim to Venezuela if they want a safe and legal abortion or even a miscarriage? Who? Moi—that's who! You think that doesn't take money?? Paying off Clarence Thomas, Sam Alito, AND John Roberts? I've held up my end. You hold up yours."

The preachers take Trump's hands and, one by one, kiss the diamond-encrusted Super Bowl ring that was a gift to Trump by the owner of the New England Patriots. Trump smiles, "Okay ... okay. I bless all of you. Now go and spread the gospel—the greatest news ever." He stands and swivels his hips, punching the air with his little fists, as he sings, "From the mountains to the prairies to the oceans white with FOAAAM! TRUMP IS THE SECOND COMING! JESUS CHRIST JUNIOR IS HOME!!!"

The preachers leave the office in a daze and Stephen Miller closes the door. Trump looks at him and sighs. Before he can speak, the door opens again and Melania drags herself into the Oval Office and flops on the couch. She wears sweatpants now and a sweatshirt that reads *Sorry I'm late. I didn't want to come.* She grabs the remote off the coffee table.

Trump looks at her and sniffs. "What do you want?"

"The TV in Family Living Quarters is on fritz. I'm going to watch TV in here. My show is on in five minutes. So get out."

Miller scurries out of the room.

Trump stands his ground. "Use the TV in the dining room."

"Barron is watching *RuPaul's Drag Race* in there. He likes fancy clothes."

"Jesus...."

The phone rings. Trump raises a hand. "I have to take this. It's on my official line. It might be about Greenland."

Melania sneers. "I give you two minutes. Talk fast."

Trump picks up the phone and says, "This is President Donald J. Trump, leader of the free world. The Chosen One...."

"Donald, it's Roger Stone."

"Yeah."

"I saw your Press conference. Nicely done.

"Where are you?"

"At the Trump Hotel. The War Room."

"What's up?"

"You know that show? The Baby Honey Show?"

"Yeah. Melania watches it." Trump looks at his wife who glares back. She mouths One More Minute.

"Well, the star of that show ... she's planning to take down your presi-dency."

"How the fuck is she going to do that?"

"Doesn't matter. We have something on her."

"Cool."

Melania yells, "Time's up! Get off phone, Donald."

"I'll call you later, Rog." Trump hangs up. He crosses to Melania and takes a seat. "Maybe I'll sit and watch it with you this week."

Melania grimaces. "Just don't talk during kissing part. That's my special me-time with myself."

Chapter 27 — The Arrest

The following day, Trump met Roger Stone, Steve Bannon, Stephen Miller, and Marjorie Taylor Greene at his favorite McDonald's—the one at 750 17th Street NW—not far from the White House. The four squeezed into a booth. Secret Service agents sat at neighboring tables.

Trump stuffed French fries into his mouth and said, "Mmmm good, huh? This is where all my food comes from. And I've never been poisoned. Because nobody knows which McDonald's I use."

Marjorie wiggled in her seat with excitement. "Thanks, y'all for taking me out on a date. I've never done a foursome before."

Roger hunched over his Diet Sprite and said, "Okay—let's get to the point. Marjorie here has discovered something devastating." The men turned to her expectantly.

Marjorie nodded, then took a bite of her fish filet, a sip of her Coke, and a second bite of her fish filet while the men watched. She chewed thoroughly and swallowed loudly. It seemed to take forever. Trump grew impatient. "WELL?"

Marjorie wiped her mouth with her napkin and leaned in. "Baby Honey is missing, sir. And I think Julie might of kidnapped her. "

Trump looked at Roger. "Huh?"

Roger winked at Trump. "The baby on the show, sir? Baby Honey? She's missing, sir."

Trump frowned. "From the TV show?"

"Yes. And in real life."

"The actress or the baby?"

Bannon spoke now. "Baby Honey is America's Sweetheart, Mr. President. This is a crisis. We have to take immediate action."

Marjorie said, "Are you going to eat your pickles, Mr. President?"

Trump shrugged. "Go ahead." He watched Marjorie slurp down the shiny discs and said, "Maybe the kid was renegotiating its contract?"

Bannon looked at Trump and said, "We had every episode subpoenaed for Ms. Greene to study. She's an expert."

"I am the president of the Baby Honey Fan Club." Marjorie said proudly; then started to cry. "I'm telling you. That baby's gone. And probably dead. It's pretty fucked up when you think about it."

Trump opened the wrapper on his second Big Mac. He removed the pickles and put them in Marjorie's outstretched palm. "Thanks a ton," she said through her tears.

Trump mumbled to Stone. "So what's the plan?"

Stone said, "We arrest the mother."

Trump chewed. "The TV character?"

"No, the star. We arrest Brenda Beacon and charge her with kidnapping. And maybe murder."

Marjorie nods solemnly. "She would have been the last to see Baby Honey. I guess she's nothing but a damn B-I-C-H."

Trump looks at Stone again. "You think we can make that charge stick?"

"Who's gonna stop us?"

"True," Trump said and farted. Immediately Stephen Miller leaped out of his seat and announced to the restaurant. "That was me! I was the one who farted! You did not hear the President fart! That was me!"

———————

One week later, back in New York City, Brenda was arrested at her local greengrocer.

Standing there with a Honeycrisp apple in one hand and an organic cinnamon stick in the other, Brenda had just turned to Kip and observed, "It's finally Autumn. I think I'll make us a pie," when suddenly she was approached by an officer of the Court of New York, and taken into custody right there in full view of the other shoppers. The elderly woman, who owned the stand, shouted, "Run, Brenda, run!" But Brenda was regal. She calmly surrendered and allowed the officer to accompany her to the waiting police car. She got in, without coercion. Kip followed, calling, "I'll meet you at the station, Babe!"

Sandy had had another dream about Trump just days before, and this time, Brenda was also in the dream. So Brenda already knew what was going to happen. She was prepared.

Brenda was taken to a central Manhattan precinct and booked for the kidnapping and murder of Baby Honey. While she sat in a jail cell waiting to be arraigned, a steady stream of police officers and staff took turns visiting with her behind bars. In every case, they were charmed by her, and all of them left with an autograph, some with a selfie.

In the Ladies' room, two cops tried to make sense of the charges.

"She didn't kill that baby. No way. Not Brenda."

"You're right, Renee. Brenda's not the type."

"She's genuinely perfect."

"She's the nicest perfect woman I have ever met."

"The baby's probably at the gramma's like always."

Later that afternoon, Brenda made her first appearance before the Judge. She was flanked by Kip, Eleanor, Mark, and the Rowlands.

JUDGE: Do you know why you have been summoned, Ms. Beacon?

BRENDA: Actually, I don't. I'm basically law-abiding.

JUDGE: The court is attracted by guilt, Ms. Beacon. Therefore, when we followed you, it was proof that you are guilty. We had no choice but to take you into custody.

BRENDA: That doesn't seem fair.

JUDGE: Fair enough for these times. The trial will begin on December 5, 2018.

BRENDA: That was a year ago, your Honor.

JUDGE: Don't be fresh, Ms. Beacon. I understand your parents live in the future?

BRENDA: Yes, they are in Buenos Aires, a time zone one hour ahead of New York.

JUDGE: And yet you have maintained contact?

BRENDA: I only talk to them on Sundays. Otherwise, I live in my own time.

JUDGE: I suppose now you are going to argue that there are more damnable crimes in the world than killing off a TV character?

BRENDA: Baby Honey wasn't killed, your honor. She has yet to be born.

JUDGE: How do you plead?

BRENDA: Innocent.

The judge set bail at ten million, and Speaker of the House Bob Rowland wrote a check. He then took the opportunity to hold an impromptu press conference on the steps of the courthouse. Standing in the white sunshine of that cold November morning, Speaker Rowland cut a dashing figure. His months in Congress had clarified not only his raison d'être, but his personal style as well. He looked great. Dark sunglasses, shoulder length silver hair, a cashmere scarf, undulating in the wind. He raised his leather-gloved hands to quiet the murmuring of the crowd before him. "C'mon, people! When has it ever been the case that an individual was booked on charges of kidnapping and killing a TV character? Open your eyes! Smell the coffee! For the love of God—Come to Your Senses, America."

Chapter 28 — The Trial

"Somebody must have slandered Josef K., for one morning, without having done anything wrong, he was arrested."
Franz Kafka, *The Trial*

Day One: Wednesday

The trial—*People Who Want to Make America Great Again versus Brenda Beacon*—finally got under way on Wednesday, December 5, 2019. The Judge immediately declared that there would be no evidence permitted in the trial because what is the point? Americans no longer trust their own eyes. The Judge advised the attorneys on both sides of the aisle to prepare to make their arguments based on feelings and hunches rather than reason. Brenda was of course well prepared for that.

Mr. Rowland volunteered his services as Brenda's defense lawyer, but Brenda knew that Mr. Rowland was too logical to be persuasive to an American jury in 2019. And having Mr. Rowland bribe all of the jurors—which he also considered doing—would be considered bad form. Especially if he got caught. So, Brenda thanked him effusively and chose Eleanor instead. Brenda figured Eleanor would deliver a passionate, albeit confusing, defense. Which would prepare the jury for Brenda's final summation. As always, Brenda was confident in her acting skills.

Brenda and Eleanor sat shoulder to shoulder at the Defense Table, passing notes and whispering. The rest of the Family, including Vivian, who had come down from the Farm, and Jacques and Bill, who had closed the Day by Day Café for the duration of the Trial, huddled directly behind Brenda and Eleanor, whispering encouragement.

Susana Rowland had smuggled a lethal dose of Polonium-210 into the courtroom. It's what the Russians use when they want to kill off a journalist. She bought it off the Dark Market. Untraceable. She would wait for an opportunity to get close to Trump.

Of course, there was no way I was going to miss this trial. I stood in line for hours with the public and snagged a single seat at the back of the courtroom. I took careful notes.

Trump arrived at the Courthouse wrapped in an American flag—the new Trump version, the one stamped with Trump's likeness over a field of red stripes. Mike Pence stood shoulder to shoulder with his boss. Trump was selling the flags during the trial for the discounted price of $1,776.99. When the two men reached the top step, they turned to face the crowd. Trump raised his right hand in his signature thumbs-up salute. There was a loud ripping sound. Trump looked over his shoulder. The back of the flag had split over his large posterior. Trump swore, "Fucking Chinese shit." He pulled the flag off his shoulders and tossed it down the steps. Then stomped into the building. Pence ran to catch up.

The Prosecutor, a slender, exhausted-looking man, chose not to speak during the trial. I couldn't ascertain if he was being muzzled by threats or was simply speechless with grief, watching the corruption that had overtaken the Justice Department since Trump ascended to the presidency. The Prosecution's case would therefore be presented by two of Trump's most notorious henchmen—Rudy Giuliani and Stephen Miller. Sitting directly behind them were the Prosecution's witnesses—Marjorie Taylor Greene, Steve Bannon, and Roger Stone.

Trump demanded that his chair be placed next to the judge at the front of the courtroom so he could face the proceedings and intimidate Brenda Beacon. He glared at her. She stared back, confidently moving her eyes from his pitted orange complexion to his pig-pink ears to his reptilian eyes. She looked at him so intensely, with such unflattering curiosity, that Trump became self-conscious. He told the judge that Brenda was trying to bully him, and the judge said, "Keep your eyes down, Ms. Beacon." Brenda nodded innocently and dropped her gaze.

The jury was composed of Twelve Americans all of whom, like their fellow citizens, had been brewing in a toxic tea of lies for the past three years. Truth be told, they were every bit as victimized by Trump as Brenda. Brenda had nothing but compassion for them.

The judge gaveled the court to order and nodded to Rudy Giuliani who rose, adjusted the crotch of his slacks, and performed the Prosecution's opening statement. A squat-looking elderly man with sticky hair the color of potting soil, and seven Rolex watches encasing the full length of his left sleeve, Rudy was already sweating. He faced the jury and screamed, "OF COURSE SHE KILLED THE BABY! THE BABY COULDN'T HAVE LEFT ON ITS OWN. I MEAN THE BABY COULDN'T DRIVE!!" Now a trickle of inky hair dye ran down the side of his face. He looked at Trump who applauded. Rudy sucked on his teeth, which appeared to have shifted in his mouth. After a moment, he continued, "So, my fellow Americans—the question is WHY? WHY? WHUH...." Rudy's dentures flew out of his mouth. He scrambled on all fours to locate them under the Prosecution's table as Stephen Miller suavely slipped out of his seat and faced the jury.

Miller's voice was a high, nasal whine. "As my esteemed colleague has so clearly established—Brenda Beacon is a pedophile. Don't let her ravishing good looks fool you. She is an Ambitious Female! She will try to tell you that Baby Honey doesn't exist. She will try to tell you that it was all an illusion. That it was just TV. But don't be fooled. She is a Leftist Communist ACTRESS. And we will prove that she has plans to steal the next election from President Donald J. Trump!"

At this point Trump rose from his seat with an audible grunt and waved to the jury. Miller applauded politely and resumed, "But before Brenda Beacon could make her move to interrupt the RIGHTEOUS DYNASTY of the Trump family, Brenda Beacon had to take care of business. To wit—she HAD to arbitrate and nullify her CONTRACT at NBC vis a vis. SO, she had to RUIN *The Baby Honey Show* forthwith. Hence—there was ONLY ONE WAY OUT. And she took it. SHE KILLED BABY HONEY—so the show would be CANCELED! And she would be free—full-time—to STEAL THE NEXT ELECTION!"

The witnesses for the Prosecution rose as one, and applauded. Rudy, who by this time had found his teeth and slipped them back in place, grinned broadly at Miller. They belly-bumped.

Rudy turned to the Defense table and, with his eyes bulging, incredulously, said, "Take it away, Bitches!"

Roger Stone, noticing Rudy's seven watches, stood up and said casually, "Hey, anybody know the time?" The courtroom erupted in laughter. Rudy gave Stone a dirty look.

Eleanor now rose and energetically crossed to the jury. "Good morning, ladies and gentlemen," she said, pleasantly. Rudy stood and caviled, "I object. She's looking at the jurors, your Honor."

The judge shrugged, "Overruled." Rudy sat down again and winked at Stephen Miller.

Eleanor resumed. "Members of the jury, you haven't lost your collective minds and no one is going to accuse you of mistaking Baby Honey for a delusion. I know that you have seen her. We have all seen her. I have seen her. And therein lies the magic of being chock-full of atoms. Which we are. Even in this difficult time when neighbors don't speak to neighbors, when families are torn apart—Americans can still be united by the one fundamental thing we all have in common. Atoms!"

The courtroom hushed. There were confused looks at the Prosecution's table. The jury prepared to take notes. Eleanor continued. "I'm going to tell you a story. The neatest story ever told. And it's true! First, does everyone know what an atom is?" The jury looked generally uncertain, so Eleanor said, "That's okay. I brought props."

Rudy stood. "I object."

Eleanor said, "They aren't evidence, your Honor. Just hand-drawn representations of atoms. I did them myself. They are just for purposes of clarification." She picked up one of the posters and held it up for the judge to see. It was a brightly colored crayon drawing of an atom with everything identified. The nucleus, the proton, etc.

The Judge nodded. "I'll allow it."

Kip and Mark set up three easels and Louise and Sandy placed large handmade posters, one to an easel. One illustrated the Atom. One illustrated a Molecule. And the third was a simple drawing of the Solar System. When Kip, Mark, Louise, and Sandy had returned to their seats, Eleanor resumed. "Now look at your hands, everyone."

Rudy's hand shot up. "Objection!"

The Judge said, "Shut up, Rudy. Let the woman talk. I want to hear this."

The jury looked at their hands, as did the Judge. Even Rudy lifted his palms close to his face. Stephen Miller gave him a sharp poke in his side and whispered, "Don't help her." Rudy obediently put his hands back on the table.

Eleanor continued. "You are made up of atoms. So am I. So is your chair. So are your clothes. The window glass ... the door ... the air we breathe! Your pets. Everything in our universe is composed of atoms. Tiny atoms ... so small they can't be seen with the naked eye but they can be seen with a microscope so we know that they do exist. Now you are probably wondering—where did these atoms come from? Well, they came from The Beginning." Eleanor paused dramatically, then continued. Eleanor spoke for the next thirty minutes, with great enthusiasm, about the wonders of science and the thrill of the Big Bang. From time to time, Eleanor referred to a poster.

Several of the jurors wrote feverishly on their paper tablets. Trump fell asleep in his chair and snored loudly. Eleanor took a quaff from her bottle of spring water, then turned back to the jury. She held up the bottle. "Water, by the way, is chock full of atoms and I just ingested a ton of them. Cool, huh?" The jury nodded.

Eleanor continued. "And here's the really nifty thing— atoms don't die or decay. Other things die of course and then their atoms go into the ground or get repurposed. The point is they are deathless unless a nuclear bomb goes off. But that's rare. Most atoms just get recycled. Over and over. For billions of years, the same atoms just keep getting reused. Think about it. You are a repository of billion-year-old atoms. You carry the history of the universe in your body! You are full of the Milky Way!"

A couple of the jurors gasped in awe. Eleanor smiled warmly at them and resumed her story. "So look at your hand. You are the story of life!"

Marjorie Taylor Greene jumped up and yelled, "LIAR!"

The judge gaveled the bench and said, "Order in the court!"

Rudy said, "Objection, your Honor!"

And the Judge said, "Mr. Giuliani, you can't object to me. Sit down."

Trump woke up and moaned. "Jesus ... how much longer is this going to take?" The Judge looked at Eleanor and said, gently. "Wrap it up, young lady."

Eleanor nodded and turned back to the jury. "We are stardust, Ladies and Gentlemen. We are a miracle. And so is Baby Honey."

At this point, Steve Bannon shot out of his chair and shouted "I knew it! Your Honor, Eleanor and Brenda Beacon are trying to seduce the jury with a new religion! That is dirty pool!" He glared at Eleanor. "You are a heretic in addition to being a Marxist!"

Eleanor spun on him. "No, sir, YOU are a heretic. Do you realize that over the millions of years on Earth that mankind has existed, there have probably been hundreds and hundreds of thousands of gods worshipped. And for you to pick out your one god and worship him above all the others is not only ludicrous, it means that you are the atheist from History's point of view. So you are the heretic!"

Bannon's face looked scalded. "Let me tell you something, lady—in Trump's second term, we will imprison non-Christians like you. And we will deport your illegal alien friends, too." He turned and stared at Sandy who stared back. Mickey put a protective arm around her.

Eleanor said, "Oh yeah? You will fail like you fail at everything else! You are weak!"

"There it is, your Honor. She admits that the Baby Honey Family is planning to Steal the Election. I rest my case."

The Judge rubbed his jaw. "First, Mr. Bannon—you are not the prosecuting attorney therefore you have no standing in this court to argue the case let alone rest it. Secondly, Ms. Beacon isn't on trial for stealing an election that hasn't happened yet. We're here because Baby Honey was allegedly murdered. So, chill!"

Eleanor raised her voice. "Give me liberty or give me death." The Baby Honey Family stood and cheered. As did an entire section of the Courtroom. I recognized many of the faces from the Day by Day.

Now the Judge stood up and shouted at Eleanor, "You have two minutes. Finish your opening statement!"

Eleanor nodded. "Yes, your Honor." She turned to the Jury. "Now close your eyes one more time. Imagine the whole room is full of atoms. The floor. The walls. The air. The chairs. The Judge. You. All of us. We are all the same. Just atoms." Eleanor paused. "Okay, now open your eyes. Do you see them? See the atoms. Everything is Oneness. Can you find Baby Honey in the Oneness—of course, you can't! You can't even find me. But you know I'm here. You've seen me. You've seen Baby Honey. She's *not* dead. You *aren't* crazy. You're Stardust. You're cool! And we are all One." Eleanor went to the Prosecution table and took her seat. Brenda patted her arm.

The courtroom was agog with wonder. Except for the prosecution team. They slumped in their chairs. Trump, looking very bored, whined, "Are we ever going to break for lunch?"

The judge gaveled the bench and said, "Guess this is a good enough time to call it a day. Court dismissed until 9:30 tomorrow morning."

Day Two: Thursday

Marjorie Taylor Greene took the stand on the second day of the trial. She placed her hand on the Bible.

"Will you solemnly swear to tell the truth, the whole truth, and nothing but the truth?" asked the clerk.

Marjorie solemnly swore, "Yes, God damn it."

Her testimony was predictably paranoid. She claimed that the earth has been sucked into a big black hole, that the Denver International Airport is the headquarters of a Pedophile ring with underground tunnels guarded by giant lizards. She insisted that the moon is hollow and Italian Jewish Space Lasers had cost Trump the popular vote in 2016. Finally, she declared that spaghetti noodles are indeed made from worms. By the time she relayed her experience discovering that Baby Honey was missing, the jury had stopped listening. But Trump was wide awake and loving the show.

Steve Bannon took the stand next. He looked at the jury and said, "Brenda is not what she seems. She's a smart aleck and a communist. And a non-believer." Bannon ended his testimony with this observation. "Brenda killed that baby. But that was just the icing on the cake. Brenda Beacon's real crime is that she's a traitor. She plans to run for president so she won't be voting for Trump in the next election and that is against the law."

Roger Stone, looking like the Devil Himself, testified that he had not met Brenda before this trial and had never seen *The Baby Honey Show*. "And, for the record, I can't stand kids. But even I wouldn't kill one. Cause I'm pro-life." There was a ripple of applause at the back of the courtroom. Stone continued, "I am merely on board to traduce Brenda Beacon's character on any basis—honest or dishonest. In defense, I will add that Trump has every constitutional right to decimate any potential opponent. Using any means. So, that is what we are doing. As my good friend, Tricky Dick Nixon, once said, 'If you can't stand the heat, get out of the get-away car." Stone laughed as he was excused. He returned to his seat.

Day Three: Friday

The next morning, the streets surrounding the Courthouse were unpassable. A throng of women filled center Manhattan, carrying photos of Brenda Beacon, By one count, there were more than a million of them.

Word of Brenda's plight had spread from Victory Farm to Victory Farm and, after days of traveling, the Sisterhood of American Women was finally arriving. Those who could pressed into the courtroom and filled the hallways and steps. Many more filled the park across the street. Women took turns making eloquent speeches. All were glued to their phones, following the trial.

Inside the courtroom, the Family was in its usual position at and around the Defendant's table. Well-wishers pressed in to hug Brenda and Eleanor and wish them success. Today, Brenda Beacon would take the witness stand.

The Prosecution team and their goons were in their usual spots. Trump had moved from his perch next to the Judge to a seat on the aisle, behind Rudy. He eyed the increased number of women in the room and chatted sternly with Bannon. Remarkably, Henry Kissinger had dropped by that morning to observe the trial. He sat directly behind Trump and feasted on the female flesh that surrounded Brenda.

Susana Rowland now had a dilemma. She had that one dose of Plutonium-120 in her handbag. Enough to kill EITHER Trump OR Kissinger. Not both. She had to make a choice. She reasoned that Trump would continue to show up at the trial so she would presumably have another chance at him. But Kissinger? This might be her only chance to be this close.

Susana got up and crossed the aisle. She warmly greeted Kissinger and asked for his autograph. Trump turned around, took one look at Susana and sniffed. "Don't trust her, Henry. She's Speaker Bob Rowland's wife. Another bleeding heart liberal." Kissinger laughed. "I'm a realist, Donald. Politics takes a backseat when a beautiful woman is before me." He leered at Susana and said, "Do you have a pen?"

Susana slipped her hand into her purse, grabbed a ballpoint pen and the tiny vial of Plutonium-120. She handed the pen to Kissinger and watched him pull a business card from his wallet. He wrote "best wishes" and his name and cell phone number on the back. He handed Susana the card. Then he returned her pen. Susana took the pen; then, as if it was a casual after—thought, said, "Please, Dr. Kissinger, you keep the pen. Others may want an autograph as well." Smiling flirtatiously and looking in his eyes to keep him from looking away, she slipped the pen into his breast pocket and simultaneously dropped the poison vial into the pocket as well. She then patted the pocket several times and thought she heard a slight hiss of a seal being released. "Well, I better get back to my seat," she said. "Good-bye, Dr. Kissinger."

"All rise." The judge entered the room and the third day of the trial was underway. Brenda took the stand. She wore her signature heraldic blue. She looked as gentle as a spring breeze. And as cool as a cucumber. She smiled serenely at the jury. They smiled back. Rudy Giuliani immediately objected.

The Judge said, "What are you objecting to now? She hasn't even spoken yet."

Rudy's eyes bulged like golf balls. "SHE'S TRYING TO HYPNOTIZE THEM, YOUR HONOR."

The Judge grinned at Brenda and said, "Are you trying to hypnotize the jurors, Miss Beacon?"

Brenda laughed airily. "Of course not, your Honor."

Trump was on his feet now. "THIS TRIAL IS RIGGED! I DEMAND THAT YOU RECUSE YOURSELF, JUDGE!"

And the judge said, "No." He turned back to Brenda. "Why don't you tell us what happened, Miss Beacon."

Brenda nodded. She suddenly felt a cramp in her stomach. She clutched her abdomen and softly moaned. But she quickly recomposed and began her testimony. "All of my girlfriends want to have a baby, but the country under President Trump is not hospitable to Life. So, we have had to defer our dreams until a better day dawns in America. Which will only happen when Trump is gone."

The Prosecution team was now on its feet. "I DE-MAND ... I OBJECT...."

The jury, as one, turned to them and said, "Shush! We want to hear what Brenda has to say." Trump looked incredulous. He crossed his arms over his chest and steamed. Kissinger laughed at the spectacle of it all.

Susana saw that Kissinger was still alive and was ready to cross the aisle and throw herself against him when suddenly Brenda moaned again louder. Brenda panted and twisted slightly in her chair, to the left, to the right. She continued, "We have prayed that Trump would have a heart attack. Or a stroke. Or get shot. Or just be impeached? Maybe even twice? I know it's not nice. And that perhaps is the most awful thing that Trump has done. He has infected all of us with his meanness. And we are all sick inside. We long to go back to being normal. We want to have babies and raise our families in a society where no one would ever think of calling a fellow American *Nigger or Jew or Bitch*. Where no one would ever think of shooting up a school. Or bombing a synagogue. We thought all was lost until Baby Honey arrived. She gave us hope."

Trump stood again and screamed, "WHAT THE HELL IS SHE TALKING ABOUT? THIS IS SHIT!"

Marjorie Taylor Greene yelled, "LIAR! LIAR!"

The forewoman of the jury stood now and faced the President of the United States and his posse. A recently retired elementary school teacher, it seemed Destiny had tapped her on the shoulder as she sat there listening to Brenda Beacon. She felt in her bones that everything Brenda was saying was true. And, as the court watched in amazement, this normally self-effacing woman began to grow. Her spine stiffened and elongated, and within seconds, she towered over the courtroom. Her voice was womanly, soft but strong. She looked directly at Trump and sternly declared, "Donald Trump, either you and your friends settle down and listen to the Defense respectfully ... or you and your comrades will be forced to stand in the corners of this building and you will not get to join the others when Court recesses. Is that clear?"

The president sunk back into his chair. Roger Stone made a snide comment about the giant woman's double chin to Bannon and the woman crossed to him. She bent down and looked him in the eyes. "What was that, Roger?"

"Nothing," he said sheepishly.

The woman nodded to Brenda. "Please continue, Ms. Beacon."

Brenda stood up now, she seemed to be in great discomfort. She grabbed her sides and wrenched forward and backward. She squirmed and moaned more loudly. But somehow she continued her testimony. "Baby Honey was everyone's baby. She reminded us of what America might be again if we got rid of this poison in the White House. Holidays with our families would be fun again! We could have backyard parties with our neighbors. But the dark forces battled on. The anger and the ugliness increased. So, finally I hid Baby Honey. Yes, I hid her for her own protection. And I waited for a sign. And I think I just got it." Brenda grabbed her belly and half-laughed and then screamed. "Vivian! Vivian! I need you. I need a midwife! I'm going to have my baby!"

The *Baby Honey* Family now raced to Brenda. Kip reached her first. "Brenda. Darling, tell me what to do...." He wrapped her in his arms and kissed her passionately while the others piled coats on the floor to create a birthing bed. Eleanor called 911. "We need an ambulance at the Courthouse immediately. Brenda Beacon is having a baby!" Susana took Brenda's hand and smiled at her lovingly, while the others kneeled around her. Vivian began coaching her through the labor. And Brenda Beacon began to give birth.

There was stunned silence at first, and then a whoop of joy echoed through the courtroom and into the street as the baby's head crowned and everyone knew it was real! Trump jumped out of his seat, screaming in terror, "EEEEUUUU! UGH! STOP! THAT'S DISGUSTING! NO ONE WANTS TO LOOK AT THAT! GET ME OUT OF HERE! NO!!! NO!!! STOP DOING THAT! I'M GOING TO BE SICK! UGH! I'M GOING TO PUKE! GROSS!" He pushed his way into the aisle, roughly slapping his hands against Kissinger's chest as he frantically shoved him and everyone else out of his way. Kissinger immediately grabbed his heart and gasped. His eyes rolled up. He collapsed, face-down on the floor. Vice President Pence jumped over Kissinger's body and raced to catch up to Trump.

The Trump crowd was now rushing out of the building to follow the president while Brenda's supporters were rushing in from the street, hoping to get a closer look at the Miracle at the front of the court room. Miller and Giuliani tried objecting, but no one could hear them now. So, they headed for the door, jumping over Kissinger's corpse on their way out. The Judge remained behind his bench, smiling down at Brenda.

I was personally swept up by Bannon, Stone, and Greene as they pushed everyone in front of them toward the exit. That's how I ended up outside on the steps. That's where I witnessed firsthand President Trump–still screaming "EEEEUUUU! GROSS ME OUT!"—with Vice President Pence close behind him, become tangled in the discarded Trump flag as he ran down the steps. He stumbled, and fell headfirst into the street. Mike Pence's own head now was firmly shoved up Trump's behind. And in full view of an astonished crowd of onlookers, the two men were immediately hit by the approaching ambulance and crushed to death.

By the time, Brenda was placed in that ambulance about ten minutes later, her baby was born. She cradled it in her arms. Kip slid in next to her and said, "So what shall we name her, Honey?" And Brenda said. "Let's call her Grace. After all she is born on a Tuesday. Tuesday's child is full of Grace." And Kip said, "Actually, Honey, today is Friday." And Brenda said, "Well, at least it isn't a Thursday."

The Family gathered around the ambulance as it readied to pull away. They waved to little Grace and blew kisses to Brenda. They wiped their tears of joy, and promised to meet at the hospital as soon as they could find a cab.

Eleanor said it was Destiny. Everyone got what they deserved. Brenda Beacon was acquitted of all the charges. Trump's death was ruled a suicide and he was soon quickly forgotten. Pence became a source of international snickers. Kissinger's murder was blamed on Melania Trump who was accused and convicted of securing the lethal dose of Polonium-120 from her Russian friends. Rudy Giuliani lost his license to practice law and went bankrupt. He had to sell all of his Rolexes to pay his legal fees. Marjorie Taylor Greene never got to be a Representative in the House of Representatives. She returned to Georgia and got a stocking job at a local Walmart and was fired within the first two weeks for being obstreperous. Stephen Miller moved back in with his parents in California. Steve Bannon moved to Hungary and became a monk in a creepy medieval monastery. He was required to take a vow of silence, and was never heard from again. And Roger Stone simply slithered away.

And Speaker of the House Bob Rowland, as the next in line after the President and Vice President, per the Constitution, became the 46th President of the United States. But he immediately issued an Executive Order and handed the presidency to Brenda Beacon. He liked being in Congress. He liked getting things done. And he knew the country would be in fine hands with Brenda in charge.

Chapter 29 – Nolens Volens

I heard someone say that the most reliable form of pleasure is the pleasure of anticipation. And so, the Family gathered at the Day by Day Café on New Year's Eve to anticipate together what the future would bring. Their guesses were pretty accurate. They all lived happily ever after.

Mark and Eleanor were married on February 14th. Mark, ever the romantic, wanted Eleanor to wear a diaphanous gown of white with a long veil and carry a bouquet of long-stemmed, Valentine-red roses. Not really her style, but when you love someone as she loved Mark, you compromise. She wore it all and added her red flip-flops so she would always remember, throughout their very long marriage, who she was. After the wedding, she and Mark honeymooned in an undisclosed location, and when they returned, Eleanor was pregnant with a little girl whom they would name Mary.

Sandy and Mickey set up a small film company that worked out of the Dollar Store basement, and partnered with Mark and Eleanor on a series of films about random thoughts. The following autumn, Sandy had a baby girl. Mickey was the happiest father anyone had ever seen. The biggest surprise that spring was when Louise and Roger announced that they, too, were expecting. Twin boys.

Meanwhile Bill and Jacques had officially tied the knot and, soon after, sold the Day by Day Café and moved into the Victory Farm in Vermont at Bob and Susana's invitation. Jacques began developing condiments that he would sell out of the Barn. They were very popular. People came for miles to purchase Jacques' mole-catsup and raspberry chutney. And he spent his days developing unusually delicious mustards that flavored his pickled-vegetable concoctions. The following summer his chow-chow won a blue ribbon at the Vermont State Fair.

In the years to come, Jacques would develop a Vermont accent, and a small hitch in his left leg. People in the town would completely forget that this tall, black, gay man had come from a place across the sea. Jacques was able to reinvent himself as a native New Englander because his neighbors, like most Americans, were good-natured, tolerant, and had short memories. Louise said, "Jacques has finally evolved into who he was always meant to be."

Speaking of Louise, she and Roger and the twins moved to the Farm as well. Louise helped Jacques turn the Barn into a charming country store that sold beautiful kitchenware and tableware as well as Jacques' gourmet condiments. Louise added stunning tea towels and embroidered French linens that she had designed herself. And even though the plan to overturn *Roe vs. Wade* had been interrupted when Trump threw himself in front of that ambulance, Louise kept a supply of the Victory Garden aprons on hand just in case. And she personally tended the small plot of Highland Flagg and Pennyroyal that grew on the furthest field of the Farm.

Roger was busy, too, recording birds singing at different times of the day and cricket chirps, the sound of wind in the pine trees. The sound of tomatoes ripening. He overlapped it all with the sound of his little boys laughing. And he gave the CDs away to anyone who asked. They were especially popular among those who were filled with remorse about their MAGA cult participation during the Trump years. The recordings, it was said, helped people find their sleep rhythm again. They say it helped people forgive themselves and heal.

Vivian now lives in Manhattan in Bob and Susana's wondrous apartment. She and Susana had become extremely close during their months on the Farm and Susana invited her to live in the apartment for free. Susanna wanted a wise woman to be nearby to help the "kids" as they embarked on raising the next generation of The Family. Susana said she would come into the city on weekends maybe twice a month to see Vivian, which would be great fun for both of them.

In the meantime, Vivian began to explore and discover the parts of her life that had been unexamined to date. She bought lovely clothes at Bergdorf's. Beautiful Italian wool slacks and oyster-colored silk shirts. A gold cuff bracelet, gold earrings. Very understated, of course, but elegant. Vivian felt more attractive at eighty-five years old than she had at any other time in her life. She spent her days now moving slowly through art galleries and museums. She had the luxury of time now to just look. She told Susana that she was used to the splendor of natural beauty, having lived in the country all of her life, but now she wanted to know human-made beauty. She discovered that she loved it every bit as much and that restored her faith in human beings.

Speaking of Susana, she and Bob were now permanently living in Washington, D.C. They hosted small dinner parties at their elegant townhouse with the most interesting people in the city. Susana took a teaching job, her first since her post-college days in Buenos Aires. She tutored young children for whom English was a Second Language. Her weekdays were therefore joyous. She always loved children. And on weekends, she and Bob would fly up to the Farm or to the apartment and spend time with the Family there. Bob, as Speaker of the House, continued to be a repository of civility and reason. He became the compass that brought the government back to a safe center after years of extremes.

Brenda and Kip moved into the White House and listened to the advice of the best and the brightest minds and hearts they could find. Brenda brought Baby Grace to work every day and set standards for workplaces to provide childcare on the premises so Mothers and Fathers could take their lunch break with their kids. President Beacon-Barrett also created a universal health care system based on that in Canada. Americans relaxed knowing that they would be cared for even if their job went away. But jobs didn't go away. Brenda increased taxes on the wealthiest and invested the money in green energy and think tanks to solve the critical problem of Climate Change. She established term limits for Congress and the Senate. And she did the same for the Supreme Court and made it retroactive.

Kip was offered a job at Georgetown University right there in the city of Washington. He taught free-wheeling courses in American Studies. His classes were soon the most popular on campus, and Kip would augment his classroom teaching by hanging around after class and engaging with the students in vigorous and intelligent dialog. He always came home happy. He would scoop little Grace up and kiss her until she cooed. And then he would kiss Brenda until she cooed, and say, "My students are so great, Babe! They are all educatable! Every single one of them!"

Finally, Brenda and Kip initiated a weekly live podcast much like President Franklin Roosevelt's "fireside chats" during the dark days of World War II. It comforted the nation and brought them together. And it became almost as popular as *The Baby Honey Show* had been. Each week, the President and her husband introduced a Truth. They began with the basics. That the earth is round. That the earth is 4.543 billion years old. That dinosaurs preceded humans on the planet. That the moon is not hollow. They made the Truth not just plausible, but enjoyable to know. In fact, there is simply nothing as miraculous as the Truth. As Brenda pointed out—every time we embrace a Truth, the ground beneath us becomes more solid. And as evidence of that fact, she noted that while Trump was in office, there were 1,455 earthquakes. And yet, you hardly ever hear about them now.

Brenda named her program, *Nolens Volens*. A Latin expression that translates to "Like it or Not." She anticipated pushback from some of the folks who still clung to the old MAGA conspiracies. But Brenda never wavered in her conviction that the Truth would set them free. She acknowledged that Truth can be elusive. It can be confounding. It can be annoying and it can be offensive. But, at the end of the day, because the people trusted Brenda and Kip to tell the Truth, and more than that—because they loved Brenda and Kip—the MAGA cultists followed them out of the Darkness and into an era of Happiness.

You ask about Bill? Well, Bill finished writing his novel. It was published by a small press in Oregon which means very few people ever read it. But he held public readings in the Barn at Heritage Farm every Thursday evening and people really seemed to enjoy listening to his story about an old man who reinvented himself at ninety. Bill was also very proud to place a copy of the book on the bookshelf in the Day by Day Café. Right next to *My Friend Whitey*. Look for it if you ever stop in. It's called *Slowly I Turn*.

Speaking of the café, I bought the Day by Day from Bill right after he and Jacques retired. He came to me first with the proposal. After all, I had been a patron for decades. I knew that the café required an owner with patience and a sense of wonder. And I have that in spades. I'm a writer, after all.

I've changed nothing in the café. Not the hours, not the days. Not the tables with the little lamps or the pale pink shades that focus such flattering light on the patrons—a light that makes them feel beautiful and unself-conscious, and frees them to imagine what might have been and what might still be.

I do the cooking now. Standard breakfast fare. You know, French toast and poached eggs. That kind of thing. I did trim the *Philodendron*. Oh my, it was taking over. I think it looks much better now. I spoke firmly to it. I said, "*Philodendron*, anything that lives forever needs some radical change every now and again. Just to stay fresh." I think it understood my reasoning. It looks quite buoyant again.

The bookshelves remain as do the books. And the Family—one or more of them drop in every day. It's usually Mark and Eleanor with their little girl, Mary. All of the kids are good parents. Their babies are thriving. I also see Mickey and Sandy a lot. They have a wonderful little girl, and a boy on the way. By the way, Brenda and Kip also welcomed a little boy last month. Eleanor says it's evidence that the world is back in balance. She declared, "Three little girls born into our Family. Three little boys born ... you see? As Confucius would say, 'Women hold up half the sky. And men hold up the other half.'"

I open the café promptly at 3 a.m. every morning and turn on the lights. I brew myself a good cup of coffee, and take my seat by the window to wait for the world to bring me my next story. Because this story is done.

The End

Acknowledgements

I want first to thank my longtime friends Katie Kraemer and Cathy Fuller for their unflagging support of my writing, in general, and for their contributions to *The Baby Honey Show* in particular. Their many readings and smart critiques as the story evolved helped me home in on what I needed to say. And their laughter buoyed me through periods of doubt. I treasure their steadfast love and affection and return it many times over.

Among my other dear friends who also provided generous support to this project, I especially want to thank Jay Reilly, Steve Andersen, Maggie Pastaar, Joyce Paxton, Wes Cutter, Lou Salerni, Nat Fuller, Jenni Runte, Dulcie Arnold, Sally Krupich, David Kwiat, Barbara Sloan, Susanne Egli, Mark Benninghofen, Signe Pretzel, Paul Meshejian, Bill Schoppert, Tara Guy, Andre Bergeron, Russ West, Amy Reasoner, Jason Reasoner, and Fred Reasoner. Thank you, Shane Warnick for the lovely art work. And thank you, Wendell Ricketts, for everything else! You all make my rockin' world go round.

Finally, I am grateful to Kurt Vonnegut for the pleasure of reading his work. For fifty years, he has entertained me, provoked my imagination, and influenced my writing. Wish he was still around. I would love to see what he would make of America in the twenty-first century.

About the Author

Nancy Bagshaw-Reasoner spent thirty-five years on the professional stage as an actress, producer, and playwright. Then she spent fifteen years overseeing construction and facilities-maintenance at Metropolitan State University in Saint Paul, Mn. In 2015, she returned to writing full-time. She has written seven plays. All but two have been professionally produced. Her most recent is *The Gathering Up*. She has written for American Public Radio, and for Sue Scott's podcast, *Island of Discarded Women*. Her novels include a fictionalized memoir—*Philip Roth Loves Me*—which was published in 2023 and *The Baby Honey Show*—a darkly funny fantasy about Trump's first term in office. Nancy lives in St. Paul, Minnesota with her wonderful husband of forty-eight years, Fred Reasoner, and their beloved border collie, Jack.